D1589224

THE FAMILY

Tonino Benacquista

Translated by Emily Read

BITTER LEMON PRESS
LONDON

BITTER LEMON PRESS
www.bitterlemonpress.com

First published in French as *Malavita* by
Éditions Gallimard, Paris, 2004
This edition published in 2013 by Bitter Lemon Press,
37 Arundel Gardens, London W11 2LW
First published in the United Kingdom in 2010
as *Badfellas* by Bitter Lemon Press

This book is supported by the French Ministry of Foreign Affairs, as part
of the Burgess programme run by the Cultural Department of the French
Embassy in London (*www.frenchbooknews.com*) and the French Ministry of
Culture (Centre National du Livre). Publié avec le concours du Ministère
des Affaires Etrangères (Programme Burgess) et du Ministère Français
chargé de la Culture- Centre National du Livre.

Liberté • Égalité • Fraternité
RÉPUBLIQUE FRANÇAISE

© Éditions Gallimard, Paris, 2004
English translation © Emily Read, 2010

A CIP record for this book is available from the British Library
ISBN Paperback 978-1-908524-21-8
ISBN eBook   978-1-908524-22-5

Typeset by Alma Books Ltd
Printed and bound in the United Kingdom by
CPI Group (UK) Ltd, Croydon, CR0 4YY

The Family

1

They took possession of the house in the middle of the night.

Any other family would have seen it as a new start. The first morning of a new life – a new life in a new town. A rare moment that shouldn't take place in the dark.

For the Blakes, however, it was a moonlight flit in reverse: they were moving in as discreetly as possible. Maggie, the mother, went in first, tapping her heels on the steps to scare away any lurking rats. She went through all the rooms, ending up in the cellar, which appeared to be clean and to have the perfect level of humidity for maturing wheels of Parmesan, or storing cases of Chianti. The father, Frederick, who had never felt at ease around rodents, allowed his wife to go ahead. He went round the outside of the house holding a flashlight, and ended up on a veranda piled high with old and rusty garden furniture, a warped ping-pong table and several shapes that were almost invisible in the darkness.

The daughter – Belle, aged seventeen – went upstairs into what would be her bedroom, a square, south-facing room looking out onto a maple tree and a bed of miraculously persistent white carnations – they looked like a constellation of stars in the night. She turned the bedhead to the north wall, moved the bedside table and began to visualize the walls covered with all the posters that had travelled with her over so many years and across

7

so many borders. Belle's mere presence made the place come alive. This was where she would henceforth sleep, do her revision, work on her movement and posture, sulk, dream, laugh and sometimes cry – all the things she had done every day of her adolescence. Warren, who was three years younger than her, checked out the next-door room without any real curiosity; he had no interest in views and harmonious layouts. All that mattered to him was having a supply of electricity and his own telephone line. Then, in less than a week, his complete mastery of the Internet would enable him to forget the French countryside, and even Europe, and provide him with the illusion of being back home, on the other side of the Atlantic, where he came from, and where he would one day return.

The villa had been built in 1900, of Norman brick and stone, decorated with a checked frieze across the façade, and festoons of blue-painted wood along the roof, which also had a sort of minaret overhanging the east–west angle of the house. The wrought-iron curlicues on the entrance gate made one want to visit what looked from a distance like a small baroque palace. However, at this time of night, the Blakes couldn't have cared less about the aesthetics of the place, and were only concerned with its comfort. Despite its evident charm, the old building couldn't conceal its shabbiness, and was certainly no substitute for the little jewel of modernity that had been their home long ago in Newark, New Jersey, USA.

All four of them now gathered in the drawing room, where, without a word, they removed the dust sheets which covered the armchairs, sofa, coffee table and as-yet-empty cupboards and shelves. Inside the

8

red-and-black brick fireplace, which was big enough to roast a sheep, there was a plaque depicting two noblemen wrestling with a wild boar. Fred grabbed a whole lot of wooden knick-knacks from the cross-beam and threw them into the hearth. He always wanted to smash useless objects.

"Those fuck-ups forgot the TV again," Warren said.

"They said they'd bring it tomorrow," said his mother.

"Really tomorrow, or tomorrow like last time?" asked Fred, just as worried as his son.

"Look, you two, I hope you're not going to attack me every time there's some object missing in this house. Why don't you just ask *them.*"

"The TV isn't just some object, Mom, it's our connection to the outside world, the real world, outside this crumbling shack in this rat hole full of peasants we're going to be lumbered with for years maybe. The TV is life, it's my life, it's us, it's my country."

Maggie and Frank suddenly felt guilty and couldn't answer. They didn't even challenge his bad language. They realized Warren had a right to be homesick. He had been just eight years old when events had forced them to leave America; of the four of them, he was the one who had suffered the most. Changing the subject, Belle asked what the town was called.

"Cholong-sur-Avre, Normandy!" Fred replied, making no attempt at a French accent. "Think of all the Americans who've heard of Normandy without knowing where the fuck it is in the world."

"Apart from our boys landing here in '44, what's Normandy famous for?" asked Warren.

"Camembert," the father ventured.

9

"We used to get that at Cagnes-sur-Mer, but we had the sun and the sea as well," said Belle.

"We used to get it in Paris too, and that was Paris," said Warren.

They all had happy memories of their arrival in the capital, six years earlier. Then circumstances had forced them to move down to the Côte d'Azur, where they had stayed for four years, until Fate had struck again, and they had ended up here in Cholong-sur-Avre in the Eure.

They then split up to explore the rooms they had not yet seen. Fred stopped in the kitchen, inspected the empty fridge, opened a few cupboards, put his hand on the ceramic ring. He was satisfied with the layout – he needed a huge amount of space for when he fancied making a tomato sauce – he stroked the wood of the butcher's block, the tiling by the sink, the rush seats on the stools, and picked up a few knives, testing the blades with his fingernail. He always began by touching things, treating new places as if they were women.

In the bathroom, Belle struck poses in front of a splendid, slightly spotted mirror in an ancient mahogany frame surmounted by a little matt-glass rose-shaped lamp holding a naked light bulb. She loved her reflection there. Maggie, for her part, opened her bedroom windows wide, pulled the sheets out of their bags, pulled the blankets down from the top of the cupboard, sniffed them, decided they were clean, and unrolled them onto the bed. Only Warren went on wandering from room to room, asking:

"Has anyone seen the dog?"

The ash-grey Australian Cattle Dog, christened Malavita by Fred, had joined the Blake family as soon as it had arrived in France. Maggie had had three reasons

10

for adopting this little hairy animal with sticking-up ears: she would be a popular welcome present to entertain the children, as well as a cheap way to buy their forgiveness and make them forget their exile. Thanks to her astonishing tact and discretion, she had easily made herself popular. She never barked, ate neatly, mostly at night, and spent most of her time asleep, usually in a cellar or laundry room. Once a day they thought she was dead, and the rest of the time just lost. Malavita led the life of a cat and no one could argue with that. Warren finally found her, as expected, in the cellar, between a boiler on pilot and a brand-new washing machine. Like the others, the animal had found her corner, and had been the first to go to sleep.

*

Life in France had not put an end to the breakfast ritual. Fred got up early in order to see his children go off with a full stomach, giving them his blessing, sometimes parting with some extra pocket money or an invaluable piece of advice about life, before going back to bed with a clear conscience the minute they were out of the door. At almost fifty, Frederick Blake had almost never had to start his day before twelve o'clock, and he could count on one hand the days when he had failed to achieve this. The worst of those particular days had been the funeral of his friend Jimmy, his companion-at-arms from the earliest days of his career – nobody had dared show Jimmy disrespect, even when he was dead. The bastard had chosen to have himself buried two hours away from Newark, and at ten in the morning. It had been a tiresome day, from beginning to end.

"No cereal, no toast, no peanut butter," said Maggie. "You'll have to make do with what I've got from the local baker – apple *beignets*. I'll do the shopping this afternoon, so spare me the complaints for now."

"That's perfect, Mom," said Belle.

Warren looked peeved and grabbed a *beignet*.

"Could somebody explain to me why the French, who are famous for their patisserie, have failed to invent the doughnut? It's not hard, it's just a *beignet* with a hole in the middle."

Half-asleep and already exasperated by the thought of the day ahead, Fred asked if the hole added to the flavour.

"They've learned about cookies," said Belle. "I've had some good ones."

"Call those cookies?"

"I'll make some doughnuts on Sunday, and cookies too," said Maggie, to keep the peace.

"Do we know where the school is?" asked Fred, trying to take an interest in a daily routine that had hitherto passed him by.

"I've given them a map."

"Go with them."

"We'll manage, Mom," said Warren. "We'll even go faster without a map. We've got a sort of radar in our heads – you find yourself in any street in the world with a satchel on your back, and a little inner voice warns you: 'Not there, it's that way', and you meet more and more shapes with satchels going the same way, until you all plunge into a sort of black hole. It's a law of physics."

"If you could only be so motivated in the classroom," said Maggie.

12

That was the signal to go. They all kissed each other, said they'd see each other at the end of the afternoon, and the first day began. Each one, for various reasons, held back the thousands of questions on the tips of their tongues, and accepted the situation as if it made some sense.

Maggie and Fred found themselves alone in a suddenly silent kitchen.

"What about your day?" he asked first.

"The usual. I'll look around the town, see what there is to see, find the shops. I'll be back about six with the shopping. What about you?"

"Oh, me…"

Behind that "oh, me" she could hear a silent litany, sentences she knew by heart even though they were never actually spoken: oh me, I'll just spend the day wondering what we're doing here, and then I'll pretend to do something, as usual, but what?… That's the problem.

"Try not to hang around all day in your dressing gown."

"Because of the neighbours?"

"No, because of your morale."

"My morale's fine, Maggie, I'm just a bit disorientated, I always take longer to adapt than you."

"What will we say if we run into any neighbours?"

"Don't know yet, just smile for the time being, we've got a couple of days to come up with an idea."

"Quintiliani says we mustn't mention Cagnes, we must say we came from Menton; I've told the kids."

"As if that creep had to spell it out."

To avoid a painful conversation, Maggie went upstairs while Fred made himself feel good by clearing the table. He could now see the garden in daylight through the

13

window: it had a well-kept lawn apart from a few maple leaves, a green metal bench, a gravel path and a lean-to sheltering an abandoned barbecue. He suddenly remembered his nocturnal visit to the veranda and its strange, rather pleasant atmosphere. He suddenly had to see it again in daylight, before doing anything else. As if there was anything else to do.

It was March, and the weather was mild and bright. Maggie hesitated for a moment over a suitable outfit for her first visit to the town. She was very dark, with a matt complexion and black eyes, and normally wore brown and ochre colours. Today she chose beige jodhpur-style trousers, a grey long-sleeved T-shirt and a cotton cable-stitch sweater. She went downstairs, with a little knapsack over her shoulder, glanced around briefly, looking for her husband, shouted, "See you this evening!" and left the house, unanswered.

Fred went onto the already sunny veranda, where he detected a soft smell of moss and dry wood – a pile of logs left behind by the previous tenants. The blinds over the bay window made stripes of sunshine along the length of the room. Fred pretended these were rays from heaven, and entertained himself by exposing his body to them. The room gave onto the garden, but was protected from the elements and covered pretty well forty square yards. He went over to the dump in the corner and started clearing out all the old stuff cluttering it up and blocking off space and light. He opened the French windows and started throwing all the forgotten possessions of the unknown family out onto the gravel: a television set from another era, some plates and copper pans, grubby telephone directories, a wheel-less bike and a pile of other objects, quite

14

understandably abandoned. Fred took great pleasure in chucking it all out, muttering "Trash!" and "Junk!" each time he hurled a piece out of his sight. Finally he picked up a small grey-green bakelite case, and was about to hurl it out with the gesture of a discus-thrower. But then he suddenly felt curious about its contents and, placing it on the ping-pong table, prised open the two rusty fasteners and opened the lid. Black metal. Mother-of-pearl keys. European keyboard. Automatic return. The machine had a name too: Brother 900, 1964 model.

Fred now held a typewriter in his hands for the first time in his life. He weighed it as he had done his children when they were born. He turned it around, examining its contours and angles, and its visible machinery, which was both splendidly obsolete and strangely complicated, full of pistons, sprockets and clever ironmongery. With the tips of his fingers he stroked the surface of the keys – r t y u – tried to recognize them just by feel, and then with his whole hand he caressed the metal frame. He held the spool and tried to unwind the ribbon, sniffing it to see if he could smell the ink, which he couldn't. He hit the n key and then several others, faster and faster until they tangled together. He excitedly untangled them, then placed all his fingers haphazardly on the keys, and there, standing in the pink light of the veranda, with his dressing gown half open and his eyes shut, he felt overcome by a strange and unknown feeling.

*

In order to retain a semblance of dignity in the playground, surrounded as they were by a thousand curious stares, Belle and Warren chatted to each other

15

in English, exaggerating their New Jersey accent. Speaking French wasn't a problem for them; after six years they spoke it a great deal better than their parents, and had even begun to replace English expressions with French turns of phrase. However, in exceptional circumstances, such as those of this particular morning, they found it convenient to revert to a more private way of talking – it was a way of reminding themselves of their own story and where they had come from. They had arrived on the dot of eight at Mme Arnaud's office; she was the education advisor at the *Lycée* Jules-Vallès, and she asked them to wait in the playground for a moment before introducing each of them to their class teacher. Belle and Warren were starting at the school at the end of the second term, when everybody's fate had long been decided. The third term would just have to be a springboard for the following year, when she would do her *baccalauréat*, and he would go into *seconde*. Belle had kept up the academic standards of her early years at Montgomery High School in Newark, despite all the upheavals. It had been clear to her, from her earliest youth, that body and soul should enrich one another, exchanging energy and working in harmony. She was curious about everything at school, and concentrated on every subject. No teacher in the world, nor even her parents, could guess at her reason for this – which was to beautify herself. Warren, for his part, who was eight at the time, had learned French in the way you learn a tune, without thinking, without even wanting to. Psychological problems due to his uprooting had meant a year repeated as well as sessions with a child psychiatrist, who was never told the real reason for their leaving America. Nowadays he bore no trace of this, but

16

he never missed an opportunity to remind his parents that he didn't deserve this exile. Like all children of whom much is demanded, he had grown up faster than others, and had already established certain principles about life, from which he never departed. There lay within him, beneath the values that he preserved as the precious inheritance of his tribe, an old-world solemnity, in which were mingled both a sense of honour and an instinct for business.

A group of girls from Belle's class approached her, curious to inspect the new arrival. Mr Mangin, the history and geography teacher, came over to fetch them, and greeted Miss Belle Blake with a touch of ceremony. She left her brother, wishing him luck with a gesture incomprehensible to anyone not born south of Manhattan. Mme Arnaud came to tell Warren that his class didn't start until nine and that he was to wait in the homework room. He chose instead to nose around the school, casing the joint and establishing the contours of his new prison. He went into the main building of the school, a circular building with spokes, known as "the daisy", with a hall designed like a beehive, where the older children could hang out away from the homework room, smoke, pick each other up, put up posters and organize meetings – a sort of training ground for adult life. Warren found himself alone there, in front of a hot-drinks dispenser and a large sign advertising the school fête, which would take place on the 21st of June. He wandered down the corridors, opened a few doors, avoided some groups of adults, and ended up in a gymnasium where a basketball team was practising; he watched them for a while, intrigued as ever by the French lack of coordination. One of his

17

happiest memories was going to a game between the Chicago Bulls and the New York Knicks, and seeing the living legend Michael Jordan flying from one basket to the other. It was enough to make you pine for your homeland for the rest of your life.

A hand on his shoulder put an end to the daydreaming. It wasn't a monitor or a teacher charged with bringing him back in line, it was a boy, about a head taller than he was, accompanied by two acolytes in loose, too large clothes. Warren was built like his father – small, dark and wiry, with controlled gestures and a natural economy of movement. You could see gravity in the still fixity of his stare. He appeared at first as the contemplative type, the sort whose first reaction is not to react. His own sister had assured him that he would one day become a handsome, greying, experienced-looking man, but that he would have to work hard to achieve that sort of appearance.

"Are you the American?"

As if brushing off a fly, Warren pushed off the hand, which belonged to the one he correctly guessed to be the leader. The two others, apparently his lieutenants, waited cautiously. Warren, despite his youth, recognized that tone of voice, the slightly unsure aggression, the attempt at authority on the off-chance that it might work, the testing of limits. It was the most cautious form of aggression, practised by cowards. Surprised for a moment, the American boy hesitated before answering. In any case, it wasn't really a question, and whatever it was that these three wanted, they certainly weren't there just by chance. *Why me?* he wondered. Why had they picked on him, as soon as he had arrived? How had he, in less than half an hour, become the object of this

18

vague and foolish threat, which was about to become more concrete, encouraged by his silence? He knew the answer, with a knowledge that was beyond his years.

"What do you want from me?"

"You're American. You must be rich."

"Cut the bullshit and tell me how your business works."

"What d'your parents do?"

"None of your fucking business. What's your little racket? Extortion? Piece work or contract work? How many of you – three, six, twenty? What do you reinvest in?"

"?…"

"Nil organization. Thought so."

None of the three could understand a word of what he had said, nor where this confidence came from. The leader felt somehow insulted. He looked around, pulled Warren to the end of an empty corridor leading to the refectory and pushed him so hard that he fell onto a low wall.

"Don't fuck with me, new boy."

Then all three got together to shut him up, with knees in his ribs and wild punches in the general direction of his face. Finally one of them sat on his chest, went through his pockets and found a ten-euro note. They then demanded from a red and breathless Warren the same sum the next day as an entrance fee to the *Lycée* Jules-Vallès. Holding back tears, he promised not to forget.

Warren never forgot.

*

19

Cholong-sur-Avre is an old medieval stronghold, lying like a jewel in the bocage. It reached its apogee at the end of the Hundred Years War, at the beginning of the sixteenth century, and nowadays counts seven thousand inhabitants. With its half-timbered houses, eighteenth-century mansions and streets bordered by canals, Cholong-sur-Avre is a remarkably well-preserved architectural gem.

Maggie opened her pocket dictionary to look up *colombages*, and then checked it with the real thing by walking down Rue Gustave Roger; most of the houses, with their framework of beams, were unlike anything she had ever seen before. As she found her way to the centre of town – Cholong was shaped like a pentagon edged with four boulevards and a highway – Maggie walked down several streets built entirely of half-timbered houses, and she very much admired the prospect. With half an eye on the guidebook, she eventually, without really looking for it, found herself in the central square, the Place de la Libération, the heart of Cholong, a large space out of proportion with the narrow streets surrounding it. There were two restaurants, several cafés, a bakery, the tourist office, a newsagent and a few old buildings around the edge of a huge rectangular space, which served as a car park on non-market days. Maggie bought some local papers and settled down on the terrace of the café Roland Fresnel, ordering a long double espresso. She closed her eyes briefly and sighed, enjoying this all too rare moment of solitude. Time spent with the family was, of course, at the top of her list of priorities, but time away from them came a close second. Cup in hand, she leafed through a local newspaper, the *Dépêche de Cholong*, then the *Réveil Normand*, (the Eure edition); it was one

20

way of getting to know her new home country. On the front of the *Dépêche* was a photo of a gentleman of sixty-five, a native of Cholong, who had once been a regional middle-distance running champion, and who was now taking part in the Senior Olympics in Australia. Maggie was amused by the thought of this character, and read the article. She understood the main drift of it: here was a man with a lifelong passion for running, who had only just fulfilled his dream right at the end of his journey. As a young man, Mr Christian Mounier had been a just about passable runner. Now that he had reached retirement, he had become an international champion, competing on the other side of the world. Maggie wondered if life really could offer a chance to catch up, a last-minute opportunity to distinguish oneself. She dwelt on this problem just long enough to turn the page. There was a long list of local news stories: petty crimes, an attack on a garage owner, several burglaries in a neighbouring housing estate, one or two domestic quarrels and a few absurd pieces of hot air. Maggie couldn't always follow the details, and wondered why editors always put all this gloomy and banal daily misery on the front pages of the paper. She deliberated over various possible answers to the question: perhaps local violence was what most interested those readers who loved to whip up feelings of fear and indignation in themselves. Or perhaps readers liked to feel that their town wasn't quite as boring as it seemed, and had just as many incidents as any other. Or perhaps rural dwellers liked to be reminded that they suffered from all the inconveniences of town life without any of its advantages. And of course the final reason, the saddest and eternal truth – that nothing is more entertaining than the misery of others.

21

Back in Newark she had never read the local or national papers. Just opening one was too much of a challenge for her – she was much too afraid of what she might find leaping out at her, that she would come face to face with an all too familiar name or face. Uncomfortably reminded of her previous life, she leafed nervously through the rest of the papers, glancing at the weather forecast and the forthcoming events in the area, fairs, car-boot sales, a small art exhibition in the town hall. She gulped down her water. She was suddenly overcome by a sense of oppression, which was accentuated by a huge shadow that was darkening the square as the sun moved. It was that of Sainte Cecile, a church described as a jewel of Norman Gothic art. Maggie had pretended to ignore it, but now turned to face it.

*

The Brother 900 had been placed in the middle of the ping-pong table, which was itself now in the centre of the veranda, a geometrical symmetry carefully arranged by Frederick. He sat in front of the machine, gathering his thoughts, with the sun behind him. He slid a piece of paper – the whitest thing he had ever seen – into the carriage. One by one he checked the mother-of-pearl keys, now sparkling – dusted and then cleaned with liquid soap. He had even managed to soften a ribbon that had become as dry as hay by holding it over a pan of boiling water. He was now ready to make contact, alone and face to face with the machine. He had probably never opened a book, had always spoken in direct and unadorned language, and had never written anything more complex than an address on the back of

22

a matchbook. *Can you say anything on this machine?* he wondered, without taking his eyes off the keys.

Fred had never found an interlocutor he could respect. *The lie is already in the ear of the listener,* he thought. He had been obsessed with the idea of telling his version of the truth ever since the result of the trial which had obliged him to flee to Europe. Nobody had really tried to understand his evidence, not the psychiatrists, not the lawyers, not his ex-friends, nor any of the other well-intentioned people: everybody just saw him as a monster, and felt entitled to judge him. This machine wouldn't do that, it would take everything on board, the good and the bad, the inadmissible and the unsayable, the unjust and the horrible – because they were all true, that was what was so incredible, these lumps of fact which nobody wanted to accept were all real. If one word followed another, he could select them all himself, with nobody suggesting anything. And nobody forbidding him anything either.

In the beginning was the word; somebody had said that to him long ago. Now, forty years later, he had been offered the opportunity to verify that saying. In the beginning there would certainly be one particular word; all the rest would follow.

He raised his forefinger and hit a light-blue, just visible g, then an i, then looked around for an o, then a v, and, getting bolder, found an a with his little finger, then two ns, with two different fingers, finishing off, with the forefinger again, with an i. He read it through, pleased that he hadn't made any mistakes.

giovanni

23

*

The young Blakes had obtained permission to have lunch together. Belle searched for her brother in the playground, and finally found him under the covered part, with his new classmates. It looked as though he knew them; in fact he was interrogating them.

"I'm hungry," she said.

He followed his sister to a table where they found two plates full of mixed crudités. The refectory was so exactly like the one in Cagnes that they had no comment to make about it.

"We're not far from home," he said, "we could go home for lunch."

"And find Mom with her head in the fridge, wondering what to give us, and Dad in his pyjamas in front of the TV. No thanks."

Warren began to eat, starting with what he liked best, the cucumber, while Belle started with what she liked least, the beetroot. She noticed a blue mark on her brother's eyebrow.

"What's that on your eye?"

"Oh nothing – I was just showing off on the basketball court. What are your classmates like?"

"The girls seem quite cool, not sure about the boys. I had to introduce myself. I…"

Warren didn't listen to the rest, his mind was far away, puzzling over questions that had been bothering him ever since the attack. He had made enquiries and gathered information, not so much about the small-time racketeers, but about others, the ones who might help him turn the predator into prey, the executioner into a victim, just as he had seen it done by so many of

24

his uncles and cousins before him. It was in his blood. He had spent the rest of the morning asking innocuous questions about everybody. Who was that one? What was that one called? Which one is his brother? Then he had struck up acquaintances with some of them, obtaining information without them noticing. He had even taken a few notes to remind himself of the picture he was building up. Bit by bit the accumulation of detail was beginning to make some kind of sense, but only to him.

The one with the limp has a father who's a mechanic, who works in the garage of the father of the one in 3C, who's about to be chucked out. The captain of the basketball team will do anything to get a better mark in maths, and he's friends with the big guy in 2A3 who's in love with the class rep. The class rep is best friends with the motherfucker who took my 10 euros, and his sidekick is scared stiff of the tech teacher, who's married to the daughter of the owner of the office where his father works. The four guys in Terminale B *who always hang out together are organizing the end-of-term show and want the limping guy's sound stuff, the smallest one is good at maths and is the mortal enemy of the shit who hit me.*

The problem had been solved, at least according to his logic, before the pudding came. And Belle hadn't stopped talking.

*

Still sitting on the terrace, reading the guidebook, Maggie ordered a second cup of coffee.

The tympanum is decorated with paintings of the Virgin Mary and the martyrdom of Saint Cecilia, who was beheaded

25

in Rome in 232 AD. The massive wooden doors are carved with representations of work in the fields in the four seasons. The porch is surmounted by a pinnacled double tower.

She could have simply got up and gone over to the church, all of whose details she now knew, walked into the nave, faced the crucifix, spoken to the figure of Christ. She could have prayed and contemplated in the way she used to before meeting Frederick, in the days when he was still called Giovanni. After marrying him, there was never again any question of raising her eyes before a cross, or even of entering a holy place. By kissing Giovanni on the lips, she had spat in the face of Christ. By agreeing to marry the man of her life, she had insulted her God, and her God had a reputation for never forgetting and for liking to be repaid.

"You know, Giovanni, when it's very hot in summer, I like to keep a very light blanket over me," she often used to say to him. "You think you don't need it, but you do, especially at night. Well, believing in God, for me, was that light blanket, and you've taken it away from me."

Now, twenty years later, she was very rarely tempted to re-engage in any sort of dialogue or negotiation with God. She didn't quite know if it was her who had changed or God. In the end she had felt that she no longer needed that light blanket.

*

In a concrete shed next to the stadium, the gymnastics teacher, Mme Barbet, searched the games-equipment cupboard for something for the new girl to wear.

"They didn't tell me I had to bring my gym things."

26

"You weren't to know. Here, try that."

Belle was given a pair of navy-blue boy's shorts. She put them on, tightening the cord. She kept her running shoes on, the same sort as she had been used to wearing in Newark, and pulled on a lemon-yellow vest with the number 4 on it.

"It comes down to my knees."

"I haven't got anything smaller."

Despite her efforts, Belle couldn't prevent her red bra from showing under the vest straps. She hesitated before joining the others.

"It's only girls," said Mme Barbet, who didn't think it was important.

Belle followed her onto the basketball court, where the girls were already practising, looking forward to seeing an American in action. They threw her a ball; she bounced it two or three times on the ground, as she had seen them do, and passed it to the nearest team mate. Belle had never taken any interest in sport, and hardly knew the rules of basketball. So where did it spring from, this grace of a champion, this ease in new situations, this natural gift for hitherto unknown movements? Where did her natural elegance come from? The casual way in which she could put on clothes that didn't suit her and then look fantastic in them? The relaxed way she dealt with situations which others would have found stressful? In her absurd, almost ridiculous outfit, Belle looked superb, right at the centre of the game.

The four tennis players in the distance didn't miss a trick. They stopped their game and came over to grip the netting and gaze at the quivering red bra, which undulated innocently with every one of Belle's movements.

27

*

It was nearly four, and there was no longer any point in Frederick getting out of his dressing gown. It was no longer the symbol of his idleness, it was his new work uniform. Now he could exhibit himself with impunity – untidy and unshaven, trailing around in slippers all day – and soon there would be many more little allowances to be made. He took a few steps out into the garden, walking with the demeanour of the Sun King towards the sound of secateurs coming from behind the neighbouring hedge; he could distinguish the shape of a man pruning his roses. They shook hands through the trellis and examined one another for a moment.

"Roses – they need attention all the time," the man said, to break the silence.

Frederick didn't know what to say, except:

"We're American – we moved in yesterday."

"…Americans?"

"Is that good or bad?"

"Why did you choose France?"

"Me and my family, we travel a lot, because of my job."

This was what Frederick had been working towards. He had come out into the garden with the sole purpose of saying a word, a single word. Since finding the Brother 900, he couldn't wait to introduce the world to the new Frederick Blake.

"So – what's your job?"

"I'm a writer."

"A writer?"

There followed a delicious moment.

"That's fascinating, a writer… Novels, I suppose?"

Fred had anticipated the question:

28

"Oh no, that might come later. For the moment I write history. I've been commissioned to write a book on the Normandy landings, that's why I'm here."

As he spoke, he stood slightly turned away, with an elbow on the fence, and a false air of humility, intoxicated by his new and rapidly inflating status. By introducing himself as a writer, Frederick Blake thought he had solved all his problems. A writer, that made perfect sense, why hadn't he thought of it before? In Cagnes, for example, or even in Paris. Quintiliani would think it was a brilliant idea.

The neighbour looked around for his wife so that he could introduce the new writer neighbour.

"Yes, the landings... You never get tired of hearing about those days. Here in Cholong we're a bit far away from where the main operation was."

"The book will be a sort of homage to our marines," said Fred, to cut the conversation short. "And by the way, my wife and I are going to organize a barbecue, to get to know everyone, so please pass the word around."

"Marines? I thought there were only GIs in the landings."

"I want to write about the whole army, starting with the navy. Anyway, don't forget about the barbecue, eh?"

"I suppose you'll have a chapter about Operation Overlord?"

"?..."

"There were something like seven hundred ships, weren't there?"

"A Friday would be perfect, next week if you like, or the one after, we'll be expecting you."

Fred slipped back towards the veranda. He was beginning to wish that he wrote novels.

29

*

At around five, when school was over, Warren was still seething over the loss of his pocket money. All the things he could have done with the money... Well, what exactly? He could have chewed some gum, read an intergalactic war comic called *Gamefight*, gone to see another American film full of "fuck"s – but what else? As a passport to minor pleasures, the ten euros didn't amount to much, he had to admit that. On the other hand, it meant an enormous amount in terms of humiliation, pain and loss of dignity. After leaving the gates of the *lycée*, Warren mingled with different groups, recognizing some of the faces, getting himself introduced to new ones, shaking hands and making deals with some of the "big ones" from the senior form, the football team especially, who had become local heroes since their victory in the regional league.

Give them what they need most.

Warren, from the vantage point of his fourteen years, had learned one lesson from his elders. To Archimedes' proposition: "Give me a fixed point and a lever, and I will lift up the world", he preferred a variation perfected by his forebears: "Give me some money and a gun, and I will rule the world". It was just a question of time and organization. In order to achieve synergy and increase complementarity, all he needed to do was to know how to listen, discover each person's limits, spot the gaps in their lives, and decide how much to charge for filling them. The more solid the base he could build up, the quicker he would rise to power. The pyramid would build itself and raise him up to the stars.

30

For the moment it was a question of wielding the carrot – the stick would come later. Most of the pupils left the gates, some of them trailing towards the café, a few lingering to wait for the ones who came out at six. Amongst those was a group of seven boys gathered around Warren.

The biggest one needed better marks in maths so as not to repeat the year, but his parents couldn't afford private lessons. The toughest, a winger in the rugby team, would do anything to be friends with Laetitia's brother, who was standing next to Warren. The brother in question would do anything to own the autograph of Paolo Rossi, which was in the possession of Simon from 1B. Simon from 1B was quite willing to surrender it in exchange for help with a personal vendetta against the boy who had targeted Warren. Another one, regarded as the *lycée* oddball, a mostly gentle boy who sometimes suffered from violent explosions, would give anything he had to be included in a group, any group, to be part of a gang, to no longer be the eternal outsider – and Warren was offering him this possibility. And the last two had joined the group for reasons they preferred not to divulge in front of Warren, who couldn't have cared less what they were.

The rugby player knew where the three gangsters always hung out after school – a park, which they regarded as their private territory and to which they controlled access. Less than ten minutes later, the three were on the ground. One had vomited, the other was writhing in pain, and their leader was on his knees, sobbing like a baby. Warren told them to bring a hundred euros the next morning, by 8. The sum would double with each half-day's delay. Terrified of angering him again, they

31

thanked him, keeping their eyes to the ground. Warren could see already that these three would become his most faithful sidekicks if that was what he wanted. Once an enemy had paid homage, you had to allow this escape route.

If Warren hadn't been able to build up the foundation of his enterprise that evening, he would have sorted things out with those three on his own, with just a baseball bat. And he would have explained to anyone who had tried to stop him that life had offered him no other choice.

*

Maggie went into the shop in the avenue de la Gare, picked up a red basket, pushed through the gate and looked for the refrigerated section. She was tempted to buy some escalopes with cream and mushrooms to make a change from her usual cooking. Unlike Frederick, Maggie was one of those people who, when in Rome, did as the Romans did. Having immersed herself in the local press and architecture, she was now prepared to explore local cuisine, and risk the fury of her family at the dinner table. But she did, by reflex, go to the pasta shelves, and studied the no. 5 and no. 7 spaghetti, the green tagliatelle, the penne and a whole range of shells and vermicelli that she had never quite seen the point of. Feeling slightly guilty, she picked up a packet of spaghetti and a tin of peeled tomatoes, in case her menfolk complained. Before heading for the cash desk, she asked a shop girl where she might find peanut butter.

"What?"

32

"Peanut butter. Perhaps I'm not pronouncing it right."

The young woman called the manager, a man in blue overalls.

"Peanut butter," she repeated. "*Peanut butter.*"

"I understood."

Like every morning, this man had been up at six to receive the deliveries and unload them into the storeroom. He had then logged the staff arrivals, motivated his troops and greeted the first customers. In the afternoon he had met two wholesalers, and been to the bank. Between four and six, he had personally rearranged the chocolate and biscuit section and checked the resupply, which hadn't been properly done. In other words, the day had gone smoothly. Until now, when this unknown woman had come in asking for a product he hadn't got.

"Put yourself in my place, madam. I can't stock all the odd things people ask me for. Tequila, surimi, fresh sage, buffalo mozzarella, chutney, peanut butter, God knows what else. It would just rot in the storeroom until it got past its sell-by date."

"I just wondered. So sorry."

Maggie went off to the back of the shop, embarrassed at having created a sense of awkwardness over something that wasn't worth it. The peanut butter wasn't the slightest bit urgent, her son had plenty of time to make fancy sandwiches – she had simply wanted to do something nice for him on the first day of school. She quite understood the manager's point of view. Nothing was more exasperating than tourists with their food fads, and all those others who turned food into some sort of nostalgic icon, or stupid chauvinistic symbol. She had

33

hated the sight of her compatriots in Paris crowding into fast-food outlets, complaining that they couldn't find the sort of food they stuffed themselves with all the rest of the year. She saw it as a sign of terrible disrespect for the country they were visiting, particularly if, as in her case, it was providing her with an asylum.

She thought no more of it, and continued around the shop, filling her basket, stopping at the drinks shelf.

"Peanut butter…"

"And then you wonder why one American in five is obese."

"And Coca-Cola…"

The voices were close by, just behind the stack where Maggie was reaching down for a pack of beer. She couldn't help listening to the hushed conversation between the manager and two of his customers.

"I've got nothing against them, but they certainly make themselves at home wherever they are."

"Of course there were the landings. But we've been invaded ever since!"

"In our day, and for our generation, it was nylon stockings and chewing gum, but what about our children?"

"Mine dresses like them, enjoys the same things, listens to the same music."

"The worst thing is the food they eat. I cook something they like, and all they can think of is to leave the table as quick as they can and rush off to McDonalds."

Maggie felt hurt. By treating her as a typical American, they had cast doubt on all her goodwill and efforts at integration. It was a cruel irony, particularly for somebody who had been cast out of her country and had lost her civic rights.

34

"They've got no taste in anything, that's for sure."

"Barbarians. I know, I've been there."

"And if you tried to settle there," the manager concluded, "just imagine how that would go down!"

Maggie had suffered enough in the past from all the sidelong glances, the muttering behind her back, the general sarcasm when she appeared in public, the wild rumours which were impossible to disprove. This unlucky threesome had unwittingly stirred up all these memories. The paradox was that if they had invited her to join in their conversation, she would have agreed with a lot of what they said.

"And they want to be the masters of the universe?"

Without revealing anything, she went over to the household-goods section, added three bottles of paraffin and a box of matches to her basket, paid at the cash desk and went out.

Outside, the last rays of the sun were disappearing and afternoon was fading into evening. The staff were beginning to feel tired, the customers were hurrying along, everything was as usual on this March evening at six o'clock, the same rituals, the same sleepy atmosphere.

So what was that smell of burning rubber that was just beginning to reach the nostrils of the cashiers?

One of the customers gave a great scream. The manager looked up from his order book and saw a strange curtain of fire undulating over the shop window. An impenetrable curtain of leaping flame began to spread into the shop.

A warehouseman reacted first and called the fire brigade. The customers looked for an emergency exit. The cashiers just disappeared, while the manager, for

35

whom the shop and his life were one and the same thing, stood paralysed, hypnotized by the red-and-gold light dancing before his eyes.

The Cholong-sur-Avre volunteer firemen were unable to save the awnings, the display or the merchandise. In fact nothing was saved from the fire, except a case of slightly bruised Granny Smiths.

*

Belle and her classmates left the *lycée* at the last bell. A few diehards leaned against the gates, cigarette in the lips or mobile in hand, in no hurry to go home, while others rushed off as quickly as they could. She walked some of the way with Estelle and Lina, and then continued on her own along the boulevard Maréchal Foch, without any hesitation about the route. Belle was one of those people who walked with her head high and a light step, curious about everything around her, convinced that the horizon would always be more interesting than the pavement. This attitude summed up her whole personality, this way of always going forwards, confident both in herself and others. She was the opposite of her brother, who would always be marked by the wounds of his childhood; she was able to stay one step ahead of her past, never allowing it to catch up with her, even at the most difficult moments. Nobody except her knew where this strength came from – the sort of strength that is so often lacking in those who have seen their whole lives turned upside down overnight. And even if she was still feeling the tremors from that earthquake, she certainly had no desire for victim status. Instead of wasting energy on regrets, she turned it towards her

36

future development, no matter what problems there were to surmount. And nothing and nobody would stop her.

An old metallic grey Renault 5 drew up alongside her. Inside it, some young people were trying to attract her attention. They were the seniors who, that same afternoon, had been so overcome by the sight of the new girl's red bra. They had been determined to get to know her, to make her welcome and show her the sights.

"No thanks, boys…"

She walked on towards her house, amused by the thought of being picked up on the first day in the school. However, she had no need for reassurance about her charms – they had been there for ever, since the day she was born. Her parents had called her Belle, not realizing how apposite the name would be. So much resonance in such a small word. How were they to know that the name would be a problem in France? At that time neither Maggie nor Fred quite knew where France was.

"Oh, please, please, Miss America!"

They were so insistent that Belle began having doubts about the way home.

"Where do you live?"

"Rue des Favorites."

"It's that way! Jump in, and we'll drop you at your house."

She let herself be persuaded, and climbed into the back. The boys were silent for a moment, surprised at their success. They had expected a refusal, and were thrown by this unexpected turn of events. Perhaps this girl was less shy than the others, a bit more daring?

37

Americans were so advanced in every way, especially when it came to morals. They glanced at each other surreptitiously and allowed themselves to dream.

"Look, boys, we seem to be going the wrong way."

Instead of answering, they bombarded her with questions about her life before Cholong. They were tense compared to her, and filled the silences with random remarks; they sought to demonstrate their coolness and savoir-faire, to show that they were sophisticated men of the world; she was amused by such childishness. The car slowed down at the edge of the forest of Vignolet, by the main road that led towards Brittany.

"Why are we stopping?" she asked.

Night had suddenly fallen. The chatter had been replaced by suspicious silences. Belle once again asked them to take her home. The boys got out and quietly exchanged a few words. With a bit of luck they wouldn't have to try very hard and it would all be like in a film, with a kiss from the new girl, perhaps a few caresses, you never knew, why not. And if it was no good, they could easily play the innocents. Belle was thinking about all the things she had to do when she got home: filling out the forms for the school records, working out her timetable and comparing it with her brother's, labelling all her school books, making a list of what was missing – it would be a long evening. She stood leaning against the car door with her arms crossed, waiting for one of these two cretins to understand that the outing was over. Before giving up, they made a last attempt, and one of them put a cautious hand on Belle's shoulder. She let out an exasperated sigh, picked up a tennis racket from the back seat, and with a perfect forehand smashed the side of the racket on the daring one's nose. The

38

other one, shaken by this sudden and violent gesture, backed away, but was unable to avoid a sort of backhand volley that nearly took off his ear. Once they were on the ground, their faces covered in blood, Belle knelt down to look at them, with the professionalism of a nurse. She had quite recovered her sweet smile and her goodwill towards her fellow man. She got into the car and, turning towards them once more, said:

"Boys, if that's the way you go about it, you're never going to get anywhere with girls."

She drove off towards the main road whistling a Cole Porter tune, then left the car a hundred metres from the Rue des Favorites and walked the rest of the way. She met her mother at the gate coming back at the same time, and helped her carry in the shopping. Warren, arriving at the same time, shut the gate behind them and all three went into the house.

Frederick, who was feeding the dog, with one knee on the ground, wasn't surprised to see his entire family coming in at once. He said:

"So – anything new today?"

As if they had rehearsed it, all three replied in chorus:

"Nothing new."

2

How much is one man worth? What price a human life? To know what one is worth is like knowing the date of one's death. I'm worth twenty million dollars. It's a lot. But much less than I thought. I must be one of the most expensive men in the world. To be so valuable and to live a life as shitty as mine – that's the worst misery. If I had that twenty million dollars, I know what I'd do with it: I'd give the whole thing away in exchange for going back to my previous life, before I was worth that much. The man who blows my head off, what will he do with the money? He'll put it in property and go off to hang out in Barbados for the rest of his life. They all do that.

The irony is that, in my previous life, I sometimes had to take care of someone with a price on his head, like I have today ("take care of" with us means stopping the guy in question from doing any more harm). Liquidation of witnesses wasn't my speciality, I was sidekick to a hitman (a contract killer as outsiders call them) who had been told by my then bosses to whack that snitch Harvey Tucci, for two hundred thousand dollars – unheard of. We had to scratch our heads for weeks to find a way of preventing him from going before a grand jury, and I'm talking about a time when the FBI hadn't quite got the hang of guarding the stool pigeons (we showed the Feds a thing or two, but that's another story). Anyway, the contract on me is a hundred times bigger than that ass Tucci's. Try and imagine for a second what it's like to be exposed to the flower of organized crime, the most determined killers, the greatest professionals, all ready to drop you on any

41

street corner. I should be scared stiff. Fact is, deep down, I'm quite flattered.

"Maggie, make me some tea!"

Fred had shouted loud enough from the veranda to wake Malavita, who gave a little growl and went straight back to sleep. Maggie heard, too, but felt no sense of urgency, and remained slumped in front of the television screen in the bedroom. Fred, irritated by the lack of response, risked losing the thread of his inspiration, and left the typewriter.

"Didn't you hear me?"

Lying back on the bed, annoyed by her husband's intrusion just at the denouement of the soap plot, she paused the cassette.

"Don't play the macho Italian with me, will you?"

"But… I'm working, sweetie…"

Maggie had to suppress her irritation at the word "working", irritation which had been mounting ever since they had arrived in Cholong a month earlier.

"Might we know what it is you're doing with that typewriter?"

"I'm writing."

"Don't fuck with me, Giovanni."

She only used his real name in extreme situations, either very tense or very tender ones. He was going to have to confess to what he had been doing on the veranda from 10 a.m. onwards, bent over a bakelite antique, and explain to them the full urgency of this project which had filled him with such unusual energy and plunged him into such delicious confusion.

"You can make fools of the neighbours if you like, but please spare me and your kids."

42

"I've TOLD you, I'm WRITING, for Christ's sake!"

"You can hardly even read! You couldn't even write down the things you say! The neighbour at number five told me you were hatching something about the Normandy landings! I had to nod like an idiot... The landings? You don't even know who Eisenhower was!"

"Fuck the landings, Maggie. That was just a pretext. I'm writing something else."

"Might I know what?"

"My memoirs."

At that, Maggie realized that all was lost. She had known her husband for ever, and now it seemed he was no longer the man she had known a month ago, the man whose every gesture and intonation she knew by heart, and understood.

And yet Fred wasn't lying. He had, with no regard for chronology, been going back, as the whim took him, over the happiest period of his life, the thirty years he had spent at the heart of the New York Mafia, and then the most painful – the time when he turned government witness. Captain Thomas Quintiliani had, after tracking him for four years, succeeded in cornering clan boss Giovanni Manzoni, and had forced him to testify at a trial which had brought down three of the biggest gang leaders, the *capi* who controlled the East Coast. One of them was Don Mimino, *capo di tutti i capi*, the head of all the "five families" in New York.

There had followed the period of the Witness Protection Programme, "WITSEC", those stinking arrangements that supposedly protected those who had snitched from reprisals. Reliving the most shameful moments of one's existence was no doubt the price anyone would have to pay for embarking on the writing of their

43

memoirs. Fred would have to spell out every letter of every forbidden word: snitching, flipping, ratting out on your friends, condemning the oldest of them to sentences ten times their great ages and a thousand times their life expectancy (Don Mimino had copped three hundred and fifty-one years, a number everyone found perplexing, including Quintiliani). Fred would not duck out of it, he would go right to the end of his confession; that was one thing you could count on – he never did anything by halves. In the days when he was in charge of eliminating troublesome types, he would never leave any identifiable pieces lying around; if he was in charge of protection in some particular district, no shopkeeper was allowed to escape his payoff, not even the man selling umbrellas in the street. The hardest part of the story would be reliving the two years spent preparing for the trial; it had been a period of total paranoia, when he moved hotels every four days, surrounded by agents, and only saw his children once a month. Up until that famous morning when he had held up his hand before all of America and taken the oath.

Before reaching that point, however, he would relive gentler memories, rediscover the best part of his life, the happy days of his youth, his first gun, his baptism of fire and his official reception into the brotherhood of Cosa Nostra. The blessed time when it was all in the future, a time when he would have strangled with his bare hands anyone who had suggested that he would one day be a traitor.

"Quintiliani thinks it's a good idea, being a writer."

Tom Quintiliani, the old enemy who had nonetheless been responsible for the safety of the Blakes for the

44

last six years, had given him the green light. They knew from experience that anyone living under guard would sooner or later attract the attention of the neighbours. Fred would need to justify some kind of sedentary activity to them.

"I thought it was a good idea, until you actually started doing it, you shit!"

The fact was that the whole neighbourhood now knew that an American writer had come to live amongst them in order to write a great masterpiece about the Normandy landings. Being known as the writer's wife gave Maggie no pleasure. On the contrary, she felt that Fred's deception would eventually bring nothing but trouble. Not to mention Belle and Warren who, when filling in their class registration forms, had left blank the space that said "parents' profession". They would have greatly preferred to tell their friends and the whole staff that their father was a model-maker, or the European correspondent of an American fishing magazine, anything that wouldn't arouse any real curiosity. There was no doubt about it – their father's sudden literary vocation was going to cause complications.

"You might have thought of something more discreet," Maggie said.

"Like architect? Like in Cagnes? That was your brilliant idea. People kept asking me how to build swimming pools and pizza ovens."

They had had this conversation a thousand times, and a thousand times they had nearly come to blows. She held Fred responsible, with some justification, for the constant moving, for their inability to settle anywhere. Not content with having exiled them to Europe, Fred had managed to attract attention as soon as they had

45

arrived in Paris. He had always been used to having wads of cash for everyday spending, and then he had decided that the protection programme wasn't giving him enough to live decently. There he was, a top-class witness who had put away the top criminals, forced to live like a third-rate bag-carrier. Never mind. Since Quintiliani refused to increase his allowance, Fred had bought a huge deep freeze on credit, and filled it with luxury items bought with bouncing cheques, which he then resold to the neighbours. (He had managed to pass himself off in the building as a wholesaler in frozen goods who would retail lobsters at ultra-competitive prices.) His little trade had been so unforeseeable, and so unlikely, and so discreetly carried out, that the Feds had only found out about it when the bank started complaining. Tom Quintiliani, the great witness-protection pro, had been able to fend off all threats, head off all possible connections with Mafia circles, and keep the Blake relocation secret, even from some of his own colleagues. He had foreseen everything. Except the comings and goings of shellfish in the Saint Fiacre building at 97 Rue Saint Fiacre, Paris 2.

Tom had been hurt by such an odious betrayal of the protection programme. To take such risks when such exceptional measures had been set in place, when he was the only witness ever to have been relocated to Europe – that showed the full extent of Fred's thoughtlessness and ingratitude. They had had to leave Paris for a small town on the Côte d'Azur. Fred, realizing that it had been a close shave, had finally calmed down.

Three years later, the Blakes had at last managed to blend into the background. In Cagnes, the children had reached their previous scholastic level; Maggie was

46

doing a correspondence course, and Fred was spending his afternoons on the beach, swimming in summer and walking in winter, alone apart from the distant presence of one of Quintiliani's agents. During those long hours of solitude, he had mulled over all the stages that had brought him to this point, those twists and turns of fate which would, he thought, have made a good story. In the evenings he sometimes went down to a bar for a game of cards and a pastis with the locals.

Until the fateful day of the pinochle game.

That evening his card partners began talking about their lives, their small worries, but also their small professional successes: a raise, a free cruise, a promotion. They had had a bit to drink, and began to laugh at Fred the American architect's silence; they started to gently tease him about his apparent idleness – the only things they had seen him build were sandcastles and card houses. Fred had taken all this without flinching, but his silence only encouraged the sarcastic remarks. Late in the evening, pushed to the limits, he had finally cracked. He, Fred, had never had to wait for good marks or raps on the knuckles from his bosses! He had built his own kingdom with his bare hands, and he was the absolute master! He had raised armies! He had made the mighty tremble! And he had loved his life, a life no one could understand, least of all these assholes in this dump of a bar!

After his hurried departure for Normandy, a rumour went round the little quarter of Cagnes-sur-Mer that the American had gone home to get treatment for his nervous troubles.

"Here, Maggie, they'll leave me in peace. They leave writers in peace."

47

At that she left the room, slamming the door, with the firm intention of leaving him in peace until death.

*

Mme Lacarrière, the music teacher, regarded Miss Blake's late arrival in her class as a miracle. Belle, unlike those who regarded her class as an opportunity to finish a maths exercise or read through an essay, took the lesson very seriously and joined in on everyone else's behalf. She was the only one who knew major from minor, or that Bach came before Beethoven, or who could even sing in tune. The tragedy of Mme Lacarrière's twelve-year teaching career had hitherto been that she had never found *the pupil* – the one who would have discovered music through her, who would have continued with the subject, who would have played and composed, and who would have made her role as a teacher, so often put into question, entirely worthwhile.

"I say, Miss Blake…"

All the teachers, disconcerted by the name Belle, preferred to address her as "Miss Blake".

"The *lycée* is organizing an end-of-term concert, with parents and graduates invited. I'm in charge of the choir, which is going to sing Haydn's *Stabat Mater*. I would very much like it if you could join us."

"Out of the question."

"What?"

"You can count me out!"

She had given the same answer to the French teacher, who was putting on a sketch written by the pupils. Ditto to Mme Barbet, who was choreographing a modern dance tableau.

48

"But... Think about it... Your parents will be there, I should think... And the mayor, and the local press..."

"I've thought about it."

Belle got up and walked out of the class, without permission, before the amazed stares of her classmates; she decided to go and work off her rage in the playground. The local press... Just thinking of Quintiliani's reaction made her give an uncharacteristic groan. The witness-protection programme strictly forbade protected families from appearing in any photos or making any public appearances. Belle began to resent those who even suggested that she play any part in this damned end-of-term show.

"You're just being shy, Belle. Appearing in public might help! A lot of people have conquered their shyness by acting in plays."

Her, shy? She had the confidence of a film star! She was as bold as a saloon-bar singer! But she was forced to conceal the real reason for her refusal from those who were urging her to appear on stage: *I'm not just a little idiot waiting to be begged – it's just that I can't show myself anywhere, the United States of America have forbidden me. Apparently I would be risking my life and my family's life, and it'll be like that for as long as I live.*

Still ten minutes till the lunch bell. Belle was getting impatient – she wanted to see Warren. He was the only one she could complain to, he who had long since given up complaining himself about this curse they lived under. She went back into the main building and sat down on the ground, opposite the classroom where her brother was having a history lesson.

Since early childhood, Warren had had an annoying habit of picking and choosing his educational options.

49

By carefully planning for his adult life he had made a certain number of choices, making it possible, in his view, to concentrate only on essentials. For him the only two subjects which deserved a little of his attention were history and geography. The first was out of respect for his origins, the second in order to defend his territory. He had always felt the need to understand how the world worked, and how it had been organized before he was born. Even back in Newark he had been curious about his background, his descent, the history of his history. Where had his family come from and why had it left Europe? How had America become the United States? Why did his Australian cousins have that weird accent? How come the Chinese had built Chinatowns all over the world? Why had the Russians now got their own Mafia? The more answers he could get, the better he would be able to run the empire he intended to reconquer. Other subjects? What other subjects? Grammar was for lawyers, maths was for accountants and gym was for bodyguards.

The year's curriculum included, amongst other things, a brief overview of international relations before the Second World War, and the main events of the War itself throughout Europe. That morning the teacher had described the rise of fascism in Italy and the way in which Mussolini had seized power.

"The march on Rome took place in 1922, and Mussolini took over the government. In 1924, after the assassination of the socialist Matteotti, he became dictator. He installed a totalitarian state in Italy and, dreaming of a colonial empire built on the model of ancient Rome, sent troops off to conquer Ethiopia. When France and Great Britain condemned his African invasions, he drew closer to the German Führer. He

50

supported Franco's troops during the Spanish Civil War. He met with no more opposition until the end of the War. At the same time, in France…"

History continued its march under the bored eyes of twenty pupils more interested in thoughts of the Friday lunch of fried fish. It was even warmer than the day before, one of those days when summer seems to have come early. Concerned with historical accuracy, Warren raised his hand.

"And what do you make of Operation Striptease?"

The word "striptease" at this unexpected moment made the class sit up, wide awake now. All saw it as a splendid and timely intervention – they expected no less from the little new boy who had managed to control boys three times his size.

"What do you mean?"

"You said that Mussolini met with no opposition until the end of the War. What about Operation Striptease?"

The lunch bell rang, but everybody miraculously remained seated. Mr Morvan had no objection to learning something on his own subject from a pupil, and asked Warren to carry on.

"I think I'm right in saying that the Americans planned to land in Sicily by 1943. At the time the CIA knew that the only anti-fascist force in the country was the Mafia. The boss was Don Calogero Vizzini, and he had sworn to kill the *Duce*. The Americans wanted him to take charge of the landings, but to get that to happen they had to get into Lucky Luciano's good books, and he had just been sentenced to fifty years for tax evasion in the toughest prison in the United States."

Warren knew perfectly well what happened next, but he pretended to search his memory. Mr Morvan urged

51

him on; he was both intrigued and amused. Warren wondered if he hadn't gone too far.

"They got him out of prison, put him in the uniform of a US army lieutenant and took him to Sicily in a submarine, with some Secret Service people. There they met Don Calò, who agreed to prepare the ground for landings three months from then."

He had hardly finished talking; several of his classmates rushed out, others asked questions, thrilled that a gangster could have played a part in helping the Allies. Warren claimed not to know any more; he may have had an interest in obscure corners of American history, but he preferred to pass over certain details in silence. When the boys asked him what had become of Luciano, Warren heard another question: could a criminal end up in the history books?

"If you're interested, there are plenty of Internet sites that tell the whole story," he said, as he left the classroom.

Mr Morvan called him back, and waited until the room was empty.

"Is that your father?"

"What do you mean, my father?"

Warren had almost shouted. What on earth had made him talk about the exploits of Luciano himself, his greatest idol after Capone? How many times had Quintiliani exhorted them to avoid sensitive subjects, whatever the circumstances? They had been expressly forbidden to mention the Mafia, or its American affiliate that originated in Sicily, the Cosa Nostra. Just for the sake of showing off in class, Warren had probably condemned his family to take to the road again only a month after their arrival.

52

"I gather your father's a writer, and he's come to Cholong to work on a book about the Second World War? Did he tell you all this?"

The boy grabbed the lifeline that was being held out; his father had saved his bacon. A father who didn't know a single date, not those of the Second World War any more than his children's birthdays, a father who would be incapable of drawing a map of Sicily, or even of being able to say why Luciano was called Lucky. But his status as a self-proclaimed author had pulled his son out of an awkward moment.

"He tells me some things, but I don't remember it all."

"What became of Luciano after that?"

Warren realized that there was no escape.

"He started the great heroin pipeline that still pours into the United States."

*

At the beginning of the afternoon Maggie began gathering her strength to embark on preparations for the barbecue to which Fred had invited the whole neighbourhood. *What better way to get to know them, eh, Maggie? To blend in, get accepted?* She was forced to agree – going out to meet the neighbours would spare them a lot of mistrust and create a good atmosphere. But all the same she was suspicious that what her husband really wanted was to live out his new fantasy in public – the fantasy of being a writer.

"Maggie!" He yelled again from the end of the veranda. "Are you making me that tea, yes or no?"

With his elbows resting on either side of his Brother 900, his chin on his crossed fingers, Fred was pondering

53

the mysteries of the semicolon. He knew about the period and the comma, but the semicolon? How could a sentence both come to an end and carry on at the same time? It was creating a blockage in his mind, this idea of an end that could continue, or an interrupted continuity, or the opposite, or something between the two, who knew? Was there anything in life that corresponded to this idea? Blind fear of death mingling with metaphysical hope? What else? A good cup of tea would have helped him to think. Against all probability, Maggie had decided to humour his demand, but only because she wanted to sneak a look at the pages that he had been covering all day. On the whole Fred's crazes never lasted long and usually vanished as fast as they had appeared; this performance he was enacting to himself was different. Fred decided to try out a semicolon.

To see an enemy croak is much more agreeable than making a new friend; who needs new friends?

On reflection, he found the semicolon so unclear, so ambiguous, that he tried to remove the comma with his Tipp-Ex, without touching the period.

Then he heard Maggie's terrible scream.

He got up, knocking his chair over, and tore into the kitchen, where he found his wife standing, horrified, with the kettle in her hand, staring at a thick gush of water from the tap – a brown and muddy liquid, which spread a graveyard stink into the basin.

*

54

At five o'clock exactly, Maggie completed her list of salads and accompaniments for the barbecue. She only had the coleslaw left to do, and the tureen of ziti, without which no barbecue in Newark was worthy of the name. She stopped for a moment, feeling guilty, looked at her watch, and then glanced over towards the house at number 9, directly opposite theirs. An immobile figure stood silhouetted behind the first-floor window like a papier mâché *trompe l'œil.* She grabbed an aluminium container and filled it with marinated peppers, put a couple of balls of mozzarella in another, and the whole lot into a basket, along with a bottle of red wine, a country loaf, some paper napkins and some knives and forks. She left the house, crossed the road, made a discreet sign to the figure in the window, and went in by the garden entrance. The uninhabited ground floor smelt disused, not having been properly aired by the three new tenants who had moved in at the same time as the Blakes. There was a bedroom for each of them on the first floor, a bathroom with a shower cabinet, a useful laundry room with washer and dryer, and a very large sitting room, which was the centre of operations.

"You must be hungry, boys," she said.

Lieutenants Richard Di Cicco and Vincent Caputo welcomed her with grateful smiles. Neatly dressed in grey suits and blue shirts, they hadn't spoken a single word for the last two hours. The living room, which was entirely given over to the surveillance of the Blake house, was equipped with a listening table, two pairs of 80/20 binoculars set on tripods, a separate telephone for communication with the United States, and several parabolic microphones of varying strength. There were also two armchairs, a camp bed and a trunk with a locked

55

bolt, which contained a machine gun, a telescopic rifle and two hand guns. Richard, woken up by Maggie's arrival, had been sipping cold tea all afternoon, not thinking about anything, apart from his fiancée, who would now, given the time difference, just be arriving at her airfreight control office at Seattle airport. Vincent, on the other hand, had numbed his fingertips playing his video game. And yes, if it encouraged their visitor, yes, of course, they were hungry.

"What goodies have you got in that basket, Maggie?"

She pulled open the container with the peppers, which was on her knees. The boys were suddenly silent, overcome by foolish emotion. The smell of the garlic-laden olive oil on the peppers took them straight back to their native land. Maggie's gesture reminded them of their mothers. Di Cicco and Caputo clung onto such moments in order not to feel entirely orphaned by having accepted this overseas mission. For the last five years, they had had three weeks' rest and recuperation every two months, and the further they were from the next leave, the more miserable was the expression of homesickness in their faces. Di Cicco and Caputo had committed no crime, had done nothing to deserve such an exile and so little prospect of going home for good. To Maggie they were victims rather than spies snooping on her daily life, and she felt it was her duty to nurture them in the way that only a woman could.

"Marinated peppers just the way you like them, with plenty of garlic."

Maggie took care of them as though they were her nearest and dearest, which in a sense they quite literally were; they were never more than thirty steps from the front door, and took it in shifts to watch over them at

56

night. They knew the Blake family better than the Blake family knew themselves. One Blake could have secrets from another Blake, but not from Di Cicco and Caputo, and least of all from Quintiliani, their boss.

They shared the food out and ate in silence.

"Did Quintiliani tell you about the barbecue later?"

"Yes, he liked the idea – he may come by at the end of the evening."

Unlike his agents, Quintiliani was constantly on the move. He went to and fro to Paris, made regular visits to Quantico, the headquarters of the FBI, and sometimes a quick trip to Sicily to coordinate anti-Mafia operations. The Blakes knew nothing about his movements – he would just appear and disappear at moments when they least expected it.

"We should have had a barbecue in Cagnes, got all those nosy people together and got rid of them once and for all," said Di Cicco.

"Try and come too," Maggie said. "I've made ziti and Fred's in charge of the steaks and *salsiccia*."

"You'll have a lot of people, the whole neighbourhood knows about it."

"There'll always be enough for you two – you can count on me."

"Is it still the same olive oil? Can you get it here?" Vincent asked, mopping up the pepper juices.

"I've still got a tin from the little Italian in Antibes."

There was a short silence at the thought of the shop, La Rotonda, in the old town.

"If anyone had ever told me that one day I'd end up in a country where they eat cream," said Richard.

"It's not that it's not good, I've got nothing against it, but my stomach isn't used to it," his colleague added.

57

"In the restaurant yesterday they put it in the soup, then on the escalope and finally on the apple tart."

"Not to mention the butter."

"The butter! *Mannaggia la miseria!*" Vincent exclaimed.

"Butter's not natural, Maggie."

"What do you mean?"

"The human body wasn't made to absorb such fatty substances. Just thinking of that stuff on my stomach lining makes me sweat."

"Try the mozzarella instead of talking rubbish."

Vincent helped himself, but continued on his theme.

"Butter impregnates the tissues, it blocks everything, it hardens, it forms a sediment, it turns your arteries into hockey sticks. Olive oil only touches on your insides and slides through, just leaving its scent."

"Olive oil is in the Bible."

"Don't worry," Maggie said. "I'll go on taking care of you with my home cooking. We'll hold the line against butter and cream."

Following a little ritual established two or three years earlier, Maggie broached the subject of the neighbours. For security reasons, the FBI had the records of almost all the residents of the Rue des Favorites and surrounding streets. Maggie couldn't resist asking questions about one or two of them – she was curious about the lives of the people she passed in the street every day; she wanted to get to know them without having to associate with them. Was it just the curiosity of a busybody? The fact was that no other busybody in the world had such technical expertise at her disposal.

"What's the family at number 12 like?" She asked, pointing a pair of binoculars towards their house.

58

"The mother's a kleptomaniac," Di Cicco said. "She's not allowed into the shopping mall at Evreux. The father's having his third bypass. Nothing much to say about the children, except the little one's going to have to repeat his year."

"Life has been hard for them," she said, with a little sadness in her tone.

Fred, who was in the cellar looking through the window onto the street, could guess at the scene taking place opposite. It drove him mad, seeing his wife being so civil to those two dung beetles, and even feeding them. Despite all these years living alongside one another, those two would never be on the same side as him, and for as long as he lived he would make sure they were reminded of it, and keep them at a good distance.

"Tell them to get fucked, Maggie…"

Malavita, lying amongst her pillows, seemed to be wondering why her master was making such a racket in the basement. Fred was holding an adjustable spanner and experiencing one of those moments when a man finds his virility being put to the test. He had the preoccupied, pouting expression of someone obliged to peer into the engine of a car, or pretending to understand what he is looking at as he gazes at a fuse box. He was poking around the pipes and the water meter, trying to find some explanation to give his wife about the foul water that had been gushing into the kitchen sink. Like many others before him, he had hoped to solve the problem on his own, and thereby perform a small domestic miracle that would earn him the respect of his family. In the same way as one might kick a tyre, he banged the spanner against the pipe, scratched off a bit of rust, and tried to make some sense out of the spaghetti of pipes disappearing into the moss-covered stonework. He considered cooking as an activity to be a lot less degrading than DIY, even though he had spent a lot of time in hardware shops for other reasons – in the past he had found drills, saws and hammers a great deal more useful for destructive rather than constructive purposes. He returned to the kitchen, where Maggie was back at work, spoke the words he had dreaded having to say ("Have we got a number for a plumber?"), and then helped himself to a plate of peppers, which he took away with him to eat on his veranda.

As soon as the children got back from school, Maggie gave them jobs to do: the younger one chopped vegetables, and the older one took charge of the garden, the table setting and general decoration. She was expecting more than thirty people, which was about a third of the number of regular guests at the barbecues in the old days in Newark – one a month, from April to September, and nobody would dream of missing them. On the contrary, there, new faces kept turning up – people who saw an opportunity of getting their foot in the door.

"What do Normans put on their barbecues?" Warren asked.

"I'd say lamb chops," his mother replied. "With potato, radish and *fromage blanc* salad on the side."

"My favourite!" Belle said, as she passed through the kitchen.

"If you tried giving them that, it would be a disaster," said Warren. "We have to give them the sort of American barbecue they expect."

"What's that?"

"American swill. Big fat American swill. We mustn't disappoint them."

"That sounds delicious, my son. Makes me really want to try it."

"What they want is pornographic food."

Maggie stopped dead with her cheese grating and, unable to think of a comeback, forbade him to use that word.

"Mom," Belle said, "your son isn't using the word pornographic in the sense that you think."

"The French are fed up with refinement and healthy eating," Warren continued, "that's all they ever hear about. Steaming, boiled vegetables, grilled fish, fizzy water. We're going to free them from guilt, Mom, we're going to give them fat and sugar – that's what they expect from us. They're going to come and eat here as if they were going to a brothel."

"Watch your language, boy! You wouldn't dare talk like that in front of your father."

"Dad agrees with me. I caught him playing the stupid American in Cagnes, and people were begging for more, he made them feel so clever."

Maggie listened to her son holding forth as she continued to put the final touches to her Tex-Mex potato salad, toss the Caesar salad and drain the ziti before dropping them into the tomato sauce. Warren fished one out and tasted it, still boiling hot, from the giant transparent plastic salad bowl.

"The pasta is perfect, Mom, but it's going to betray us."

"?..."

"They'll realize that we were Italians before we became American."

Fred rolled into the kitchen with an air of abstraction. Warren and Maggie stopped talking. With the same gesture as his son, he picked at the pasta, chewed it carefully, nodded at his wife and asked her where the meat was that he was supposed to be cooking later. Not having chosen it himself, he half-heartedly inspected the merchandise, weighed up a few steaks and examined the mince. The fact was, he had left his study in order to give himself a little time to reflect on a passage he was finding particularly difficult.

The word I hate most in the world is "sorry". Anyone thinks I'm sorry, I shoot them on sight. The day I took the oath and shopped everyone, all those lawyers and judges would like to have seen me bow my head and beg for forgiveness. They're worse than priests, those little judges. Me, regret anything about my life? If it was all to do again, I'd do everything – EVERYTHING – the same, just avoiding a couple of traps at the end. Apparently, for the French, regretting is when the painter repaints his canvas. Well, let's say that's what I've done, I've covered a masterpiece with a new layer and that's all the regretting I'm going to do. A guy who regrets his life – he's worse than an immigrant who doesn't feel any more at home in his new country than in the one he's left behind. Me, I'll never be at home again with my brother criminals, and honest folk won't make space for me anywhere. Believe me, regrets are worse than anything.

Fred was getting in a muddle with his definition of regrets. He could see how clumsily he was expressing himself, but was unable to change anything. The parallel with his life was all too clear.

"I'll start the grill about six," he said. "I've got to finish my chapter."

62

He went solemnly back to his veranda, which, tonight, would not be open to the public.

"His chapter? What does he mean, exactly?" asked Warren.

"No idea," Maggie replied, "but just for the sake of the survival of the human race, it might be better if no one ever found out."

*

Three hours later, the whole neighbourhood was crammed into the garden – no one would have missed it for anything. They came prepared to stay up late, taking advantage of the unseasonable warm weather, perfect for a garden party. And they had made sartorial efforts too, the women in white or brightly coloured summer dresses, the men opting for linen and short-sleeved shirts. The buffet was laid out at the end of the garden, loaded with salads and different sauces, with two little casks of red and white wine at each end. A few yards away, people gathered around the still-cold barbecue, impatient to see it lit. Maggie welcomed her guests with open arms, pointed them towards a pile of plates, answered all the expected questions with prepared answers, and expressed her great happiness to be living in this Normandy which had been so dear to the memory of her parents. She showed them round the house, introduced each new arrival to her two children, whose job it was to divide the guests between them and entertain them as much as possible. She accepted all invitations, including the suggestion that she join an association to protest against a local building threat. She took down a great many telephone numbers. How

63

could they possibly have guessed that soon their private lives would have no secrets for Maggie?

Belle attracted more attention than her brother. Belle always attracted attention – from men and women, young and old, even from those who were suspicious of beauty, who had perhaps suffered from it at some time. She was good at reversing the roles, and playing at being the guest, allowing herself to be served, answering questions. All Belle had to do was be herself, and imagine that she was addressing her public. Warren, on the other hand, cornered by a small group of adults, was undergoing a grilling. Ever since he had arrived in France, he had been asked a million questions about American life and American culture, to such an extent that he had made a list of the most frequently asked: What's a home run? What's a quarterback? Do people really grill marshmallows over a flame? Do all the sinks have grinders? What does trick or treat mean? etc. Some of the questions were surprising, some not, and, according to his mood, he would either deny the clichés or reinforce them. That evening, against expectation, nobody asked him to play this role – on the contrary, he found himself obliged to listen to the interminable stories of those who had been over there. Starting with a neighbour who had just come back from a visit to New York for the marathon.

"After the shopping, I went to have dinner at the Old Homestead Steak House, at the corner of 56th and 9th Avenue. Do you know it?"

Warren had, between the ages of nought and six, been to New York fewer than a dozen times, to a skating rink or a toy shop, and of course that visit to the hospital to consult an asthma specialist, but he had certainly never

64

been to a restaurant, and definitely not this steak house he'd never heard of. So he didn't answer, but the man wasn't waiting for an answer.

"There were just two dishes on the menu – steak weighing less than a pound, and steak weighing more than a pound. I was being asked to choose between a piece of meat of less than five hundred grams, and one of more than five hundred grams. I was pretty hungry after running about twenty-six miles, but still I just took the 'less than a pound' and I had to leave half of that."

The other man leaped on the story in order to cap it with his own, about a lunch in Orlando.

"I had just got in from the airport, I was on my own, I went into a pizzeria and saw on the menu that there are three sizes – large, small and medium. Well, I was so hungry that I ordered the large one. The waiter asked how many people it was for and I said I was alone. He burst out laughing. Take a small one, he said, you won't finish it. And he was right – it was like the wheel of a truck!"

Warren smiled, exasperated at not being able to answer back. The size of the dishes, that was all they remembered about his country. Just to confirm this, the third man brought them back to New York, to Grand Central Station.

"They told me the seafood there was wonderful. I went to John Fancy's, which I'd been told was the best fish restaurant in town. Terribly disappointing – totally dull, you find much better seafood at the Taverne d'Evreux. I went to the station to catch a train to Boston, where I was supposed to meet my company's sales manager. It was one o'clock, I had an hour until my train, so I wandered around below ground in the huge station and

65

chanced on the Oyster Bar. Oysters as big as steaks! The shells were like ashtrays! I never saw such a thing! And in a station! Warren, do you know the Oyster Bar?"

Warren was tempted to say what was in his mind: "I was eight years old when my family was hounded out of the United States of America." He was finding it less and less bearable to be treated like a future case of obesity with an IQ lower than that of an oyster in the Oyster Bar, someone ready to sacrifice everything to the God of the dollar, an uncultivated being who felt entitled to rule over the rest of the world. He longed to tell them how much he missed his childhood home, the neighbourhood, his local friends and the star-spangled flag which his father had trampled upon all those years ago. Warren found himself caught in a strange paradox: he was moved to tears by the American national anthem while simultaneously imagining himself building a Mafia state within the state, and then settling various problems that politicians could not deal with, and – who knows? – eventually getting himself invited to the White House.

To escape from this conversation, Warren found himself reduced to joining the others in awaiting the only event capable of causing a diversion – the arrival of his father. But the great man was biding his time, shut away on the veranda with the blinds down. Maggie felt her temper rising. Fred had left her to do all the work, and the barbecue wasn't even lit. Only the guests understood his absence, knowing as they did that writers, whether American or not, always planned their entrances carefully.

They were all wrong.

Fred Blake, in the pose of The Thinker, was rereading, deeply moved, a paragraph that he had struggled with

66

for several hours. He now felt so close to those memories that the need to recount them had made him completely forget that forty-five people were waiting impatiently to meet him.

In 1931 my grandfather drove one of the two hundred Cadillacs chartered by the legendary Vito Genovese to follow his wife's funeral procession. In 1957 my father, Cesare Manzoni, was summoned, along with one hundred and seven capi *from all over the country for the Apalachin meeting, which ended in a manhunt. Quite frankly, was I really going to grow up strumming guitars with the hippies? Could you see me in front of the jig-borers in a cardboard factory? Was I about to start keeping my retirement coupons in a shoebox? Was I going to rebel against tradition and become an honest man just to enrage my father? No, I joined the family firm, and what's more I did it of my own free will, nobody forced me, I was proud to. "You only have one life," Uncle Paulie had said when he gave me my first gun. I know now that he was wrong: you can have a second one. I just hope he can't see me from wherever he is, sad fucker that I've become.*

At that precise moment, he was no longer acting a writer and playing to the gallery; he now felt that he had completed the very first stage of a job that might make sense of everything he had been through, everything he had suffered, and made others suffer.

"Go and see what your fucking father's doing!"

Belle ran up to the veranda, where she found Fred sitting still and silent, bent over the typewriter. For a moment she thought he was dead.

"Dad, we're waiting for you. Are you going to light the barbecue, or what?"

67

He emerged from his trance, and drew his daughter to him, hugging her in his arms. Writing that last page had drained him, and left him vulnerable, and for the first time in ages he drew a curious kind of comfort from the embrace of such innocence. They emerged, Fred beaming, with his arm around his proud daughter, and all heads turned towards them. He greeted his guests, apologized for being late, and said a few words to put everybody at their ease. He went over to the barbecue, where he was given a glass of Bordeaux, which he sipped delicately as he prepared the fire, surrounded by a handful of men there to lend their support. In three quarters of an hour, all the meats would be cooked and the rush would start.

Word had spread throughout the whole neighbourhood, and the freeloaders kept on coming – it was beginning to feel like a village fête. Lieutenants Di Cicco and Caputo rang Quintiliani on his mobile before taking any private initiative. The boss was on his way up the motorway from Paris and swore he'd be there within the half-hour. Meanwhile he instructed them to go over and join the gathering. So they abandoned their observation post and mingled with the guests – nobody paid any attention to them. In order to blend in, Richard grabbed a plate and started to eat, without the slightest embarrassment.

"Are we allowed to do that?"

"If you hang around like an idiot with your arms dangling, you're bound to get spotted."

The argument was carried and Vincent elbowed his way towards the ziti.

Malavita, too, was tempted to make an appearance. She was curious about all the noise that was reaching her through the basement window. She appeared to

68

think for a moment, sitting up, her eyes wide open, her tongue hanging out. But then she decided after all to go back to sleep, because all that noise could only mean something disagreeable.

The rest of the evening might have carried on in a peaceful and happy atmosphere, with nothing to disrupt it, if Fred hadn't suddenly started having regrets. About everything.

Five characters, all male, stood in a semicircle around the fire, their eyes fixed on the coals, which were refusing to light, despite the dry weather, despite the sophisticated equipment and all the efforts of the master of the house, who was, after all, an old hand when it came to barbecues.

"That's not the way to do it… You need more kindling, Mr Blake, you've put the coal on too soon."

The speaker had a cap on his head and a beer in his hand. He lived two doors away, his wife had brought an olive loaf, and his children were running around the buffet screaming. Fred gave him a cold smile. Beside him the bachelor who ran the travel agency in the middle of the town took up the ball:

"That's not the way to do it. I never use coal at all, I do it like an open fire – it takes longer, but you get much better embers."

"That's not the way to do it," added an eminent local councillor. "You're using firelighters – they're poisonous, and that's no joke. And anyway, you can see it doesn't even work."

Without realizing it, Fred was proving a universal truth, which goes like this: as soon as one idiot tries to light a fire somewhere, four others will gather round to tell him how to do it.

69

"We won't be eating that sausage before tomorrow at this rate," the last one said, laughing, and he couldn't resist adding: "You'll never get anywhere with those bellows – I use an old hairdryer."

Fred paused for a beat, rubbing his eyebrows, in the grip of a violent and mounting rage. At the most unexpected moments, Giovanni Manzoni, the worst man on earth, took over the body of Fred Blake, artist and local curiosity. When one of the five guys gathered around the fire took it upon himself to suggest that only a bit of white spirit could rescue things, Fred imagined him on his knees begging for mercy. And not just mercy – he was begging to be finished off, released from his pain. Giovanni had been in such situations several times in his life, and he could never forget the very particular moan of a man begging to be killed: a sort of long wail, rather like that of the professional mourning women in Sicily, a song whose notes he could pick out from thousands of others. It wouldn't have taken him more than five minutes to make this one sing that song – this big relaxed fellow with his arms crossed, standing only inches away, unaware of the fate being prepared for him. The local councillor, for his part, was suffering excruciating torture, crouched in his underwear inside a freezer, like Cassidy, the Irish boss of the fishmongers' union in New York. The local councillor was doing less well than Cassidy, who, with his head wedged against a pile of chicken breasts, had banged on the inside of the freezer for a good two hours before dying and finally ending the long wait for Corrado Motta and Giovanni, who had passed the time by playing cards on the lid of the freezer.

70

The man with the cap, unaware of the terrible tortures Fred was planning for him, continued:

"It'll never take, there must be some old ash in there."

Fred delved far back into the past: he had been twenty-two when his boss had ordered him to make an example of Lou Pedone, a negotiator for the "five families", who had allowed the Chinese triads to set up shop on Canal Street in exchange for a big wad of drug money. To carry out the vendetta, and in order to set an example, Giovanni had shown quite exceptional powers of imagination: Lou's head was found floating in the aquarium of the Silver Pagoda restaurant, on the corner of Mott and Canal. And the most extraordinary thing was that it took several hours for the customers to notice the glassy stare coming from inside the aquarium. Fred, who was now beginning to lose it and had started lighting hundreds of matches under scrunched-up paper, could see the man's head in the aquarium, with his ridiculous hat floating on the surface. But the ordeal was not over: another man, hitherto silent, grabbed the bellows and took over the whole situation without even consulting Fred, who had already had his virility cast into doubt that afternoon. This time it took a superhuman effort not to grab the miserable man by the hair, press his face onto the grill and stick a kebab skewer through one ear and out the other side.

"Well, well, Mr Blake, you're probably better at stringing together sentences than making fires. One can't be good at everything."

A few steps away, Warren, still trapped in the conversation about American cooking, was asked a question on a subject he had never even thought about.

71

"So, what makes a genuine hamburger?"

"A genuine hamburger? What do you mean?"

"There must be an original recipe. Do you have to have ketchup? Pickles? Lettuce? Onions? Does the meat always have to be grilled? Do you bite into it, or do you open it up and use a knife and fork? What do you think?"

Warren didn't think anything, but said what came into his head.

"A true hamburger is fatty if you want it fatty, huge if you want a blowout, full of ketchup if you're not worried about diabetes, you put onions on if you don't mind your breath stinking and mix mustard in with the ketchup if you like the colour it makes, plus a salad leaf for the sake of irony. And if you feel like it you can add cheese, grilled bacon, lobster claws and marshmallows, and it'll be genuine American hamburger, because – us Americans, that's what we're like."

Maggie, for her part, was acting her role admirably; this barbecue was nothing compared to some of the summit conferences she had had to organize on Fred's orders. Everything went through the wives, who passed the invitation on to their husbands and all concerned. A barbecue at the Manzonis was nothing less than a Mafia summit with chops on the side. Decisions were taken there that Maggie preferred not to know about. Twice she had even welcomed Don Mimino himself, the *capo di tutti i capi*, who never moved unless there was a war between the families. That afternoon there could be no problems, everything would have to take place according to a gentle ritual in an open and friendly atmosphere. She had to be more than just diplomatic, she had to use her sixth sense, keeping an eye on

72

everything and making sure the men were able to carry out their business discreetly, business which might include sealing one of their own men's fate in a block of concrete. What could possibly worry her now, so many years later, here in the midst of these French guests who were so amused by their lapses in taste?

Meanwhile the coals had finally caught, putting an end to the sarcastic remarks. The steaks were cooking alongside the sausages, giving out such an appetising smell that the guests started gathering in larger and larger numbers, plates in hands, around the barbecue. Fred was gradually beginning to relax, happy to have lit his fire, despite all the bad will around him. The man with the hat had had a narrow escape; without knowing it he had been within a whisker of a death so hideous that it would have made the peaceful town of Cholong famous. He was even one of the first to taste the meat, and couldn't resist one more piece of advice:

"It's good, Monsieur Blake, but perhaps you should have waited until the embers were hotter before putting on the steaks."

Fred had no choice now – the man with the stupid hat would have to die immediately and in front of everyone.

In New Jersey, the man with the stupid hat would not have survived more than two weeks, he would have been taught to hold his tongue from earliest childhood, or he would have had it cut off with a razor-sharp switchblade – the operation wouldn't have taken a minute. In New Jersey, faced with real bad men of the Giovanni Manzoni kind, the man with the stupid hat would have bitten back all his sly comments, and would have long since given up looking over his neighbour's shoulder purely in order to make tiresome suggestions. In New Jersey, if you had the answers to everything, you had to prove it on the spot, and idle commentators were a rare breed. Giovanni Manzoni grabbed a poker leaning against the grill, clutched it tightly, and waited for the man in the stupid hat to turn round so that he would see death coming as he was being hit full in the face.

And too bad if Fred brought everything down around him, if by killing this man he put his family in danger, too bad if he went back to prison for life. Too bad if, once in prison, his anonymity only lasted twenty-four hours and Don Mimino gave orders to liquidate him. Too bad if the whole Manzoni story got back into the headlines and if Maggie, Belle and Warren didn't survive the shame and the vengeance. The death and ruin of a family were as nothing compared to Fred's irresistible urge to silence for ever the man in the stupid hat.

Just at this precise moment a gentle hand landed on Fred's shoulder. He turned round, ready to hit anyone who stopped the attack.

Quintiliani had arrived. He was upright, strong and reassuring, with the look of a priest. He had seen Fred's temper rising, and it was something only he could control. He knew very well how to deal with that sort of rage – in fact some of his FBI colleagues saw it as his special gift. For Tommaso Quintiliani, it was not so much a gift as a matter of dealing with ancient demons. In the days when he had hung out with his gang of friends on Mulberry Street, a man's life was only worth what could be found in his pockets. If he hadn't been drawn into the ranks of the FBI by some innate good conscience, he would have joined those of the Cosa Nostra with the same steely determination.

74

"Give me a drink, Fred."

Fred heaved a sigh of relief. The ghost of Giovanni Manzoni vanished like a bad dream and Frederick Blake, the American writer living in Normandy, reappeared.

"Come and try the sangria, Tom," he said, dropping the poker.

*

The party had dragged on and Maggie was in bed, yawning, ready to drop off to sleep as soon as her head touched the pillow. Fred took his pyjamas off the chair by the bed, put them on, lay down next to his wife, kissed her on the forehead and switched off the bedside light. After a moment of silence, he gazed up at the ceiling and said:

"Thanks, Livia."

He only used her real name when he felt he owed her. Within that thanks, there was a long unspoken sentence that went like this: *Thank you for not leaving me, despite everything you've been through, because you know that without you I wouldn't last long, and thank you too for...* lots of other things that he would rather not say out loud – saying thank you was, on the whole, beyond his strength. He sensed her dropping off to sleep, waited for a moment, and then got out of bed, put on his dressing gown, and crept down to the veranda like a burglar. All the exhaustion of the day had melted away. He sat down in front of the typewriter, turned on the light and reread the last lines of his chapter.

How I miss the town where I was born and where I won't die. I miss it all, the streets, the nights, my freedom, those

75

friends who would cheerfully kiss you warmly on both cheeks one evening and just as happily put a bullet in your eye the next day. Yes, I can't understand why I even miss that lot. All I had to do was help myself, everything belonged to me. We were kings, and Newark was our kingdom.

3

The plumber had twice put off the appointment and Maggie had finally persuaded him, practically on her knees, to come by that morning. However, that same morning her long-awaited appointment in Evreux was finally confirmed. Fred was fed up at the thought of having to deal with a plumber on his own, and took refuge in the veranda.

"Leave the door open – it would be so stupid to miss him," she said, as she left the house.

So he kept an ear out for the doorbell, and returned to his notes, which would eventually form a complete plan of the second, third and fourth chapters of his memoirs. They went roughly like this:

2.   *The "*sciuscià*" years.*
– My four years working with Jimmy.
– The greyhound stadium.
– The Schultz haulage company.
– The Pearl Street vegetable market.
– Profits reinvested in excavation business.
Description of people I worked with at the time: Curtis Brown, Ron Mayfield, the Pastroni brothers.

3.   *The "*a faticare*" years*
– The front company, Excavation Works and Partners, and its subsidiaries.
– The local girls at Bonito Square.

77

– The trip to Miami (non-interference pact and consequences).
Plus: Little Paulie, Mishka, Amedeo Sampiero.

4.   The Family years.
– Meeting Livia.
– Don Mimino.
– The Esteban contract.
– Loss of the East End.
Plus: Romana Marini, Ettore Junior, Cheap J.

He was in his stride now and felt ready to press on to the next chapters, but just then the doorbell rang, cutting him off in full flow – another reason to hate the miserable workman waiting behind the door. Fred began to miss the good old days, when he had been the hero of the New Jersey building unions. By bending and intimidating the biggest businesses in the area to fall in with his family's interests, Giovanni Manzoni had unintentionally advanced those of various unions, one of which was the plumbers'. As a result bathroom fittings and general upkeep at the Manzoni home in Newark were henceforth maintained to a standard worthy of the White House.

He let in a tall, rather portly man in threadbare jeans and a bleached sweatshirt, who set off to inspect the kitchen, leaving a trail of plaster dust behind him. Didier Fourcade could always, by a careful calculation of factors, assess the limits of a new client's technical knowledge.

"The lady said something about a problem with dirty water?"

Fred had to turn on several taps in order to convince him.

"Well, you're not the only ones round here."

78

"What is it?"

"How long's it been like this?"

"Five or six weeks."

"Some of the ones I've seen, it's been four or five months."

"What is it?"

The man turned on the kitchen tap and let the brown water gush out.

"Can I see the cellar?"

Fred had dreaded hearing what he then heard as soon as the man set eyes on the pipes: a low whistle of horror, which said everything that could be said about the gravity of the situation, the amount of work needed, the irresponsibility of the owners, the danger involved in not taking action, the astronomical sums this action would cost and the general disastrousness of the situation. This low sound had been a part of his training, a moaning blood-curdling whistle, repeated if necessary. The client, racked with fear and guilt, would go to any lengths not to hear it again. For Didier Fourcade, this sound represented his monthly paycheque, a better car, his daughter's education.

The trouble was, Fred didn't like it when people tried to scare him. If he had one single gift, it was the ability to resist intimidation. Trying to frighten him was like trying to bite a rabid dog, or scratch a mad cat, or hit a fighting bear. And once he had been provoked, he feared neither humiliation, pain or even death.

"So what about this filthy water, then?" he said. His patience was running out.

"What about it, what about it... What can I tell you? It could be lots of things. See the state of these pipes? Completely rusty. You've let them go."

79

"We only moved in two months ago!"

"Then you'd better complain to the previous owners, they've let the pipes get into this state, look at that…"

"What's got to be done?"

"My poor fellow! It all needs redoing. This plumbing must be more than a hundred years old."

"Is that why the water's that colour?"

"Might be. Or it might be coming from outside, but that wouldn't be my job."

Fred would have settled for very little, one hopeful word, one sincere smile, even an unkept promise. Anything rather than this abuse of power in the face of a helpless victim. Fred recognized that language all too well.

"So what are you going to do?" he said, in a last appeal to the plumber's goodwill.

"Well, I can't do much at the moment. I came because your lady seemed to be in trouble, but you can't say it's an emergency. I've got two jobs on at the moment, and they're a bit of a way away. And there's a flooding at Villers, they're waiting for me, can't be everywhere at once. Can't do everything myself."

"…"

"Make another appointment. See about it with my wife – she deals with all that. That'll give you time to decide with yours whether you want to get things done properly here."

He had done the main part of his job: you create anxiety, and then you walk away. Didier Fourcade planned to leave the unhappy man to himself, expecting any minute to hear those frantic pleas which always came as music to his ears. He started up the stairs, but Fred Blake, or rather Giovanni Manzoni this time, stopped

80

him by slamming the cellar door, and reached for a hammer from the work bench.

*

During the ten o'clock break, bunches of children played as children do, full of long-pent-up energy, letting out long-repressed yells, excited by the sun and the prospect of the summer holidays. The little ones played at war, the bolder ones at love; the older ones, busy with their mobile phones, arranged their social lives. The noisy playground teemed with this vibrant mixture, and nobody, not even the teacher on duty, was the slightest bit suspicious about the curious gathering that was taking place in a corner of the playground shelter.

About ten boys of all ages were waiting patiently in front of a bench, sitting in a row along the white games line. Warren sat alone on the bench, his arms stretched along the back, with a rather tired and yet thoughtful expression. The only boy standing was the plaintiff, his arms crossed, gazing at the ground. The others waited their turn, listening to their comrade's complaints, as he chose his words with a mixture of embarrassment and concentration. He was only thirteen and had not yet learned how to complain, at least not like this.

"I tried to do well at first. I don't mind maths, and I even had quite good marks at the beginning of the year, but the teacher left, and then the new one came…"

Warren, slightly annoyed by the noise coming from the playground, sighed quietly, still paying attention. He nodded to the boy, encouraging him to continue.

81

"He hated me straight away. The others will tell you that's true. I was the punchbag for that creep. He'd put on a special nasty smile when he told me to come up to the blackboard... And scribbles in the margins to humiliate me... He once gave me two out of twenty, and he put: *could do better*, but with a question mark for me, not like for the others. And lots of other stuff like that, just to humiliate me. I've got them, I can show you!"

Warren waved off this suggestion.

"Dunno what he's got against me... I must remind him of someone... I even asked him once; I wanted to sort things out. And he punished me! He gave me twenty exercises to do over the weekend! Twenty! Stinking bastard! My mother even went to see him, so that he could explain, and the creep pretended there was nothing wrong. He twisted my mother round his little finger! And who do you think she's going to believe, him or me? So I really worked hard, kept my mouth shut, even when he insulted me... And then at the last class meeting he blew me up. You should have seen my mother's face when she saw the report... 'We suggest he repeats the year'... I'm not going to start the third year again because of that prick!"

The words choked in his throat, with the cracked voice of innocence brought down by cruel injustice.

"I can see you're telling the truth," Warren said. "But I don't see what I can do for you. What exactly do you want?"

"If I have to stay down, I'm going to kill myself. I'll never get over it. It's just too unfair. I want him to change his mind, and agree to let me go into fourth, that's all I ask. Just for him to change his mind, that's all."

Warren raised his arms helplessly.

82

"Do you realize what you're asking? He's a teacher!"

"I know. And I'm ready to make some sacrifices. I demand justice, do you understand?"

"Yes, I understand."

"Help me, Warren."

And he bowed his head in allegiance.

After a moment's thought, Warren said:

"We're quite far into the term, but I'll see what I can do. Don't go out for the next few days, except to come to school, spend your spare time with your family. I'll deal with the rest."

The boy clenched his fists, holding back a gesture of triumph, beaming.

"Next!" shouted Warren.

A little boy with glasses got up and stood at the exact same spot as the previous one.

"What's your name?"

"Kevin, 2B."

"You wanted to see me?"

"Someone's stolen the money my mother puts aside in the cupboard. I know who it was – it was my best friend. My parents think it's me. He says it wasn't him. My dad doesn't want to quarrel with his family, he says I'm a coward and I made it up. But I know it's true. I can't leave it like that."

*

The writer's wife. Maggie might have acquired a taste for the title if she hadn't for so long been known as the gangster's wife, married to the head of a family, a mafioso – Giovanni Manzoni, that snitch Giovanni Manzoni. After being married to all that, there was no

83

way she could embark on a new role, especially that of a writer's wife. What made her incandescent with fury was the odious way Fred thought that he could somehow redeem himself by listing his crimes in black and white. Could there be any more perverse method of clearing one's conscience? Nor could she understand the relish with which he shut himself away on that stinking veranda, when, unlike the rest of his gang of thugs, he had never previously had any interests beyond his own position in the hierarchy at the heart of the Cosa Nostra. Some of the others liked fishing or sport, others bred dogs or tried to lose weight at the Turkish baths. Not him. His only hobby was finding new business ventures, new schemes to enable him to fleece new victims, who would only realize what had happened once it was too late. Why now, so many years later, did he have to feel this urge to shut himself away for eight hours at a time in front of a rotten old typewriter? Was he trying to give a new and cynical definition to the whole concept of confession? Or did he just want to relive his old battles, and make some claim to immortality? It was as though he was experiencing some sort of nostalgia for evil. He was dipping his pen into the darkness of his soul – and that ink would surely never run dry. The neighbourhood might have accepted this imposture without a murmur, but Maggie was not taken in.

She was ten minutes early, and parked the car in Rue Jules Guesde in Evreux. She lit a cigarette to pass the time, and tried to imagine how her husband would have jeered at her if she hadn't lied to him about where she was going.

"What are you trying to prove, my dear Maggie? You want to salve your conscience? Redeem your sins? Well,

84

take it from me, I don't regret anything, and if things had gone differently we'd still be back there, with the family and all my team, and we'd be living just the same life, the life we were born to, instead of mouldering here, so let me tell you, it's a real hoot to see you playing the holy saint."

The Eure branch of Secours Populaire is looking for a volunteer for administrative work. A small ad in *Le Clairon de Cholong.* All that was needed was a bit of time, a bit of practical ability and plenty of motivation. Maggie felt she had been chosen. It couldn't have been the hand of God – she had turned her face away from him, and no longer believed in his mercy any more than in his anger. The ways of the Lord remained impenetrable, and the cruel pleasure He seemed to take in muddying the issues no longer fascinated her, it just left her weary. To have to always remain a mystery to human eyes must inevitably affect your motives. So much gravity, transcendence, excessiveness, eternity, and all in the most profound silence – well, Maggie just gave up. The truth was, and she could hardly bring herself to confess it, God simply didn't move her the way he used to – the crown of thorns, the Sistine Chapel, the White Lady, the great church organs, none of them had the effect on her that they had in the past. Nowadays the only real miracle which touched her heart could be summed up in one word, a word which covered so many others: solidarity. The phenomenon, for her, had made itself felt in the most mundane of circumstances, walking past a television set, or coming out of a film, or turning on the radio for some background noise. The first time had been seeing a television ad for an insurance company, which fearlessly proclaimed its high moral

85

status and its mission to help others to a crescendo of violins; Maggie had felt tears welling up, idiotic real tears in front of the screen; she felt a fool for having been so taken in, but every time the ad came on, the same thing happened. And then there was the Hollywood film where the young man finds his true love thanks to the benevolence of an anonymous crowd; there, too, obvious strings were being pulled, and she wasn't proud of her reaction, but all the same it did make her heart beat faster. Every time she heard something on the news about groups of individuals uniting to help another, she felt a personal call. Gradually she began to analyse these feelings, identifying their components, until they mingled together: team spirit, appeals to public generosity, defence against injustice, empathy for one's fellow man, the list could go on for ever – it didn't matter, the most important thing was to serve the high ideal of solidarity, in so far as one could. It would be a way of showing God that men could do the job for themselves.

They asked her to wait in a little room with a low table covered in magazines. Before she had made the appointment, Quintiliani had expressed some reservations.

"A charity? It's a deserving cause, Maggie, but pretty risky. You never know, there might be stuff in the papers, photos, I don't know…"

"I'll be careful."

"What does Frederick think?"

"I haven't mentioned it to him."

"I'll see, but I can't promise anything. You know your name and picture must never appear."

All the same, Quint thought Maggie's initiative was a good one: she was integrating herself into the community at the same time as keeping herself busy – both activities encouraged by the protection programme. A few days later, he gave his permission in principle, for a trial period. Then they'd see.

Maggie had another, more personal reason for wanting to make herself useful to the poor. Destiny was offering her an opportunity, many years later, to pay a sort of tribute to her own modest origins, to revisit them, after having tried to deny them during the time of the Manzoni excesses. Unlike Giovanni, who was a natural son of the Cosa Nostra, brought up in the tradition of ever increasing financial profit, Livia had been born into a family of workers, who had remained workers all their lives. Now that she was nearly fifty, she began to remember her early youth again – it felt as though she had only just left that part of the East Side where, before they began killing one another, people from all over the world formed a single nation – the immigrants. She wondered why particular images would come back to her from her unconscious mind, like that of the moment on Friday nights when her father would hand his pay packet to her mother, a white envelope that had to keep them going until the following Friday. She remembered, too, how she had envied her elder sisters going off to their typing courses; Livia would follow as soon as she was old enough. She remembered almost hour by hour the long anxious night after her older brother, who worked for a chimney sweep, had stolen a box of jewellery from an apartment full of marble fireplaces. In the early morning, her father had gone down to the police station to fetch him, and young Aldo's career as a burglar had ended. She also remembered, too, the sad day when she had been bitten by a dog in a smart area of town; there had been

87

no way of getting compensation, or even complaining. Above all, she remembered her mother, who had lived in daily fear of some new danger threatening her children, and her father, who had always kept his head down whenever there was an incident in the area. Livia had married Giovanni in order to escape from all that.

They asked her to come into the office. The interview took less than ten minutes.

"When could you start?"

"Straight away."

*

Al Capone always said: "You can get much further with a kind word and a gun than you can with a kind word alone." That simple phrase, to me, explains the continuing success throughout the ages of the phenomenon that is the Mafia.

Fred stopped typing in order to think for a moment, but the last sentence didn't seem to lead on to anything else. What could he add to something that said so much in so few words? He supposed that was what was called literature. How could he explain to his future readers the magic he saw in these words? All his friends in Newark would have got the message straight away. By quoting Capone, Fred saw how useful it was to have his words backed up by the thoughts of a master. He threw the carriage back, and tackled a new paragraph.

A few yards away, Belle stood stark naked in front of the bathroom mirror, with a seamstress's tape measure, measuring the vital statistics of her splendid body, without missing out a single curve. She knew the basic measurements – chest, waist, hips, her body mass index

88

(20), the hip/waist ratio (7), but she was curious about the rest: wrist, neck, calf, foot, forehead, thickness of arms, shoulder blade to armpit, distance between nipples and so on. Each time she found she was the perfect size.

Maggie, in the kitchen, was busy at the stove. *Pasta aglio e olio.* It was all very well spaghetti with garlic and oil being her speciality – neither her husband nor her children would contemplate a plate of pasta without tomato sauce. Fred just fiddled with his food when he was faced with sophisticated meat or herb sauces, or luxuries like truffles or lobster – what he called fancy food. Pasta, for him, meant red sauce, nothing else.

"You know I don't like that," he said as he passed through the kitchen.

Maggie was at that crucial moment when you toss the spaghetti and garlic together in the pan before adding the fresh oil.

"What makes you think it's for you? If you want tomato sauce, you can make some this afternoon, between chapters."

"So who's this pasta for?"

"Those two poor guys who are so far from home. Unlike us, they've done nothing to deserve it."

He shrugged and asked what she was punishing him for. Maggie didn't deign to answer and, covering the dish with foil, left the house and went over to join Richard di Cicco and Vincent Caputo, who were playing cards, with earphones on their heads.

"Someone ringing my house?" she said.

"Yes – it's someone called Cyril," said Vincent. "I don't want to spill the beans, but he's been ringing Belle every day for a week."

89

"Never heard of him. Let me know if she falls in love, boys."

Instead of just suffering their presence, Maggie had learned to make use of the FBI. Quite apart from the true respect she felt for Quintiliani and his men, she now felt she was being protected rather than spied upon. Only heads of state normally got such treatment. No need to look through her husband's pockets or go through her children's drawers. The FBI could deal with it, and Maggie was safe from all the dangers that wives and mothers live in dread of. She wasn't proud of it, but neither was she ashamed of having made use of the high-tech methods at the Bureau's disposal to sort out her domestic problems. Fred's little acts of cowardice, Warren's little side-slips, Belle's little secrets – Richard and Vincent kept her informed.

"I've made you some *pasta aglio e olio*," Vincent.

"Even my wife can't make it like you do, don't know why, maybe she puts the garlic in too soon."

"How is she?"

"She's missing me, she says."

This conversation highlighted the absurdity of their situation. Did those three have nothing better to do in life than hang out in an empty house in the middle of a little Norman town thousands of miles from home? Overcome with silent homesickness, they ate the pasta with little appetite. Maggie's presence was even more of a comfort than her cooking – just the fact of a woman looking after them, sometimes like a wife, sometimes like a sister. They knew she was sincere, and that trust had, over the years, become a valuable link between them. She would appear, and a wave of comfort and reassurance would help them to forget another silent

90

day of boredom and regrets. Maggie helped them to hold fast and to continue to test the limits of their professional dedication.

In order to understand how Caputo and Di Cicco had come to be there, you had to go back six years, to the end of the "five families trial" as it had been known in the papers. The Manzonis had been taken in hand by the Witness Protection Programme. They had become the Blakes, a little family with no story, who had left the Big Apple to go and live in Cedar City, Utah, a town of eighteen thousand inhabitants, in mountainous country in the middle of a desert. The town ticked the right boxes – it was small enough not to have a crime syndicate but large enough to allow a modicum of anonymity. The Blakes settled into a residential area of rich retirees, and began adjusting to their new life of idleness as best as they could. It was a strange environment, a sort of imprisonment, but completely relaxing after all those stressful months. The shopping was delivered to the house, they signed up to correspondence courses, and they lived like recluses, ignored by the neighbours. Quintiliani had stuck with Fred since the end of the trial. He had been picked for his incredible tenacity as well as his Italian origins, and he had chosen Di Cicco and Caputo as his lieutenants for the same reasons. All three knew the Manzonis better than anyone, having followed them and listened in on them unceasingly for the four years until Giovanni was finally trapped. The Witness Protection Programme had set two goals to establish their reinsertion into society: schools for the children in Cedar City, and a job for Maggie, as long as their identity remained secret.

But they hadn't reckoned on the determination of the five families who controlled the state of New York.

91

Each one of them had lost two or three men by the end of the trial, not to mention Don Mimino himself, whose battalion of lawyers had been reduced to silence in the face of the mass of evidence supplied by Giovanni Manzoni as to his position as supreme leader of the Cosa Nostra: Brutus had plunged the knife into Caesar's heart. And so the five families had got together – money no object; anyone who could supply the smallest accurate piece of news about the whereabouts of the Manzonis could claim a reward of twenty million dollars. After this announcement had been made, squads of four or five hitmen had been assembled for the sole purpose of tracking down the Manzonis. Enzo Fossataro, who was acting boss of the families until Don Mimino named his successor, had made deals with the families in Miami, Seattle, Canada and California, and had created a countrywide network of information and surveillance. He had even, quite openly, placed barely disguised advertisements in several perfectly respectable papers which, although not in the pay of the Mafia, were happy to see the resulting huge increase in their circulation, thanks to this real-life soap opera. Very soon a phenomenon was observed that had hitherto been unknown on American soil: death squads, or "crime teams" as the *Post* called them, began methodically dividing up the country, visiting the smallest townships, asking questions in the seediest bars, leaving tips and mobile-phone numbers wherever they went. The FBI itself had never come across such a thorough investigation, or such huge means deployed for a single operation. The trackers followed a recognized sequence: two men went into a bar, and put a newspaper on the bar, folded to show a

92

photo of the four Manzonis posing with smiles on their faces at the Newark grand parade. The men didn't need to say anything, or ask any questions; this simple crumpled piece of newspaper was the instant equivalent of a cheque for twenty million dollars.

If the five families were prepared to spend their last cent on the operation, it was because for them it was more a question of survival than one of vengeance. The blow struck by the Manzoni trial had cracked the very foundations of the organization, and threatened a total collapse in the medium term. If one grass could cause such damage, and then escape with the blessing of the court and spend the rest of his days in protected surveillance at the taxpayer's expense, the whole concept of the family, and therefore the Mafia itself, was thrown into question. In the past you joined in blood, and could only leave in blood. And there was Manzoni trampling on his oath of allegiance, lounging in front of the TV, probably with his ass in a swimming pool. Many centuries of secrets and traditions would perish in the face of this image. The Cosa Nostra could not allow its reputation to be sullied like this, leaving the prospect of a disrupted future. In order to prove that it still existed, and intended to stick around, it would have to strike hard: the very survival of the families now depended on the deaths of the Manzonis. And so it happened that the so-called crime teams spread out like a generalized cancer to every urban centre in the country, to remote towns, criss-crossing areas hitherto unvisited even by the census-takers. No local or national authority could prevent this deployment – wandering around a town with a folded newspaper couldn't be said to break any known law. Almost six months after the Blakes' arrival in

93

Cedar City, strangers had been spotted sitting down in a coffee shop in Oldbush, forty-five miles away, holding the famous newspaper and striking up conversations with bored locals.

"Fuck it, can't anything be done to stop them? You're the FBI, Quintiliani, for Christ's sake!"

"Keep calm, Fred."

"I know them better than you do! And what's more, if I was in their place, and I found the son of a bitch who had done what I've done, I know exactly how I'd take pleasure in wasting him. I'd probably already be behind that door, about to bust us both. I trained some of these guys myself! Your fucking protection programme... Six months, that's all it's taken them!"

"..."

"Get me out of here. It's your duty, you promised."

"There's only one solution."

"Plastic surgery?"

"That wouldn't work."

"Then what? Pretend I'm dead? They'd never swallow that."

Fred was right and Quintiliani knew it better than anyone. Ever since Hollywood had taken over that particular script, there was no point faking an informer's death. The Cosa Nostra would only believe in Fred's death once they were faced with a bullet-riddled body.

"You'll have to leave the United States," Quint said.

"Tell me you're joking."

"We're living in a cynical age, Giovanni. The whole country is now following this soap opera. It's called *How Long Will the Manzonis Survive*? It's a reality show, and three hundred million viewers are watching."

"And the end of the show is the end of my family?"

94

"Europe, Giovanni. Does that word mean anything to you?"

"Europe?"

"Exceptional procedure. Don Mimino's guys can cover this country, but they can't do the whole world. They haven't got any connections in Europe except in Italy. You'll be safe there."

"You're ready to cross the ocean to save my skin?"

"If it was up to me, I'd ring one of those crime-team guys right now, I'd do it for free, just to see a scumbag like you with a bullet in your head, which is what you deserve. But the trouble is, you dying would give organized crime twenty years of impunity, with all that crap about *omertà* and sealed lips. On the other hand, if you get out of it, I'll get a list of rats long enough to keep me going for the rest of my life and it'll pay for my retirement. It's what Washington wants. Your survival is worth a lot to us, and you're much more useful to me living than dead."

"If that's the only solution, then I want to go to Italy."

"Out of the question."

"It would give some sense to us being in exile, otherwise there's none. Let me get to know the land of my fathers, I've never been there. I promised Livia the day we got married that we'd go there some day. Her grandparents were from Caserta, mine from Ginostra. They say it's the most beautiful place in the world."

"Sicily? Great idea! You might just as well walk around Little Italy with a placard saying HAVING FUN IN JAIL, DON MIMINO?"

"Let me see Italy before I die."

"If I land you in Sicily, you'll be made into *spezzatini* in less than ten minutes. Think of your family."

95

"…"

"Talk to Maggie, we've still got a little time."

"I know what she'll say. It'll be Paris, Paris, Paris – all women dream about it."

"To be quite honest, I've spoken to my bosses, and Paris is one possibility. Also Oslo, Brussels, Cadiz, with a slight preference for Brussels – don't ask."

A few weeks later the Blakes were installed in a quiet building in the second *arrondissement* in Paris. Once past the first few months of adaptation – new life, new country, new language – they got into an everyday routine which, without really satisfying them, helped them get over the trauma of the move. That was before Fred began single-handedly undermining the protection programme.

*

Both arms in plaster, suspended by straps to the bed-head, Didier Fourcade, the most sought-after plumber in Cholong, watched his wife sleeping, not daring to wake her. The pain had subsided thanks to powerful analgesics.

He relived that morning in his mind – how, suffering the pains of hell, he had pushed open the double doors of the Morseuil clinic with his shoulder. He had presented himself at the admissions desk, with his arms in the air, like a flightless bird, torn between pain, shame and terror.

"I've broken my arms."

"Both of them?"

"It hurts, for God's sake!"

An hour later, in plaster up to the elbows, he had had to face questions from an intern who walked around him without taking his eyes off the X-rays of his arms.

"Fell down the stairs?…"

96

"I fell two floors on a building site."

"It's odd, you can see points of impact, as though you had been hit... Like hammer blows on the wrists and the arms. Look, there."

Didier Fourcade turned away to avoid another wave of nausea. He was still haunted by the sound of his own screams as that psychopath had hammered at his wrists. He was taken home in an ambulance, the straps were fixed up and he was put to bed, all under the amazed stare of his wife, Martine.

They had got married twenty years earlier, surprised at wanting to commit to each other only three months after meeting, but unable to prevent themselves. However, as though to counterbalance the euphoria of the first years, the boredom of daily life had caught up with them sooner than with most couples. Both had begun to daydream, imagining a third party entering the equation, imagining a secret life, and in the end living one for real. As long as their relationship was not poisoned by bitterness and reproaches, they had remained together, nostalgic for their lost happiness, and always ready to believe that some small incident might bring it all back. Once their physical passion had died down, they had become prudish with one another: she would lock the bathroom door, turn her back to him when doing up her bra and draw away when she touched his skin by mistake. And for the last few years both had begun to wonder whether any couple could survive this physical distance.

Now he found himself watching her sleeping, just as he had done in those early days and nights, and the sight made him thank God for having sent him Martine. She was resting at last, emotionally exhausted by this

97

accident which had forced her to perform some unusual new gestures: she had had to spoon-feed Didier, wipe his mouth, hold a glass to his lips. She, who had never smoked, had to light a cigarette, put it between his lips, and take it out to tap off the ash. How could he have had such a terrible fall? Supposing he had fallen head first? She had often dreamed of freedom, but now she had been offered a glimpse of life without him and the prospect had filled her with horror.

Didier had bravely faced all that day's ordeals, until now, at 2.17 a.m., when a horrible itch started up, down by his perineum. About ten years earlier he had picked up a skin complaint from God knows where. The doctors had assured him that the tests were negative, that it was benign, that there was nothing much you could do about it, that it would go the same way it had come, but still, at least once a day and according to ambient heat and sweatiness, he was seized by an irresistible urge to scratch between his thighs. It was an awkward place to have to scratch during the day, and he often disappeared into toilets, or went back to his car for no obvious reason, returning almost at once. The only way to achieve some form of relief was to wash the affected spot with dermatological soap, dry it thoroughly and, in times of great heat, sprinkle it with talcum powder to soak up the sweat and alleviate the friction. He, a plumber, had insisted on installing a bidet in their bathroom, to the great surprise of his wife, who couldn't see the point of it, and indeed he was the only one who used it (it was a masterpiece of a bidet, ultramodern – he had put his all into it). In the morning, when he got up, the jet of water soothed the patches which he had scratched during the night, sometimes drawing blood. On summer evenings,

98

he would sometimes take a hip bath as a late reward for a sweaty day spent resisting the temptation to put his hands between his legs in public.

By 2.23, the itch had become intolerable. He had felt it coming on since the early evening, but he had held out, like a soldier biting his belt to make pain disappear. His battle with himself had taken the form of cold sweats, a strange shuddering of the shoulders – his whole body was begging for release so forcefully that eventually all qualms were swept aside. He woke his wife, calling her name, begging her to scratch his "perineum" – a word he had learned at the dermatologist's, along with "scrotum". Such precision made her hesitate; Didier always called a cat a cat, and a tomcat a tomcat, even with people he hardly knew. This word "perineum" was hiding something, it was a roundabout way of saying "scratch my balls", but still, she was in no doubt about the urgency of the situation. Guided by her husband, she slipped her hand into his underpants, then under his testicles, a gesture she hadn't made for a long time. He yelled when she found the crucial spot:

"Harder!"

The happiness he felt at that precise moment was so intense that it was soon followed by an erection.

*

To distract themselves from the insomnia that they were both suffering from, Fred and Maggie watched a film late into the night. She was feeling guilty at lying about the *Secours Populaire*, at having secrets from this monster of a husband whom she still loved despite everything. He, for his part, felt unable to give an honest answer to

99

the question she had asked when she came home: "How did it go with the plumber?"

What he had done to Didier Fourcade could well imperil the fragile equilibrium that she and Quintiliani were trying to maintain. Fred did not even dare to imagine what would happen if the Feds got wind of the story. However, he didn't have much to fear on that front – the fear he had seen in Fourcade's eyes guaranteed total silence about what had happened in the cellar. Fred knew how to arouse that sort of terror and how to fine-tune it as one might twiddle the knobs on a radio to find the perfect frequency.

At 3.06, Maggie had finally dropped off on her husband's shoulder. When the film ended, he carefully put her head back on the pillow without waking her, and went down to the veranda. For the first time in his life he was creating rather than destroying, and even if the result turned out to be laughable in the eyes of the world, he felt that he had at last begun to exist.

In a future chapter I will show myself to be the worst scumbag who ever lived on this earth. I will spare myself nothing, I will tell as much as I can, without trying to salve my conscience or try and get forgiven. You will be given a clear picture of what a bastard I was. However, in this chapter I'd rather tell you just the opposite. If you take the trouble to look, you'll find I'm a decent man..

I don't like making people suffer unnecessarily – all my sadistic impulses can easily be satisfied by necessary suffering.

I have never despised those who feared me.

I have never wished for someone's death (the problem was always solved before that).

100

I always face up to the truth.

I would rather be the person hitting than the one taking pleasure in watching me get hit.

As long as you don't contradict me, you can expect nothing but good things from me.

I have avenged wrongs done to others, even if I always demand a quid pro quo.

When I controlled my territory, there was never a single aggression or mugging incident in the street – people were able to live and sleep in peace.

If I have lived "in contempt of the law", only those that the law itself holds in contempt will not judge me.

When I was the boss, I never lied to anyone. That's the privilege of the powerful.

I respect enemies who play according to the same rules as me.

I have never tried to find a scapegoat: I am responsible for EVERYTHING.

Fred removed the paper from the carriage, refrained from rereading it, saving that moment for later, and went back up to Maggie, where he went to sleep with all the satisfaction of a job well done.

101

4

The writer Frederick Blake had recently begun going to bed at that time of the night when insomniacs wake up, children have their nightmares and lovers separate. After long hours of work, only the prospect of reading his work through when he woke up would send him to bed. In the past his nocturnal activities varied according to the times and the seasons; sometimes he would be busy calling in debts, or loosening tongues or dealing with those individuals for whom the bell was tolling. All that effort couldn't have been conceivable without the prospect of leisure. Here the choice was between ferocious card games, women who were up for anything and, most frequently, terrifying drinking sessions from which you emerged walking stiffly, your back ramrod straight, before going home. Since turning government witness Fred had been sleeping like a hunted animal, a sleep filled with painful dreams that left him in a zombie-like state for the whole of the following day. Now his encounter with the Brother 900 had revived a forgotten taste for nocturnal activity. The excitement he felt when faced with a blank page brought back some of those past thrills, and revived that particular intensity. At such moments, he couldn't have cared less whether the words he was writing would ever be read, or if the sentences would even survive him.

Belle and Warren, on their way to school, tried to picture the scene.

"He's been shut up on that fucking veranda for three months now, he said. His whole vocabulary must get used up several times a day."

"Are you saying our father's illiterate…"

"Our father's an average American, and you've forgotten what that means. It means someone who speaks to be understood, not to make sentences. Someone who doesn't go in for formalities. Someone who is, who has, who says and who does, and doesn't need any other verbs. He doesn't dine out or have lunch – he just eats. The past for him is whatever happened before the present, and the future is what comes after – why complicate things? Have you ever tried to list the range of things your father is able to express just by using the word 'fuck'?"

"No obscenities please."

"It means much more than any obscenity. 'Fuck', coming from him, can mean 'God, how did I get into this mess', or 'That guy is going to have to pay for this one day', or even just 'I love this film'. Why should someone like that ever feel the need to write?"

"Well, I like the fact that Dad's busy, it does him good, and it means he leaves us alone."

"Well, I find it painful to contemplate. Try and imagine him, at night, on that veranda, with his fat fingers battling with that crappy pre-war typewriter. And when I say 'his fat fingers', it's probably just one single forefinger doing all the work, click, click, click, with a good ten seconds between each click."

He was wrong about this. Fred used both his forefingers. The left one did everything up to t, g and b, the right one from y, h and n – a fair distribution, except when it came to annoying words like "regrets", which he

104

typed entirely with the left finger. Slight calluses were beginning to form at the ends of the fingers. He was settling into the job.

As his children walked to school, Fred, in his deepest sleep, dreamed that he was driving his garden tractor in the garden of the Newark house. Oddly, he was mowing the lawn just while his daughter was having her first communion; she was waiting for her father to come and cut the cake, a giant cube covered with red roses, with a drawing of a chalice and two candles with golden flames and the words *God Bless Belle* written in red icing. In front of the red-brick *palazzo*, dozens of smartly dressed figures had poured out of haphazardly parked Cadillacs, a well-fed lot, the wives with little veils over their faces, the men with carnations in their buttonholes; all of them were now becoming impatient, waiting for Giovanni to deign to get of that fucking tractor and come and cut his daughter's cake – was this really the right moment to mow the lawn? Belle and Livia were becoming more and more embarrassed, and making excuses to the company, but Giovanni hadn't noticed anything and continued to parade up and down on his machine, entertaining himself by spraying newly mown grass on the ladies' dresses. He was laughing, not noticing the murmuring in the ranks, and that this lack of respect was beginning to worry them. He hadn't even bothered to dress for the occasion, and was wearing sneakers, brown nylon trousers and a white anorak with a hardware store's insignia on the back. The guests were gathering together, beginning to react, and threatening figures began to approach the tractor. A telephone rang somewhere, very close by. But where?

105

Fred groaned as he woke from this nightmare, waving his arms around nervously. The telephone didn't stop ringing. He groped for the receiver on his bedside table.

"Frederick?"

"?..."

"Whalberg. Hope I didn't wake you up, it must be about eleven in the morning where you are."

"It's fine, it's fine," Fred grunted, not sure if this was a continuation of the dream.

"I'm in Washington, this call is safe. Quintiliani isn't listening."

"Elijah? Is that really you?"

"Yes, Frederick."

"Congratulations on your election. I followed it from here. It's always been a dream for you, the Senate, you used to talk about back in the Butchers' Union days."

"That's all so long ago," the other replied, embarrassed at being reminded of those times.

"I hear you're a special adviser to the President."

"Yeah well, I've been invited to the White House from time to time, but just for social gatherings. Tell me about you, Frederick. France, eh?"

"There are some good things about it, but I don't feel at home. 'There's no place like home', like it says in the *Wizard of Oz*."

"What do you do all day?"

"Not much."

"I hear you're... writing."

"?..."

"..."

"It's a way of passing the time."

"Memoirs were mentioned."

106

"That's a big word."

"Frederick, I think it's great. I'm sure you'll do it very well. How far have you got?"

"A few pages, odd bits and pieces."

"And are you telling... the whole story?"

"How could I tell it all? If I want to be believed, I'd better steer clear of the truth, otherwise they'll say I'm just a fantasist."

"So you want people to read it."

"Well, I'm not thinking about publication, that would be a bit ambitious. At least, not yet."

"Frederick... this conversation is worrying me..."

"Don't worry, Elijah, the only real names I'm using are the dead ones. And I've changed some of details about the business with the Pan Am freight and the refrigerated trucks, you can sleep easy on that one."

"..."

"I don't want to lose the only friends I've got left, Elijah. As long as I'm being pampered by the FBI, and as long as they're keeping me safe at the taxpayer's expense, why would I go looking for trouble?"

"I understand."

"If the vets decide to come over for a millionth commemoration at Omaha Beach, come along with them and we can shoot the breeze."

"Great idea."

Fred hung up, feeling rather smug. His reputation as a writer was beginning to reach the Senate, government departments, the White House even. Uncle Sam was going to hear about him.

*

107

Warren lay stretched out on a bench, one which nobody ever challenged him for, jotting down passing thoughts in a notebook. It was 3rd June, and a wind of freedom was blowing through the school; the younger children hung about the playground, the older ones were at home revising; some sprawled on the grass playing doctors and nurses, others took over the sporting facilities for wild games of football or tennis. But according to time-honoured tradition, the most motivated amongst them devoted all their energies to the end-of-year show.

The town of Cholong-sur-Avre had, since time began, observed the feast of Saint John; in addition to the purely local festivities, a big funfair was always set up on the Place de la Libération over the weekend closest to 21st June. The school administration used the occasion to invite parents along to a big end-of-term show produced by their offspring, and everybody always made a special effort to turn up for the event. The great spectacle began with a choral concert, which was followed by a sketch put on by the members of the theatre workshop, and ended, or had done for the last two or three years, with the showing of a video film made by the sixth-form pupils. Any good idea was welcomed, all talents put to use, and those who wanted to express themselves without having to go on stage helped edit the now famous *Jules Vallès Gazette*, the school magazine. Here you could find the essays which had received the top marks that year, articles written by volunteers, games, puzzles, riddles invented by the children, and two pages of strip cartoons that had been polished up by the art teacher. People who had hitherto felt shy or inhibited found that they could express themselves

108

here, and each year, a few new talents emerged from the ranks. And this was where they were hoping to catch Warren.

"Write something for us in English. Just a few funny lines that everyone can understand, or a simple play on words – whatever you feel like."

A play on words... As if any of these Cholong brats, let alone their English teachers, even with all those diplomas, had the faintest idea about what constituted New Jersey humour! That combination of cynicism and mockery honed by fist fights and punches in the jaw, against a background of urban misery. Nothing like life in Cholong! That kind of American humour was the only thing those outcasts really possessed, their only source of pride and dignity. In Newark a good comeback could save you from a knife in the ribs, or at least soften the pain of the knife. That kind of humour didn't come from reading the classics – it had itself been the inspiration for the classics. A good dose of irony, a dash of euphemism, a splash of nonsense, a little understatement, and the joke was complete, but to make that particular joke you had to have been hungry and afraid, to have trailed in the gutters and taken some knocks. And, like a bullet that misses its target, a badly timed comeback would turn out, more often than not, to be fatal.

Feeling short of inspiration, Warren lay on his bench and searched his memory. His mind wandered back to Newark, to an uncle or aunt's house, a house full of people, which somehow didn't feel entirely welcoming, despite all the smiles.

It's probably a wedding, or some other happy celebration. There are cousins in little suits and little dresses. Warren doesn't mingle with them – he prefers

109

the company of the adults, especially those who are friends of the father he so worships. He's a million miles from suspecting their activities, but already he admires their stature, the way they hold up their heads, their gigantic corpulence. They all hang out together, laughing and mocking each other, like the overgrown schoolboys that they are. Warren already feels that he's one of them. He creeps towards them without showing himself, so as to listen to their conversation, and perhaps overhear some secrets. He lets himself be forgotten, sliding between the furniture. He doesn't go too near the centre, where a strange man is holding court, much older and thinner than the others, with white hair and a little hat on his head. If it wasn't for the little hat, he might be quite frightening. Judging from the way his father is addressing the old man, lowering his voice, Warren realizes that this is someone important. So that's him, the great Don Mimino, who is spoken of in respectful tones by even the biggest bosses. Warren is torn between fear and admiration, and he listens – they're talking about opera. His father, like the others, sometimes listens to opera. Some evenings it even brings a tear to his eyes. It must be the Italian language that does it. Don Mimino is asking what's on at the Metropolitan Opera in New York. They reply:

"You wouldn't like it, Don Mimino, they're showing *Boris Godunov*, it's by a Russian."

And Don Mimino, sharp as a razor, retorts:

"*Boris Godunov*? If it's good enough for you, it's good enough for me."

And all the men burst out laughing.

There was a sudden brainstorm in the mind of the five-year-old boy. Godunov – good enough. The words

110

had been changed and a new meaning had been invented, and all with the speed of light. Warren had experienced an almost physical sensation before the perfection of this brilliant interlocking of thought and words, along with a sudden beautiful and violent realization of his own intelligence. He had caught and understood the joke and it had been a sort of coming of age for him, this fusion of word and irony burning into his brain, causing an intense feeling of pleasure. There was no need to hide behind the sofa any more; Warren emerged to take his place with the men. His view of the little thin man with the white hair had changed in a single moment: Don Mimino had, with just that one phrase, shut everybody up, and once more proved his enduring sharpness of mind, once again reconfirming his position as boss of bosses. There was no doubt about it, once you had such a weapon you were more or less invincible. For Warren nothing was ever the same again: he could no longer ignore the power words had to conquer and ensnare. He fully intended to learn for himself this art of summing the world up in two or three short sentences, giving it a meaning so as, in the end, to put it all in perspective.

Years later, this perspective had enabled him to overcome the traumatic events surrounding his exile, by sheltering him behind a rampart of irony – this was his way of remaining a true New Yorker.

Now, with his notebook in hand, slumped on his bench, this "good enough" joke seemed a little laborious, but just good enough to fob off on that stupid magazine. The teachers would congratulate him on a tour de force, and he would probably claim authorship. After all, who would dare to challenge that?

111

*

Fred walked upstream along the Avre, pulling his feet out of sticky ankle-deep mud at each step. On the opposite bank a fly fisherman, standing ramrod-straight in a green waterproof, waved over to him. Fred took no notice and continued on his way, his face whipped by brambles, one hand on his heart; he was out of breath, unfit after so many months of sedentary life. On the pretext of a change of air and to get away from the veranda for a bit, Fred had obtained permission from Di Cicco to go for a walk in the woods. The agent had watched with a sarcastic expression as he set off in rubber boots and parka to discover the Norman countryside for the first time. Fred would have happily passed on this expedition – the thought of going into the woods held no thrill for him. In Newark, his rare rural outings had usually ended up by a hole in the ground six feet long and nine feet deep, most often with the purpose of burying a blood-soaked body that was no longer in any condition to do the digging itself. Giovanni and an acolyte would then patiently get on with the task, with spade and pickaxe, chatting to pass the time, both keenly looking forward to a bourbon back at the nightclub.

Faced with an impenetrable thicket, he left the river bank and decided, still grumbling to himself, to cut across a field of wheat. Although from an early age he had learned all there was to know about living off the wild fruits of the urban jungle, nobody had ever taught him patience and humility in the face of the natural world. Fred had always known how to reap without sowing, and to draw milk without feeding any cattle. Worried about getting lost, he now followed the local

112

road for a good half a mile before coming to the sign he had been looking for: CARTEIX FRANCE, CHOLONG WORKS, WORKS STAFF ENTRANCE.

It was a new sign, quite small and already dirty, despite its colour, chosen to blend with the mud. Two tarmac paths had been built to allow access to the parking ground, one for the trucks, the other for the employees, and there was a sixteen-foot-high fence around the whole building, preventing all access to outsiders – Fred wondered who could possibly want any access. At the top of the main building, you could see the logo of the Carteix fertilizer company – a white oval following the shape of a C.

While trying to solve the problem of the malfunctions in his plumbing, Fred had shown patience, curiosity and real dedication, and he had been thrilled to discover these qualities within himself. The plumber Didier Fourcade's unfortunate visit had been a challenge: he became determined to find out the truth about the tainted water supply. In the past, when Giovanni Manzoni had wanted answers, he would get them without necessarily having to resort to unnecessary violence. There were plenty of other possible methods, and you could always think of new ones; it was only the result that counted. How could he now accept the thought that things were being concealed from him? Of course he couldn't, not with a Mafia past like his, during which he had often had to keep the most painful secrets. Not after having got to know the inner workings of the FBI. Not after having himself become a state secret. Not after having single-handedly stirred up anxiety in the intimate circles revolving around the White House. Who, nowadays, would dare keep from him the truth about a mystery as opaque as this murky water gushing out of his taps? Fred had enquired among the neighbours, who had all agreed that the problems with the water coincided with the arrival of the Carteix factory, and at first he had questioned this theory. Maggie had gone to the town hall, which had in turn sent her on to other plumbers who all knew about the problem, but not how to solve it. She asked Quintiliani to find out about the water refinery: nothing there, it was brand new and top quality. Fred had become exasperated by all this inertia surrounding his water problem, and he had become determined to find, if not a culprit, at least some rational explanation. It was quite unbearable, the way he kept coming up against a brick wall each time he demanded explanations, and this feeling that he was speaking to hollow institutions, empty offices, agencies that just bounced you back and forth between them. This bureaucratic manner of just telling you to fuck off was driving him mad.

The local inhabitants in his area, who had suffered from the same insulting behaviour from the authorities, had drawn up a dossier of the steps they had taken so far. Even worse than the water, which often had the smell and texture of liquid manure, some of them had suffered various health problems, migraines and gastric troubles, and had formed a protest group. After several petitions, one of which had been addressed to the Ministry of the Environment, they had managed to extract, after long months of claims, the right to get the water analysed by the departmental laboratory, which found high levels of "coliform bacilli", "high bacterial pollution" and "bacteriologically unsatisfactory water". Seeing these results, the mayor found himself obliged

114

to intervene, but, instead of ordering a serious inquiry into the causes of the pollution, he simply instructed the water board to pour chlorine into the water. Consequently the next analysis pronounced the water to be "sound" and that, for him, effectively closed the case. The residents finally agreed on a hypothesis, the only possible one, according to them. They had discovered that the Carteix factory, after blending chemical and natural fertilizer, washed the containers with water from the Avre and poured the contaminated water into underground containers. It seemed that these containers had faulty linings and that their contents were leaking into the water table, which in turn was supplying Cholong with drinking water.

Despite the complaints and threats of lawsuits, the residents of the Favorites district had not been successful. A legal procedure had now been dragging on for two years without anyone being too troubled – not the mayor, who seemed strangely uninterested, not the businessmen, not even the Health and Safety people, who claimed to be powerless. The *Clairon de Cholong*, worn out, had moved on to other news items. Bogged down and exhausted, the residents themselves had lost heart and were making fortunes for the sellers of bottled water.

Fred, who still had plenty of energy, wasn't looking for a scapegoat, but more for some concrete reality to hook on to; then he would decide what to do. He was even perfectly happy to play the good citizen, conscious of his civic duty, who takes it upon himself to point out some mistake, some human error, or a technical malfunction that has escaped the experts. After all, he couldn't care less about Carteix, or its claims, or the

115

pollution it was creating. What did he, Fred, care about pollution, the state of the world and what the pursuit of profit had done to it? As far as he was concerned, the end justified the means, and the end was always the same – money – above and beyond everything, and would be so for ever. That notion had been his *raison d'être* for too long for him to think of changing it now. He didn't particularly want to go poking his nose into anyone else's business; those days were long past. All he wanted to know was this: did the Carteix factory have anything to do with the disgusting water coming out of his taps or not? The rumour was that it did, but he wanted to know for sure.

He began by walking round the factory, which seemed to be empty, although it was the middle of the week. He skirted the fencing alongside the delivery area, where he found a wall of pallets ten feet high. Then he emerged into an open-air dump filled with casks, and blue, red and white metal barrels painted with the logos of various oil and petrol companies. At the northern end of the factory, he saw carts loaded up with huge cubes wrapped in white plastic, which he took to be merchandise waiting to be loaded. A little further on, at the back of the main building, you could see three enormous metallic containers shaped like grain silos, the contents of which fed straight into the factory. Fred finished his round beside the locked gate of the staff entrance, whose car park was completely deserted.

And it seemed as though his crusade was going to end there.

Without a word, without a gesture, without a battle. No negotiation, no treaty, no convincing anyone, or being convinced. He would never find out what that

116

bulky material was, or what use it was to anyone. He hadn't seen a single soul, not even some employee, who of course would have sent him to his superior, who in turn would have sent him on to a director. Fred would have been quite prepared to go right to the top.

Overcome by a great wave of discouragement, he sat down on the gravel, leaning against the metal gateposts. He sat there for a while, with his arms crossed, thoughtful, deprived of his adversary, his plan of attack undermined. If he had learned a single thing from his career as a gangster, it was that behind any structure, no matter how forbidding, you would always find men. Men whose paths one might cross, men with names that everyone knew, men with faces, men invulnerable on the face of it, but still men, and therefore fallible.

The Carteix factory was one of many subsidiaries of a large group based in Paris, which was itself one of the subdivisions of a large conglomerate which had diversified into many different sectors, and was held in a network of other holdings, part of a web of interconnected partnerships, an empire which depended on the support of several governments, whose governing board did not even know of the existence of the insignificant Carteix factory, which could be sold off at any given moment, the victim of some random tidying up of the portfolio, some slimming down operation, some decision taken in a country that had never even heard of the Norman bocage.

Fred now understood it all: this world he was now condemned to live in, the world of so-called legality and morality, was in fact filled with traps set by faceless enemies, against whom any attempt at resistance would be pitiful.

117

And as long as this great corrugated iron wart filled with poisonous substances planted in the middle of the forest stood empty, as long as there was no hope of finding the big boss himself, Fred was faced with the one thing he dreaded the most – powerlessness.

Slumped there on the ground, he felt miserably human, small and worthless. And he hated having to face this fact.

*

Cholong-sur-Avre had never had a proper cinema. In each generation a volunteer had taken charge of a long-established cinema club housed in the main reception room in the town hall. Despite the gloomy prognostications of the officials ("It's a lost battle!"), fifty stalwarts turned up twice a month, whatever the film, and that kept the whole operation going, and the doubters at bay. A retired teacher and cinema enthusiast, Alain Lemercier, booked the films, designed the flyers and led the debates that followed the screenings. His love of film seemed to spring in a direct line from the lives of those obsessive types who had divided up the countryside in the past, showing Marcel Carne and Sacha Guitry films in barns and town halls, crazy people who would go searching for audiences in fields and farm kitchens, and inviting them to watch without any thought of box-office receipts – nobody really paid much, that wasn't the aim of the exercise. These wizards with their magic lanterns were amply repaid by the laughter at the appearance of Michel Simon in *Boudu*, and the tears at the end of *The Grapes of Wrath*. In memory of that tradition, Alain Lemercier had taken up the torch in Cholong. He would draw

118

up programmes around particular directors, showing forgotten classics, pretexts for debates which kept most of the audience in their seats after the showing. Often he would arrange for a guest to come along, someone who could shed some particular light on the subject of a film; everybody remembered the evening which had filled a good half of the room – they had shown *Chariots of Fire*, the story of the rivalry between two middle-distance runners, and Alain had invited a local celebrity, Mr Mounier, whose career as a runner had had a late spurt during the Senior Olympics. And there had been another memorable evening when he had succeeded in persuading a specialist on gifted children to come up from Paris for a thrilling debate based around a film about an apparently retarded child who turned out to be highly gifted. And if the debate flagged, Alain would act as mediator, encouraging questions, and drawing out those who might have something to say on the subject.

The arrival of an American writer in Cholong now provided an excellent excuse for revisiting an American classic. Without any hesitation, Alain had picked up the telephone to invite Fred to come along, describing to him the great interest of his cinema club.

"It would be a great honour for us if you would agree to be our next guest."

A debate in a cinema club? Fred? Fred, for whom it would be inconceivable to watch a film without a can of beer in his hand, and a "pause" button, to enable him to go and rummage around in the fridge? Fred, who was bored rigid by anything that didn't contain explosions and gunfire; who always dropped off during the love scenes; who couldn't read the subtitles and watch the film at the same time? A debate? In a cinema club?

119

"What's the film?"

"I was thinking of *Some Came Running*, Vincente Minnelli, 1959."

"That rings a bell... Is it Sinatra or Dean Martin?"

"Both."

Alain, without realizing it, had gained a point. For a New Jersey Italian, and one connected to the *Onorevole Società*, Frankie and Dino were heroes.

"Remind me of the story."

"It's a writer, an army veteran, who comes back home with an unfinished novel. Everybody regards him as a failure, except his wife, who tries to encourage him."

"Is the writer played by Sinatra?"

"Yes."

Fred, a bit perturbed, said he'd think about it. He hung up, and then stayed by the telephone, which, sure enough, immediately rang again.

"Hello, Fred?"

"Which one is this, Pluto or Goofy?"

"Di Cicco. What's this 'I'll think about it' business? Are you mad?"

"I don't talk to minions, pass that on to Quintiliani, tell him to ring me."

And he slammed down the receiver, feeling humiliated. Given the up-to-the-minute technology at Caputo and Di Cicco's disposal, Quint's return call wouldn't take more than a minute, wherever he might be on the planet. In the past, in order to trap him and force him to confess, the FBI had used parabolic antennae, lasers, satellites, microphones that could fit inside a beauty spot, cameras in spectacle arms and hundreds of other gadgets that even James Bond scriptwriters had never thought of.

"Tell me Fred, have you gone mad?" Quint said.

120

"I didn't want to offend that nice fellow and make myself unpopular."

"Unpopular? I wouldn't give much for your popularity if those people knew who you were, the great crook and murderer Giovanni Manzoni. You're not a writer, Fred, you're nothing more than a scumbag who's managed to save his skin, don't ever forget that."

Fred and Tom had long ago run out of insults for one another, and these verbal jousts were mere formalities. The game they were really playing demanded great precision and constant inventiveness.

"There's one thing that completely escapes me," Tom went on, "and that's how on earth you could take part in a debate of any sort. It's just not your thing."

He was right, of course. A debate, an exchange of ideas? It was true, the words "exchange" and "ideas" could not have been more foreign to him. For Giovanni Manzoni, eloquence sprang from the business end of a crowbar, and dialectical satisfaction was generally best achieved through the sort of sophisticated arguments deployed by blow torches and electric drills. Fred would have been happy to have sent Alain Lemercier packing, if he hadn't brought up this story about "a writer whom everyone regards as a failure". What could he say? Who else, for miles around, would be better placed than Fred to deal with such a subject? In order to become a writer, it wasn't enough to just write, you had to have genuine writer's problems. And these days Fred knew all there was to know about the sufferings of a man, alone in his lair, telling his story, searching for truths that are often too uncomfortable to be told.

"I'm going to watch the video of the film first, Tom, and I'll prepare lots of interesting things to say. And you

121

can come along to the showing, I'll say you're a friend. In exchange, I promise to give a completely accurate picture of you in my memoirs."

Quintiliani, taken aback by such a sneaky argument, just burst out laughing.

*

Maggie was not planning to come to either the film show or the debate. She had spent a long afternoon toiling over the administration at the *Secours Populaire* (processing donations, bringing the accounts up to date, planning ahead), and now she was busy working as a volunteer at a soup kitchen for eighty people in the refectory of the Evreux Technical Institute. She stood behind a counter of Formica tables, filling the plates of the hungry and wondering how much pea soup she would have to dole out before she had paid her debt to society. She felt like a Red Cross nurse on the battlefield, simultaneously serving and cooking, loading and unloading vans, greeting people and washing up, like an athlete trying to break some record. Indeed, for her, charitable work was like some sort of sporting discipline – you had to warm up, do the exercise, and then accelerate – and if you trained regularly enough, you could become a champion. When the refectory was finally empty, she had to admit it to herself: there was a certain pleasure to be had from giving one's all. Armed with a sponge, she attacked the empty containers with self-denying energy. She allowed her hands to be scratched, grazed, crushed and bruised. After all, there were famous precedents for this.

122

*

In the semi-darkness of the great room, the audience awaited Alain Lemercier's introductory speech. The fifty people, the core, who always turned up, whatever the programme, had become, in doing so, a true club. They would not have missed this ritual for anything, the sort of shared communion that you could no longer find elsewhere, as well as the emotion you could only feel in front of the big screen. And after it was over they were all the more appreciative of the return to reality and the after-show drinks. The simple act of leaving their cosy sitting rooms and TVs to go and watch a film had become, in their eyes, an act of defiance.

Thomas Quintiliani and Frederick Blake sat side by side at the back of the hall. They were finding it hard to conceal their emotions – one excitement, the other apprehension. The FBI man was dreading the prospect of his snitch having to undergo even the mildest of questioning. But at the same time he realized that Fred's insertion into the local community would be perceived as a good result by his superiors. In a perverse way, the fake respectability of this supposed writer was proof that he, Tom Quint, had succeeded in turning an ex-con into a respectable citizen, and in a country like France – in other words he had performed a miracle. Fred, for his part, had watched a video of the film several times in order to prepare for the debate, and he felt ready to expound the modest thesis he had prepared, and had prepared answers to all the questions he was bound to be asked. He had even planned to begin his presentation with a quote that Warren had found on the Internet: "Wives of writers will never understand that when they

123

appear to be just looking out of the window, they're actually working." This summed up, for him, the total incomprehension of his family for his work, and their insidious way of denigrating his status as an author. This evening, before his first official audience, he would take his revenge on all those who doubted the genuine nature of his calling. And Tom Quintiliani, his greatest enemy in the world, would be the only witness.

Lemercier had vanished into the projection room, and the film had not started; people were becoming impatient.

"Back home we would have shot the projectionist by now," Fred whispered.

Tom, despite having spent a lifetime waiting for things, rather agreed. Lemercier reappeared, his arms raised in despair, and climbed onto the stage to make an announcement.

"My friends! The film library has made a mistake. The reels I've been sent are the wrong ones. It's not the first time it's happened…"

It was true – it happened about twice every year. Last November, Michael Cimino's *Heaven's Gate* had strayed into the boxes labelled *20,000 Leagues Under the Sea* by Richard Fleischer, and a few months earlier, instead of an American documentary called *Punishment Park*, the club had had to make do with *Pink Panther 2*. But it took more than this to unsettle Alain, who was able, with skilful juggling, to justify the change in the programme, and improvise a rough presentation, even finding connections between the films. This kind of recovery from mishap had become the master of ceremonies' speciality. Quint looked at Fred with a relieved smile.

"No point staying here. We might as well go home."

124

Alain apologized profusely to his guest, and suggested making a date for another showing, while Fred, disappointed not to be appearing on stage, headed for the exit without a word. Tom suggested they go and have a drink in the town.

"At least stay for the film," Alain said. "It's another American one, you won't have wasted a trip."

Fred followed Quintiliani. He would calm his nerves with a couple of glasses of bourbon, annoy Tom with his spiel about the good old days, and they would go back to the Rue des Favorites like the close neighbours that they were.

"Do stay," Lemercier insisted. "I'm sure you'll like the film, it's Martin Scorsese's *Goodfellas*, about the New York Mafia. You'll see, it's very funny and instructive."

Fred suddenly froze, with one arm in his jacket sleeve. His face was expressionless.

As an officer in the FBI, Quintiliani had learned never to show surprise, and to face the unexpected coolly and methodically – he was the type of person who knew how to breathe with his stomach when the barrel of a .45 was suddenly pressed into the back of his neck. However, at this precise moment, and despite his usual aplomb in the face of new situations, he felt overcome by a simultaneous hot flush and an icy blast in his guts, and he broke into a sweat.

Fred betrayed himself with an evil smile.

"We're not in any great hurry, Tom…"

"I think we'd better go. Anyway, you've seen that film. What's the point of seeing it again?"

Like all mafiosi, Fred adored all the films in the *Godfather* series. They were the chronicles of their great history, they provided legitimacy, and enhanced their

125

reputations in the eyes of the world. There was nothing the wise guys enjoyed more, when gathered together, than to recite lines of dialogue from the films to one another, even miming some of the scenes. Sometimes one of them would find himself alone in front of the screen, late at night, sobbing over the death of Vito Corleone, as played by Marlon Brando. To them, all other Mafia films were totally ridiculous and full of inaccuracies, with their operetta killers and absurd costumes. Dozens of such inept films were made in America each year – they were anachronistic and grotesque, and deeply insulting for the members of the real families, who were not amused at seeing their image turned into caricature by Hollywood.

Until Martin Scorsese's *Goodfellas* came along.

Fred knew the film almost by heart, and he hated it for a thousand reasons. In it gangsters were reduced to what they really were: scum, whose only aim in life was to park in forbidden places, give the biggest fur coat to their wife and, above all, never to have to live the lives of those millions of idiots who get up each morning to earn a miserable crust, instead of sleeping late in a gold-plated bed. That was all a mafioso was, and *Goodfellas* told it like it was. Without the myth, all that was left was stupidity and cruelty. Giovanni Manzoni, Luca Cuozzo, Joe Franchini, Anthony De Biase, Anthony Parish and all the rest of the gang knew that henceforth their bad-boy aura had lost its shine for ever.

So why this film, this particular evening?

A coincidence? Just one more reversal? Another little episode to blame on human fallibility? Why not some other film, any film, from the thousands of possibilities?

126

La règle du jeu? Lawrence of Arabia? La grande vadrouille? Bitches on Heat? The Blood of Frankenstein? Why *Goodfellas*, why this horribly accurate mirror-image of Fred's life?

"I'd be delighted to see it again," he said to Lemercier, as he returned to his seat. "I don't know much about these gangster stories, but I'd be happy to try and answer a few questions during the discussion."

The MC, happy to have saved the situation, went back to the projection room. Tom, feeling unusually angry, restrained an impulse to knock Fred to the ground. Fred savoured the anger like a fine liqueur; any opportunity to see Quint in such a state was a victory gained over his misfortunes. Fred now held in his hands a way of taking his own particular kind of revenge against a film that had deprived him of his image as an honourable bandit, and had branded him as nothing more than a stereotypical loser.

"Instead of getting cross, Tom, tell me if you've seen the film."

Quintiliani was not a man who went in for leisure activities; he enjoyed neither fishing nor camping, and only took exercise in order to keep in shape. He spent his rare moments of leisure reading articles that were more or less relevant to his activities. The cinema? He had memories of drive-ins, where the film took second place to the girl on the back seat of the car, or films shown in breaks during his training, and, most of all, endless films of no interest watched on his many plane journeys. However, he had seen *Goodfellas* and all the other Mafia films, in the interests of research. He needed to know about the heroes of those he was tracking, to understand their language, and the in-jokes derived from the films.

127

"You really want to play this game?" he whispered in Fred's ear.

Fred understood Tom perfectly, and interpreted the question as: *You creep, Manzoni, if you play this trick on me, I'll make your life such hell, you'll wish you'd spent the rest of your life in jail.*

"It'll be a chance for you to ask me all the questions you've been wanting to ask all this time, and maybe today you'll get some answers. Surely that makes it worth the journey?"

A suggestion that Tom read as: *You can go fuck yourself, you fucking cop.*

The lights went down, silence fell, and a white beam of light hit the screen.

*

Maggie parked the car in front of the house and waved at Vincent, who was smoking a cigarette at his window. As soon as she came into the living room she collapsed on the sofa with her eyes closed, still overcome by the sensation of having travelled through the looking glass. On her drive home, she had been unable to stop thinking of the room lent to the Newark branch of the Salvation Army, where every day tramps and homeless people would gather. Wooden tables and benches, and all those people sitting there for hours, battling against the winter cold, the boredom, the fear of the streets and, above all, hunger. She had looked through the filthy windows on occasions, at this goldfish bowl of misery, practically holding her nose just imagining the smell. She had several times wanted to go in to experience the dizzying sight of degradation, and what had stopped her

128

was not fear of confronting such squalor, but the strange feeling that she was worse off than them in her own degradation. These filthy men and women had their own sort of dignity. Not her. By accepting the values and way of life of Giovanni Manzoni, she had renounced any kind of self-esteem. If the local hobos could have suspected that this fine lady in her fur coat felt that way, they would have been the ones to give her some charity.

*

When the credits had finished rolling, Lemercier came back onto the stage and took the microphone to make a few general remarks about the film and its director. Before asking for comments from those who had something to say, he turned to Fred and invited him to join him. There was some encouraging applause and, as usual, Alain asked the first question.

"When you're living in New York, are you aware of the presence of the Mafia, as shown in films?"

Tom, with a reflex gesture which betrayed his anxiety, reached for his holster.

"The presence of the Mafia?" Fred repeated.

He didn't really understand the question. It was too abstract, it was like asking if he was aware of the sky above his head or the earth beneath his feet. He sat dumbly in front of the microphone, feeling ridiculous, and took refuge in silent thought.

The presence of the Mafia.

Alain interpreted his silence as shyness due to the language barrier, and came to his aid.

"Might one see guys in the street like those three gangsters in the film?"

129

With this question, Fred caught a glimpse of the immense chasm which separated him eternally from the rest of humanity, the part that remains on the right side of the law. Gangsters fascinated honest people, but only in the role of fairground monsters.

Quintiliani almost raised his hand to say something. Not to put an end to this charade, but to come to the poor fellow's rescue. It was very well being clever alone on your veranda, telling your particular form of truth with an old typewriter, all very fine... But to speak for your life as a gangster on stage, holding a microphone, in front of fifty people – it was like going before the grand jury again. Fred was like a schoolboy, all excited about reciting his poem in public, who can't even remember his own name once he's up in front of the blackboard.

There were low mutterings in the audience, and a feeling of awkwardness. Alain tried to think of some quip to offer support. *Might one see guys like that in the streets?* How could one answer a question like that, which seemed so harmless, but was in fact so brutal? Faced with all the stares, Fred was tempted to lie, to claim that the criminals were invisible, and melted into the background like chameleons; he could even question their very existence, suggest that they were a scriptwriter's invention, like zombies or vampires. And then he could have made his farewells and fled back to his veranda, swearing to himself that he would never re-emerge. But in the name of the very truth that he was trying to discover by writing his memoirs, he felt he did not have the right to run away.

"At the start of the film, in the first scene in the bar, there's a guy who crosses the screen holding a glass, you

130

don't get told his name, he's wearing a grey waistcoat over a yellow shirt with rolled-up sleeves. That man really existed, his name was Vinnie Caprese, he was a regular on Hester Street at a coffee shop called Caffe Trombetta. He would have a strong espresso there every morning, like he'd done since he was eight. His mother used to make one for him before he went off to school, no bread and butter, nothing else, and the kid would go off like that after gulping down his espresso – sometimes if it was very cold she'd put a drop of Marsala in it to warm his belly. I've always thought that that sort of thing is what makes people into executioners. Just details like that."

*

Despite her exhaustion, Maggie couldn't get to sleep. She picked up the phone and suggested an evening visit to the G-men, who welcomed this unexpected distraction. Di Cicco got out three glasses for the grappa Maggie brought with her. She went over to the binoculars mounted on the tripod and pointed them towards the apartments that were still lit. Without the slightest mocking voyeurism or ill will, Maggie was now in the habit of watching the neighbours several times a week under the intrigued gaze of the two federal agents. The sample of humanity in the Favorite district was now her private laboratory – spying was her new science. If Fred regarded humanity as a grey and distant entity, Maggie refused to believe in the apparent banality of her neighbour's lives.

"What is it that amuses you in all this, Maggie?"

"Nothing amuses me, but everything interests me. When I was young, I used to spend my time putting

131

people into categories, labelled with one function – one name was enough. Now the idea that everybody is in some way exceptional helps me to understand how the world works."

She pointed her binoculars towards the little three-storey building at number 15, where four families and two single people lived.

"The Pradels are watching TV," she said.

"She suffers from insomnia, it sometimes stays on till four or five," Caputo said, sipping his drink.

"I wonder if he's got a mistress," she said.

"How did you guess, Maggie?"

"I can sense it."

"She's called Christine Laforgue, medical assistant, thirty-one years old."

"Does the wife know?"

"She doesn't suspect anything. Christine Laforgue and her husband came to dinner there the other night."

"What a pig!"

This had been a frequent *cri de coeur* in the past, at the time when Giovanni and his acolytes had had "official" mistresses. They would parade them on their arms in selected places, to such a point that the wives would try and meet them in person, hoping to scratch out their eyes. Since then adultery had been very high on her list of deadly sins.

Maggie then looked up to the top flat, where there was no light.

"Has Patrick Roux gone out?"

"No. He set off on his tour of France yesterday," Di Cicco replied.

Maggie, like an entomologist, observed the evolution of her subjects, and their interactions. Occasionally

132

she intervened directly in order to precipitate some development in their lives.

Patrick Roux was fifty-one, divorced, and worked as a bursar in a private school. He had just taken an unpaid sabbatical in order to fulfil a long-held dream – to criss-cross the country on his beautiful 900cc motorbike. Knowing that bikers were much in demand for this purpose, Maggie had persuaded him to carry an organ-donor card in his wallet. Roux thought that this would bring him luck, and in any case he had no objection to the thought of his heart beating in another man's body.

"I've got something here that might interest you, Maggie," Caputo said. "It's about the little old lady at number eleven, who looks as though she'd go straight to heaven, the one who lives with her daughter and son-in-law. Well, back in 1971, she poisoned an old neighbour's dog. He never got over it and followed the animal soon after. It was a perfect crime."

"And nobody ever knew?"

"She talked about it yesterday to a friend in Argentan. I suppose she wanted to confess to someone before facing her maker."

God... Where had He got to? Maggie felt that by observing her neighbours so closely, she was doing the work that He should have been doing for his own creatures: watching over them and sometimes showing them the right way.

"Mr Vuillemin's light is still on," she said, surprised. "He's supposed to be getting up in less than three hours..."

This was the baker in the avenue de la Gare, who had lost half his business since the arrival of a young

133

competitor. Like the others, Maggie had gone and bought a baguette from the new man, and had had the courage to give Mr Vuillemin her verdict in person: "His bread is much better." How could this be possible? Nobody had ever complained about his bread for more than twenty years. It was no more or less spongy than any other, no whiter, it stayed fresh for the same length of time, so what was it? To find out, he had tasted it too. And looking at his dough, he wondered, with a sudden burst of nostalgia, where he had gone wrong along the way. And then he had decided to set to work and show this callow youth what he was made of.

Maggie couldn't bear to miss a single detail of all these human stories unfolding every day outside her door.

*

"...Bill Clunan learned Italian in order to become a gangster. You can picture the type, both parents Irish – he studied books of Eyetie slang, ate every day at Spagho, practised swearing, even Catholic that he was, that must have stuck in his gullet, having to blaspheme like the Italians, calling the Virgin Mary a whore, that was the hardest thing, but what can you do, he wanted to join Fat Willy's gang rather than any Irish one. If you ever go to Brooklyn and you're on Mellow Boulevard around seven, you might see him; he's got long grey hair brushed back, Ray-Bans on his nose, he'll be playing Scopa with his mates, who still call him Paddy."

Tom, mortified, was desperately trying to think of a way of shutting him up. The simplest method would have been a bullet between the eyes, to put an end

134

once and for all to this Calvary Manzoni had put him through ever since their paths had crossed.

"Who's this Fat Willy you mentioned?" a woman's voice asked.

"Fat Willy? What can I say about Fat Willy?…"

No! Not Fat Willy! Tom tried to convey his thought. But Fred was only aware of his own excitement.

"Fat Willy was a *capo*, a boss, a bit like the Paulie character in the film you've just seen. His place in the hierarchy didn't matter much, Fat Willy just hated injustice. He could shed a tear when you told him your troubles, but he would also feel quite justified in smothering you if you had trimmed a bit of his profit. You could talk to him about anything, except his weight – nobody knew exactly what it was, they just said Fat Willy was a *pezzo da novanta*, somebody of more than two hundred pounds – it was the name they used for all the big cheeses, the gang leaders. He was so impressive physically that when he walked down the street it was as though he was guarding his own bodyguards. It was in nobody's interest to refer to his weight – not his sons, not his lieutenants, no one. You just had to tap his stomach and say 'Hey you're looking well, Willy!' – you could be sure those would be your last words."

Tom, horrified, nearly got up to intervene. Fred hadn't mentioned that Fat Willy was one of the first snitches to be taken care of by the FBI and the Witness Protection Programme. In order to make him unrecognizable, the FBI had placed him on a draconian diet and he had shed dozens of pounds. The first time he had been allowed into town, Fat Willy, or Guglielmo Quatrini as he was really called, had dived into a doughnut shop and eaten the equivalent of what he had shed.

135

"Willy just beamed at life," Fred continued. "He was always agreeable, always in a good mood, he always had a friendly word for the ladies, and a kiss for the babies' cheeks, always happy. He only stopped smiling once, and that was when one of his sons was kidnapped. The kidnappers had demanded an enormous ransom, but Willy had held out, right up to the end, when he had received one of the boy's fingertips in a dental floss box. He not only got his son back alive, he got his hands on the kidnappers. He shut himself up in his basement with them, with bare hands. Yes, believe it or not, bare hands! Well, no one knows what happened then, all I can say is the neighbour had to go away for the weekend to get away from the screams coming from Willy's basement."

The fifty people in the audience sat like frozen statues, hanging on the words of this man on the stage. A tremor of amazement passed amongst them, and nobody dared move or say a thing. All the rest, the discussion, the programme, all forgotten. One man was talking and they had to listen.

One spectator tiptoed out and went to ring his wife, who was down the road attending a meeting of the Green Party candidates for the next local elections. Basically, he told her to get over to the cinema club, as "something" was happening. She looked at her watch and suggested to the gathering that they might all go and see what was going on at the town hall.

*

Maggie, now tired of looking through the binoculars, was sitting at the listening table, wearing earphones,

136

absorbed in her neighbour's conversations. She had just learned that Mr Dumont, the motorbike repair man, had been taking Chinese lessons for the last ten years for no apparent reason, and that his wife wasn't really his wife but his cousin, that the unmarried mother at number 18 went and put flowers on Flaubert's tomb in Rouen every month, that the French teacher lived well beyond his means, and won fortunes playing tarot in the back room of the only nightclub in the area, that Mme Volkovitch had knocked ten years off her real age in her dealings with officialdom, and that Myriam, at number 14, spent all her spare time searching for her real father so as, in her words, "to force him to admit to his paternity".

During each of these sessions, she learned a little more about human nature, what motivated and moved people, what made them suffer – more than she could ever glean from any book or newspaper article.

"It's that young computer guy who's placing the small ads in the *Clairon de Cholong*," she said, taking off her earphones.

Giving away PC XT computer, 14" screen with jet printer in good condition. Obsolete equipment for which he could get nothing second-hand, but which could be very welcome to someone with no money. That was the sort of thing which thrilled Maggie the most, simple acts of kindness, small thoughts for others. If she felt drawn to the great humanitarian causes, she still had a lot to learn about such discreet and well-judged actions, inspired as much by common sense as good fellowship. Such actions often took the most unexpected forms. For example, her neighbour, Maurice, who owned La Poterne, the other big café in Cholong, had been on holiday in

137

Naples, where he had come across an ancient custom still practised in some of the bars over there. Given the price of an espresso taken at the counter (a matter of centimes), you would often see customers getting rid of their small change and paying for two coffees, and only drinking one themselves; the barman would chalk it up and give a free coffee to some indigent passer-by. Maurice, who wasn't a particularly generous man, and who didn't give much thought to any poverty around him, had nonetheless found the idea interesting, and had introduced it. He was the first to be surprised at how many customers played the game. And Maggie had made Maurice into one of her real-life heroes, for having introduced a custom that went against all the expectations of the times, and one you would have thought bound to fail.

*

Quint was planning his revenge. This man, who was expressing himself with all the confidence of a seasoned lecturer before his very eyes, was going to pay dearly for this performance. Tom sometimes forgot about the incredible stupidity of gangsters, and how their taste for bragging was, more often than not, their undoing.

"If you can see them in the streets? Is that what you were asking? Have you ever heard of Brownsville? It's the West Point for the made men in a sense: once you've trained there you can go to the top. In the great days, in that little area about six miles square, you might pass a Capone, a Costello, a Bugsy Siegel (the one who founded Las Vegas) in the street. Or maybe a Louis "Lepke" Buchalter, or a Vito Genovese, who was

138

Di Cicco had gone to lie down in the next-door room and Caputo sat in front of a television with the sound muted – he had forgotten Maggie was there. As for her, watching and listening to her neighbours had put the craziest of ideas into her mind. She was carried away, helped by the grappa, into a utopia in which her neighbourhood had become a free zone that no longer operated according the old laws of indifference towards your fellow man. Her cheeks blazing and her heart glowing, she began to dream of a small corner of this earth in which the highest ideals of communality in human relations reigned supreme. Just two or three remote streets in which each inhabitant had set aside his or her own selfish interests and instead taken an interest in those of their neighbours. In this little Eden, any way of reaching out to others would be acceptable. You could admit to some weakness or confess to some error instead of sinking into denial. You could affirm the eternal possibility of redemption. Approach the person you had feared without really knowing them. Help someone in distress, despite the urge to run away. Dare to explain what had gone wrong. Satisfy those who are never satisfied. Intervene and mediate in some conflict. Pay back a debt even if it was no longer expected. Encourage a family member's artistic ambition. Spread good news. Give up an unattractive habit for the sake of those around you. Pass on a piece of wisdom before it disappears for ever. Bring comfort to an old person. Make some tiny unnoticeable sacrifice. Save a life far away by forgoing some useless gadget, and all the others still to be invented.

Maggie, in this poetic trance, saw this whole little world falling into place, all it needed was her own contagious

140

generosity of spirit: she would concentrate her efforts on one neighbourhood in the hope of seeing them spreading outwards, into other areas and then into the whole town, and then the rest of the world. With a tear in her eye, Maggie offered Di Cicco a last drink – she was in no hurry to come down to earth.

*

"...Tony was famous for his energetic interrogations of suspected rats – he wasn't called The Dentist for nothing. He ended up as Carmine Calabrese's lieutenant. For made men, that was like becoming a high official. His career would never be meteoric, but he was safe from a lot of worries. It was a choice that the other wise guys respected. And yet he had the makings of a good *capo*, and God knows what he could have dreamed up to consolidate the empire."

Tom was determined to create a diversion so as to bring an end to this unbearable verbal diarrhoea, spewed out by a boastful ignoramus who was going to bring everything down around him. But what sort of diversion, for God's sake? How was he going to get this bastard to shut his mouth?

One of the spectators managed this miracle by raising his hand.

"If there's any message we get from the cinema about gangsters and mafiosi, it's something to do with the idea of redemption. As though they'd been trying to atone somehow for the last thirty years."

"Redemption? I don't suppose most of those guys know what that word means. Honestly – have you really been taken in by all that crap? Why would a man who

141

has just blown out the brains of his best friend over some incident with a bookie feel the need to play Jesus Christ? Guilt – that's a concept invented by intellectuals. Go and try it on Gigi Marelli, who was a fourteen-year-old executioner, a baby-killer as they used to call them. He was known as "Lampo", the lightning bolt. He had an average of six or seven contracts a year, that kid, and two bodyguards who watched him day and night. One day he was given a special contract: his own father – he was asked to kill his own father. The old man had been stupid, and the *capo* at the time was insistent that the son should do the job. Once he'd done it, Gigi went and told his mother. They stood together, clutching each other at the funeral. Guilt? There's a Greek tragedy taking place every day in Brooklyn and New Jersey, plenty of material for new plays and plenty of new theories for psychiatrists too."

Quint grabbed his phone, called HQ and got Di Cicco.

"Go and wake Maggie up."

"She's here."

"Let me talk to her."

In the audience, twenty impatient hands were now raised. The jungle drums had beaten around the town, and the hall was filling up. Fred was glowing. His performance was that of an actor and a raconteur, a blend of thinly disguised confession and dramatic invention. This warm glow cleared his mind of the bitterness and sacrifice of the last few years.

"So to answer the question you put at the beginning, yes, you can see goodfellas in the street. You want names? James Alegretti, known as Jimmy the Monk, Vincent Alo, known as Jimmy Blue Eyes, Joseph Amato, known

142

as Black Jack, Donald Angelini, known as The Wizard of Odds, Alphonse Attardi, known as The Peacemaker..."

Tom dreaded the logical conclusion of this list, the inevitable moment when an exultant Fred, carried away by his own confession, would finally betray himself.

"...John Barbato, known as Johnny Sausages, Joseph Barboza, known as Joe the Animal, Gaetano Callahan, known as Cheesebox, William Cammisario, known as Willie the Rat..."

The very last person to come into the hall was Maggie. She walked slowly down the aisle without taking her eyes off the man on the stage, who reminded her of another man, a certain Giovanni with whom she had fallen in love a long time ago. Why him, why that rascal Manzoni who hung around with all the other hooligans? Nobody could answer that except her. She knew him by reputation and she had seen him for the first time at the San Gennaro dance on East Houston Street. She had watched him drinking with his mates and chasing skirt until late in the evening, when a handful of girls remained, all longing to be taken home by the handsome Giovanni. Instead he had asked Maria la Ciociara to dance; she was a plain young woman who had been a wallflower all evening. Seeing him taking the overcome girl in his arms had made Livia's heart beat harder.

"Frank Caruso, known as Frankie the Bug, Eugene Ciasullo, known as The Animal, Joseph Cortese, known as Little Bozo, Frank Cucchiara, known as Frankie The Spoon, James De Mora, known as Machine Gun, and hundreds of others. Most didn't wear the pinstripe suits and garish ties you might expect – you had to be a made guy to recognize another one. Otherwise you would just

143

take them to be decent family men coming home from a day's work, which is what they were, really. And amongst all these, there's one I want to make a special mention of, a clan boss from Newark, a really special guy. He was married to the sweetest of girls, and they had two lovely kids, a boy and a girl. I must tell you about this guy, the way he took to heart every single thing that happened on his territory..."

Fred suddenly caught Maggie's eye, as she stood below the stage. There was nothing reproachful in her look, on the contrary she was gazing at him with indulgence. He stopped talking, smiled at her, and slowly woke up.

"Come on Fred, we're going home."

With this "come on Fred", he felt her take his hand.

Like an old actor relishing applause, he bowed to his audience, who clapped wildly. Alain Lemercier understood that one of the greatest evenings of the cinema club had just taken place. His struggles had all been worthwhile.

*

Tom, Maggie and Fred walked home in silence in the dark. Quint, as he left them at their door, warned Fred:

"If this evening's exhibition has any repercussions, I'm dropping you all, even if it means the FBI takes a hit for it. I'll just have to live with the painful knowledge that I have facilitated your death instead of delaying it as long as possible, which is what I've been busting a gut doing for the last six years."

Quintiliani would not have that pleasure. Fred's pointless foolhardiness would never have any consequences. But the inhabitants of Cholong would long remember

144

this extraordinary performance, which they simply took to be the outpourings of a writer's extra-fertile imagination.

Fred and Maggie didn't speak until they reached their bedroom.

"So – you made a fine spectacle of yourself?"

"And you had a good time being lady bountiful with your starving people?"

She turned off the bedside light and he grabbed his toothbrush in the bathroom. A jet of dark-brown water splashed onto the white basin. Disgusted, he went back to his bedside table and picked up the telephone.

"Quintiliani, I want to apologize. I behaved like an idiot."

"Nice to hear that, but I don't believe a word of it."

"I sometimes forget how hard you work."

"You usually come up with this sort of crap when you're trying to get something out of me. Do you really think this is the right moment?"

"I've got to tell you a story, Tom…"

"Wasn't this evening's performance enough for you?"

"A story about you."

"Go on then."

"Do you remember when Harvey Tucci couldn't give evidence because he'd had his throat shot out by a hitman? You were part of the team supposed to be protecting him, Tom. Sorry to remind you of a painful moment. You were a new boy at the Bureau."

"You were just a little squirt yourself, Fred. You were acting as cover for the hitman that evening, you told me about that."

"What I didn't tell you was that the shooter couldn't get Tucci in his sights, after several hours. There was still

145

the possibility of icing one of your people to terrorize Tucci and persuade him not to make the deal."

"…"

"It was your head that was in his sights, Tom."

"Go on."

"He asked me what he should do, and I answered, 'No collateral damage.' We waited for another ten minutes, which seemed to go on for ever, and then that fool Tucci went to smoke a cigarette at his bedroom window."

"…"

"Pretty close, eh?"

"Why are you telling me all this now?"

"This evening got me down. I need to talk to the only family member I've got left back there."

"Your nephew Ben?"

"Do me a favour, I need to know how he is."

"One suspicious word and I cut you off."

"There won't be any. Thanks, Tom."

"By the way, you never said who the hitman was. Was it Art Lefty? Franck Rosello? Auggie Campania? Which one was it?"

"Don't you think I've done enough snitching?"

Ten minutes later, the telephone rang, and woke Maggie up. She had only just dropped off.

"Hello?"

"Ben? It's Fred."

"Fred? What Fred?"

"Fred, your uncle from Newark, who lives a long way away."

Ben, at the other end, realized that it was his uncle Giovanni ringing from God knows where on the planet, and that the conversation was being tapped.

"You OK, Ben?"

146

"Fine, Fred."

"I was remembering that weekend in Orlando, with the children."

"I remember."

"We had such a great time. I think we even went to see Holiday on Ice."

"We did."

"Hope we can do that again one day."

"Me too."

"You know what I miss most? It's a good bagel from the Deli in Park Lane, my favourite, with pastrami, fried onions, raw onions and those funny sweet peppers. And some pepper vodka."

"There are two different sorts, the red and the white."

"The red."

"That's the best one."

"Apart from that, everything OK, Ben? Anything particular to tell me?"

"No. Oh yes, I kept your cassettes. All your Bogarts."

"Even *Dead End?*"

"Yes."

"Keep them. Do you still go to the races?"

"Of course."

"Well, next time, in memory of your old uncle, play eighteen, twenty-one and three for me."

"I'll remember that."

"Big kiss, my boy."

"Me too."

Fred hung up, and turned to Maggie.

"My nephew Ben is coming in two or three days to spend a weekend with us."

"How does he know the address?"

"I've just given it to him."

"You've just given him the address?"

"Yes, I've just given him the address."

"Quintiliani's going to kill you."

"It's done, he'll just have to shut up."

"Hey, Gianni, is that story about 'collateral damage' true?"

"Yes."

They switched out their lights at the same time. The day was ending as it had begun, with a transatlantic telephone call.

"Ben can make us his polenta with crayfish," she said. "The kids'll be pleased."

Fred didn't go down to the veranda that night. Maggie snuggled up in her husband's arms and they went to sleep straight away.

5

Sandrine Massart stood silently in her dressing gown, with her arms crossed, watching her husband preparing for his trip to the Far East. For Philippe, nothing was more delightful than this series of studied little movements, refined over the months: packing the laptop into its black canvas case, picking out shirts according to carefully worked-out parameters, checking the weather in South-East Asia on the Internet, wrapping up the Hermes squares to give to his clients, not forgetting a book that wouldn't be read, something connected to his destination. The simple act of changing the batteries on his Walkman, or clipping his vaccination certificate to his passport, gave him the added satisfaction of knowing the departure was imminent. Sandrine was resigned to him going away so often, but she resented the fact that he was unable to hide his happiness at leaving the house. At these moments, Philippe felt he was already in transit, far from the house in Cholong, nearly there – there, meaning anywhere else.

They had got married fourteen years earlier in Paris, where he had just landed an office job in a sewing-machine factory and where she was finishing her law degree. Two years later, Philippe was offered a position as sales manager for a new company starting up in the Eure, just at the moment when Sandrine had the chance to join a law firm specializing in employment law: a choice had to be made. Little Alexandrine was about to arrive, and so Sandrine didn't feel too bad about abandoning the bar and the robes and moving the family to Cholong so that her executive husband could pursue his career.

"It's just a matter of three or four years, darling. Maybe you can find a law firm in the area?"

But she couldn't find anything in the area, and once Timothée was born, she gave up the whole idea. She never regretted her decision for a moment; giving up her career for such a good reason wasn't a real sacrifice. Sandrine found a new kind of happiness in this big house which would shelter them all for ever.

Until the day a French engineer in her husband's company invented a crafty process which knocked twenty or thirty seconds off the assembly of the zip fastenings, and which, by saving time and manpower, could be worth huge sums to the manufacturing industry.

Most of the Asian countries had bought the patent, and the brilliant Philippe Massart was given the job of finding new markets all over the world. Unable to delegate, Philippe was in the habit of personally finalizing each contract. And so these days he went away three or four times a month for stays of three full days in each place, sometimes more if he decided to combine two destinations reachable in less than three flights. What Sandrine found worse than the absences were the effects of the jet lag, which lasted just long enough to meet up between journeys.

That morning he was leaving for Bangkok, to finalize an agreement which would allow his company to invest with the manufacturer himself, opening up new sectors – in other words the culmination of a long-term strategy that would promote him in the hierarchy without the

150

slightest risk of demotion, and thus the preparations for this departure felt even more delightful than usual. Watching all this, Sandrine felt only silent resignation at the thought of the sad outcome of their common story.

"Darling? You haven't seen my guidebook, have you? The new one, I mean."

He had been swotting up the night before, unable to sleep, excited. The days of the Rough Guide and Lonely Planet were long over, now it was all Michelin, luxurious hotels and palm-fringed beaches. He had had the time to try one out on his last trip, and he couldn't wait to go back.

"I'll see you on Tuesday, darling. If there's a change of plan, I'll ring."

All he had to do now was put on his grey flannel jacket, put his ticket in the inside pocket and kiss his wife.

"A change?"

"Perseil hinted that it might be a good idea to do a trip up to Chiangmai to sort something out with one of the suppliers. Anyway, I'll let you know."

With a gesture that was still affectionate, Sandrine straightened her husband's collar and smiled at him for the first time that morning. At the doorway, he gave her a peck on the cheek and went out to the waiting taxi.

"Darling! I nearly forgot!" she lied, grabbing a magazine from her dressing-gown pocket. "Alex has been writing for the school magazine this year, a poem they chose from a whole lot of others. He'd love you to read it. If you're bored on the plane…"

Caught out, he took the *Jules Vallès Gazette*, without quite knowing what to do with it, and put it in his briefcase.

151

*

His plane took off on time, the weather was good, business class was almost empty and the air hostess was pretty enough to eat. Bored on the plane? If Sandrine only knew... If she could only imagine... No, it was better if she didn't imagine anything. Late discoveries are often the most intense, and Philippe Massart had only just discovered, at the ripe age of forty-four, that he was made for this life, the flights, the transits, the business, the interpreters, the "fluent English speakers", the brief stays in Hiltons, the countries just flown over, the dinners just picked at – all that mattered was the speed, the distortion of time and the distances. Philippe Mansart could think of nothing finer on earth than an attaché case open on the bed of a suite in the Sydney Sheraton. Indeed, everything in his new life seemed beautiful to him, starting with all the little actions associated with travel, there were so many – those of the departure were only a start, others followed in good time, and time passed quickly between the time zones. At lunchtime, he looked at the menu, holding a glass of champagne, unable to decide between a cod steak or a rack of lamb; he spent as long as he could on this pleasant dilemma with his forehead against the porthole. As he waited to be served, he leafed through the Air France magazine, pausing for a moment to be moved by the sight of an Indian beauty in traditional costume illustrating an article on the textile industry in Madras; he remembered Sandrine's silhouette in her flannelette dressing gown. He loved her, no question about that. In their fourteen years of marriage, they had lived through a lot and surmounted a lot of

152

obstacles. *Yes, I love her.* He hung onto that statement for a moment, trying to find the evidence for it. He loved her. That was a given fact. He couldn't possibly doubt his love for her. And anyway, how did one go about doubting love? What were the signs? In any case, if he found signs, he probably couldn't trust them. What couple didn't suffer some sort of erosion of physical passion? How could affectionate gestures remain the same after fourteen years? Getting erections at the mere sight of her choosing a brassiere, kisses for no reason, public embraces which verged on the indecent. That was all over, but it had happened, that was the important thing. Yes, he still loved her, but differently. He still admired her figure, despite the passing years, indeed he found it almost more affecting than before. He loved Sandrine, no need to go on about it. *I love my wife.* Even to ask the question was absurd. He loved her, it needn't be put into question again. He loved her even if there was no longer any desire. Even if he sometimes thought about other women. Just thought about them. He had never been unfaithful to Sandrine. Or only abroad, which didn't count. He loved her, that must mean something, even nowadays, didn't it? He loved her, the problem was elsewhere. Paradoxical as it might seem, he found her somehow less present in his life. He might travel the world for the sake of his company; it was Sandrine herself who no longer seemed to be at his side. Ever since his career had taken off, she seemed to watch what was happening from afar, and seemed less and less to play the part of the partner who looks after the home base. Their team was no longer a winning one. Recently he had sensed that Sandrine was more preoccupied with Alex and Timothée's future

153

than his. It was as though he had been forgotten, now that he was away so much. It would be amazing if it were true, but it was also the most obvious explanation. And he had worked so hard, purely for the happiness of his family. As he finished off his pear charlotte, he was struck by a sudden insight: those who go off to the front are condemned to loneliness.

"Would you like a little liqueur, Monsieur Massart?"

The air hostess had already seen Philippe on a previous flight, and she remembered serving him two *poire* liqueurs as they came down to Singapore airport. It was nothing to do with fear of landing, he just needed a little burst of alcohol to launch him into his stay and to get him into the right rhythm. In Bangkok it was all a matter of timing. As soon as he was out of the airport, a taxi would take him to his hotel, the Grace, on Sukhumvit. He would take a long tepid shower, put on clean clothes, have a dry Martini on the bar terrace, in the rococo patio surrounded by fans, while he waited for Perseil and the director of FNU Thailand Ltd, whose name Philippe could never remember. They would have dinner in a bamboo pavilion at Krua Thai Law – Laotian chicken with strange spices – in order to go through current business, study the latest figures, and consider a proposal to increase the capital through the agency of the company. Then, to reward themselves, they would go and have a traditional drink in a bar in Pat-Pong, without overdoing it – they had to be fresh for the next morning. Philippe, with his *poire* in his hand, gazing out at the dark skies of the Siamese kingdom, daydreamed about the rest of the journey – a much more exciting film than what was being shown on the plane. What happened next was a light breakfast the next morning,

154

and then down to Chitlom for a massage by Absara, if she was free, if not, one of the others, although none of them was as good as Absara. Last time she'd told him he had beautiful eyes. She had a particular way with him, a way of putting him completely at ease the minute he arrived, manipulating his body until all resistance gave way to ejaculation, after a delicious penetration. Then would follow another massage which took in every single joint and vertebra, until the next erection and the "happy ending", as it was called in the establishment. After being in Absara's hands, all the physical and nervous exhaustion of jet lag disappeared, and he could at last enjoy his stay in Thailand. At the thought of this little moment of happiness, he leaned back in his seat and swallowed the last drops of the liqueur. Then, getting ready for landing, he closed his diary and put it back in his briefcase. In its pocket he noticed the dog-eared corner of the magazine that Sandrine had forced on him, which he had completely forgotten about. Curious, he pulled it out and unfolded it, fastening his seat belt at the same time.

The *Jules Vallès Gazette*... What was this?... Oh yes, the school magazine... Alex's poem... His little Alex, who had suddenly become so grown-up after the appearance of his little brother Timothée... He had written a poem... How was he going to deal with the now inevitable divorce? He'd understand. He'd have to, anyway. A poem? Well, why not. A bit old-fashioned, but touching all the same. Philippe idly leafed through the *Gazette*, not really concentrating – perfect reading matter for the landing. He passed an editorial he had no desire to read, skimmed through a strip cartoon by the pupils of the fifth form, and found himself looking

155

for Alex's poem, so as to save himself the trouble of reading it during his stay. He started planning some little compliment he could make to his son about it, so as to recapture some of the intimacy that had faded in the last few months. He found it in the contents list:

'A Hundred Ways My Father Died', by Alexandre Massart.

Philippe smiled, surprised. He felt strangely proud to be mentioned as a father, but oddly worried about the title – the word "died" leaped out at him. He turned quickly to page twenty-four, where his son's long poem was printed vertically on the page and covered a two-page spread.

A HUNDRED WAYS MY FATHER DIED

My father died without leaving an address. He didn't
have one.
My father died a hero's death, on the battlefield,
shot by an enemy only he knew about.
My father died stupidly last week.
My father died because he never told anyone he was
going to die.
My father died when he came home, like an
exhausted salmon.
My father died because he watched too many
different channels at once.
My father never got over having made me an orphan.
It killed him.
My father died because he got a memo telling him
to die.
My father died so many times that nobody believed
it the last time.

156

My father, who was terrified of ridicule, was found
                                        dead in a cupboard.
Death knocked on the door with his shroud and his
            scythe, and my father went without a murmur.
My father died to clarify things he found unclear.
My father died because he wanted the moon.
My father died for no reason.
My father died thinking that only God would
                        understand what he had done.
My father died on the other side of the world, like a
                        bird blown off course by the wind.
My father died the way he lived, without noticing
                                                anything.
Anything new? Oh yes, I'd forgotten: my father died.
I would prefer to say he was dyed.
My father died like a dog on his master's grave.

Philippe pressed his elbows on the armrests, trying to
block off a strange sense of oppression in his chest and
catch his failing breath. A second later he was pierced
to the stomach by a stab of pain. He put his hand on his
forehead and rubbed it; he can't have read this right,
his son couldn't have written this, it was a bad-taste joke,
and Alex was too young... too young, too... or not young
enough, and anyway, it was absurd, he wasn't the sort of
boy to... He was normally hopeless at French, there must
be some mistake, Alex wasn't...

My father died just outside the house, where Fate
had waited patiently for his return from the Galapagos
                                                Islands.
My father regarded life as forced labour and he died
                                                of it.

157

My father died without asking any questions about life.
My father died too young; wherever he is, he probably
                                        agrees about that.

Alex... is that you, my little boy? Tell me, it isn't you...
what did I do, Alex?

My father died without any show.
My father died and they spelled his name wrong in
                                        the death notice.
My father died so that people would mourn him.
My father died without my consent.
My father died and it doesn't even make a spoonerism.
Since my father died, everybody agrees about him.

"Monsieur Massart? We've landed, Monsieur Massart..."
And Philippe, hardly taking anything in, followed the
crowd onto the bus to the main building of Bangkok
International Airport.

My father died without seeing the shaft of light which
                                        they say takes you to the other side.
My father died without ever having done anything
                                        forbidden.
My father died the way he wanted to: in his sleep.

Carried along in the crowd as far as the transit zone, he
suddenly felt weak, and stopped to let the main body of
passengers spread out by the passport desks.

My father died too young to be worried about me
                                        having to bury him one day.
My father died a hundred times, or thereabouts.

158

My father died and it won't be front-page news.

My father died, anyone who loved him can follow him.

Philippe collapsed on a bench, exhausted, crumpling the magazine in his fists, and then, with his hands on his face, he burst into tears. His whole body shook with childish sobs.

He got up suddenly, grabbed his briefcase, stamped on the magazine on the floor, and walked down the duty-free area, looking for a telephone. He was shown an oddly exotic telephone booth with a green roof shaped like a Buddhist temple, and rang another telephone which he could visualize perfectly, a little cordless phone, midnight-blue, standing on a side table, next to a little jug of water and a holiday photo in which Sandrine, pregnant with Timothée, was turning her beautiful face into the evening breeze.

Back there in Cholong, at home, it was only ten in the morning.

"Hello... Darling... It's me, darling..."

"Hello... Who's that?"

"It's me, darling! Philippe!"

"Philippe... Where are you?"

"I love you! I love you so much!"

"?..."

"Can you hear me? I love you! I love all three of you! So much..."

"You're scaring me, did something happen on the journey?"

"You're my only reason for living, you're everything, without you my life has no meaning."

"..."

"I'm getting the first plane back, and I'm never leaving the house again without the three of you."

159

"What about Perseil?"

"He can go to hell, and the company too. Do you still love me?"

"See if you can guess."

Then there was another wave of tears, this time of happiness, which washed all the misery out of his heart.

*

A young Belgian called David Moens, arriving from Macao and bound for LA, was waiting, bored stiff with the interminable transit through Bangkok. He could no longer even remember why he had suddenly decided to set off to the Orient, just like that, on the spur of the moment. It was certainly something to do with proving something to himself and to the world, but he had completely forgotten what it was. To go... to leave... Asia... over the horizon, far away... All travellers are poets... Surely he deserved his share of exoticism as much as the next man? Or at least he had to find out what it was, and for that, the only way was to travel, alone, far away, without a bean. Life, destiny and chance would see to the rest.

To sum up the result so far: in less than a week he had lost the little he had left in some less than thrilling gambling and struck up a few random, already forgotten acquaintances; he had not experienced a single moment of excitement, and he was now desperate to get out of Asia and get to America, which might turn out to be a little less impenetrable. In fact California was his last throw of the dice – there was a couple there he was supposed to stay with, some couple he'd met in Brussels last year, with whom he had sworn friendship and exchanged addresses over several Krieks, the usual thing. But a voice inside him was already whispering that nobody would be waiting for him in Los Angeles.

Besides, David was unable to say what part disappointment in love had played in this precipitous departure. He had left Brussels, not because of a woman, but because of all women. The three last years, devoid of either love or sex, had driven him to regard women as the enemy. He saw them all in each one, and each in all, all with the same faults, driven by the same urges, so different from his own. At the risk of sliding into obvious misogynistic clichés, even those of literature, he agreed with all the usual remarks about the female sex, and felt he could sum up all women with just a few well-chosen adjectives. When he bought that plane ticket, it was because he had subconsciously decided to find out if women on the other side of the world behaved in the same way. And he had convinced himself that this was the case before even meeting one.

He found out from the only representative of his airline in Thailand that his plane would be taking off three or four hours late. He turned back, exasperated, and lay down in a corner of the transit lounge, with his head on his rucksack. If only he had something to read… A novel, a magazine, a French prospectus, anything to pass the time. When he had packed his suitcase, the thought of reading hadn't occurred to him. He wouldn't read, he would keep a diary of his travels, one or two pages a day, to record new experiences as soon as they happened. Alas, as his pursuit of the exotic ran into the ground, he became bored of the exercise. He had written four days' worth, and the last entry, Tuesday June 17th, consisted of one paragraph.

161

Wake up feeling tired. Enormous cockroach runs across the ground, where I'm lying, covered with a sheet. They advised me not to kill the insects, it just encourages more. Apparently you should just ignore them. I've turned off the fan; don't want to catch a cold, that would be absurd in this heat. The laundry girl comes by every Tuesday apparently. Where will I be next Tuesday? I'd better look around the town, otherwise no one will believe I've come this far.

Suddenly he noticed a pile of crumpled paper under a row of seats on which he spotted the black-and-white squares of a crossword. It was an odd publication, the *Jules Vallès Gazette*, goodness knew how it had got there. But David Moens wasn't concerned with that – it was in French! A chance to reclaim his language, and set his rusty brain to work again. There were texts, puzzles, drawings, lots of odd little items; he set to work at once on the crossword.

*

High above an ocean whose colour he would never see, because it was dark and he wasn't by the window, David now felt happier about his fate, safe in the aeroplane cabin, at peace with the world. Everything seemed luxurious to him, the hostesses' smiles, the cool drinks, the fragrant wipes, the air-conditioning, the sharp sweets. Safe at last, he could now concentrate on the crossword, which presented no great challenge.

The young compilers had made no attempt to limit the number of black squares, nor to make the clues particularly difficult. But they had embarked on a ten-by-ten grid, which was made it oddly complicated for

162

the crossword-solver. David dealt easily with all the three and four letter words which fitted smoothly into one another. Most of his neighbours were already asleep, and the plane travelled through the night in perfect silence, as he sipped his tepid mini-can of Coke through a straw. "Party people", eight letters? These snotty-nosed brats were beginning to slow him down. David had to admit that he was one of those occasional crossword fanciers who only enjoy it when it's easy and soon feel humiliated by clues with several layers of meaning. The easy start had too quickly made him overconfident. Once he'd found "*Noah*", the second word in the fourth vertical column ("sheltered a lot of couples"), *revellers* occurred to him for "party people". In full flight now, he got an awesome *adultery*, for "half plus a third". These kids from Cholong-sur-Avre, some dump in the back of beyond, were definitely more sophisticated than he thought. David had automatically written down the word *adultery* without wondering what the word could possibly mean to a child of twelve. What could someone of that age know about adultery, when he, David, at the great age of twenty-four, was full of self-pity about his miserable libido. Adultery? It was his dream! To be the lover of a married woman represented the pinnacle of sexual experience. He imagined passionate afternoons in a slightly seedy hotel near the Bruxelles-Midi station, a bottle of white wine on the bedside table and a fine-looking bourgeoise of fifty from the smart streets by the Chaussée d'Ixelles, pink with shame and excitement at finding herself naked in a squalid room, with a yob who made her come by treating her like a tart. Such were the images that sprang into David's mind at the very word *adultery*. Either the kids from the Jules Vallès

163

*

Two hours later, now sitting side by side, prodding each other in a familiar way, they still couldn't finish the crossword.

"Perhaps we were wrong with 'First jet', suppose it's not..." he said.

"What do you suggest?"

"*Caravel.*"

"Sorry?"

"It was a sort of ancestor to the jet. The little bastards are trying to catch us out. All these air pockets made me think of it."

"Don't forget that this puzzle has been compiled not just by little bastards, but by perverted little bastards. This jet idea isn't an aeroplane – 'first jet', at their age, must mean something different..."

"Surely not..."

"First jet – you're a boy..."

"*Wanking?*"

"Of course. We'd keep the *a* from *adultery*, but we'd have to find something else for 'bodies in fusion'."

"*Debauchery?*" she almost whispered.

"Would they have *orgy* AND *debauchery?*"

"Of course, it can only be *debauchery.*"

"'Something sensual' in four letters could be anything: *lust... fuck...* even *love!*"

"..."

"..."

"Let's allow *love*, but that means 'needs a helping hand', seven letters, would have to start with an *o.*"

"You know what I'm thinking?"

"I'm afraid I do..."

165

"I'm sorry to have to say it, but *onanism* means 'on fire', seven letters, can't be *kindled*."

"Why not *amorous*?"

"Yes, why not?"

The plane was about to land in Los Angeles. David no longer planned to call the American couple, who had probably forgotten his existence anyway; he suggested to Delphine that they might explore the city together. Twenty minutes later, the airport cleaners worked their way down the economy-class aisles, throwing all the rubbish into their binbags, including the *Jules Vallès Gazette*.

*

At the north corner of LA International Airport, the rubbish-disposal services piled up, ground and burned, in gigantic containers, the many tons of rubbish that arrived daily from the nine terminals. Some of the containers destined for recycling were waiting, that early morning, to be taken on trailers to the San Diego recycling centre. Four of the two-hundred-cubic-feet receptacles were piled high with thousands of magazines, newspapers and computer printouts, thrown out by the airlines by the pallet-load. Donny, like an insect caught in a matchbox, scrabbled around in the least full of the four.

Donny's mother was dead, and he spent as much time as he could out of the house to spare his hard-up father any extra worries. He was fifteen and no longer expected to be fed, clothed, or even given any advice on life and its many vicissitudes, all of which his father had suffered. He hardly ever went to the cinema, never

166

watched TV, and there was no decent male role model in his neighbourhood to guide him into adulthood. His father was in fact a kind of example – an example of what not to do, a perfect guide to failure in life. So Donny just got along on his own, and pretty well really, picking up tips about life here and there in his wanderings. After several jobs, most of which were only borderline legal, he had become a specialist in the recuperation of old newspapers, just as others had found their calling in old Coke cans. So, three times a week, he would visit the airport containers, and then sell his booty on to other sellers who were prospecting on behalf of collectors of strip cartoons, magazines, dailies – you could find a taker for anything. Danny had become a master of his art: the search, the redistribution amongst his contacts, the discovery of new depots, and, as long as he worked discreetly and alone, the rubbish authorities were happy to turn a blind eye to his business. There was no one like him, capable of plunging bodily into the container, pushing himself down through the layers, turning over the furthest corner, opening up a gap, leafing through, sorting, piling, and then coming up to the surface with his rucksack full of miraculous booty. LAX airport had become his exclusive territory, and he had become a familiar figure, to whom nobody paid any attention.

However, that particular morning, Danny felt he had wasted his journey: the *Vogues* were too recent, there were some fitness mags, hardly ten-dollars' worth, possibly another five for a 1972 *Playboy* which he knew a bookseller in Catalina would take. You could always find takers for these old mags, and they weren't just for nostalgic perverts; sometimes they were completely respectable people, researchers sometimes, or maybe

167

a student writing a thesis about magazines in the past. The most unlikely titles would turn out to be collectors' items, particularly *Playboy* – you really had to have money to burn to look at this outdated American myth. Naked women from 1972, what was that about?

In 1972 his mother and father hadn't even met, and there was nothing anywhere to suggest the future existence of a Donny Ray. He would only be born fifteen years later, by which time the sense of the forbidden had given way to all-powerful merchandising, and the profit motive had broken through the last taboos. For Donny, who had never touched a woman, nonetheless found their bodies a source of inexhaustible raw material, always available, with not the slightest mystery or concealment. For him nudity had always, from the very beginning, been a fact of life, like running water, or the bus, a basic human right. He had never opened a girl's legs, but he knew all about what was there. During his searches, he would glance coolly at the pin-ups in *Hustler* or *Penthouse* – to him all female shapes were equal and none aroused his curiosity any longer. Donny Ray just couldn't imagine that, back in 1972, very pretty women were already taking their clothes off in magazines to be queen for a day, and that a boy of his age would have killed to get his hands on this copy of *Playboy*. He simply leafed through it to check it was in good condition, unfolded the centrefold and found the Playmate of the Month spread out over three pages. Miss May 1972 was called Linda Mae Barker; she was posing in a bubble bath, photographed face on and from above.

Crouched in his container, Danny studied the magazine, thinking. The central photo didn't show much, not *everything* in any case. For the first time in

168

his short life, he felt that something was being kept from him. And this girl didn't look at all like the ones in the present-day magazines. Were women's bodies that different then? Intrigued by the photos of young Miss Barker, so old-fashioned, so charmingly dated, almost to the point of being kitsch, Donny left the airport, still studying the magazine. Before climbing out of the container, he had picked up a crumpled rag, hardly glancing at it – the *Jules Vallès Gazette*, what was this crap? – just the right size to hide the *Playboy* from the curious eyes of passers-by. A gesture that betrayed his age.

He took the overground railway at Aviation Avenue and settled down on a bench at the end of an empty carriage. He began to study Linda Mae Barker's body from head to foot, amazed by all of it, starting with the dark-brown hair with its darker roots, held back by a schoolgirl's red ribbon. An ordinary brunette, like any of the ones you might see in the street, no more nor less sophisticated than usual; he had passed thousands like her in real life: there was the dental technician who never looked up from her work in the little office in Placid Square, or even that social worker who was always begging him to keep appointments with the psychologist. The playmates Donny looked at nowadays had great blond manes which could have covered their whole bodies. Linda Mae Barker was a gazelle compared to lionesses like that. Donny, with infinite patience, studied her every feature, her hardly visible freckles, her sweet smile, her adorable little face. He was touched by such innocence, by the way she seemed to say so little while showing so much, her shyness at being naked, the slight vulnerability of her expression, the reason for which you could only guess at, and which was invisible to

169

those who didn't study her properly. He recognized that look in the women he saw every day; they had no pride, and were simply curious about everything, capable of being amazed by the smallest thing. The modern-day pin-ups had eliminated every shred of that naivety from their expression, gazing out as they did, beyond the photographer, at the millions of men, all connoisseurs of the power of naked flesh. You could read in Linda Mae Barker's face the challenge she had set herself – to pose naked in front of the whole of America – and her victory could be read deep in her eyes.

And the most extraordinary thing was that the rest of the body, from the shoulders down, also reflected this modesty that Donny was finding so confusing. Linda Mae Barker's breasts! High on the torso without being insolent, almost fragile despite their splendour. He searched for a word to describe them and, for want of a better one, picked "imperfect". Yes, they were imperfect, their shape slightly unfamiliar, something between an apple and a pear, and a very long way from a melon. Before discovering Linda Mae's, Donny had always thought breasts were like geometrical spheres, all the same size, pumped up until they almost leaped out at the reader's face. Linda Mae's imperfect breasts made one long to spend some time remodelling them by hand, just so that they could spring back to their original shape, which was in the end the best one. Linda Mae's chest pre-dated surgery and silicone. And the innocence was compounded by the way the whiteness of Linda Mae's breasts contrasted with the rest of her tanned body, showing a clear bikini line. Donny couldn't get over this. White breasts? It was unheard of! It was almost indecent. What, no sunbeds in 1972? No

170

instant tan? No one topless on the beach? Had Linda Mae never shown herself naked to anyone else? He got off the train at Long Beach station, still clutching the *Jules Vallès Gazette* wrapped around Linda Mae Barker's body. The more he stared at her, the more he wanted to protect her from sight. He got on a bus going to Lynwood, where his mate Stu lived, a childhood friend now working as a debt collector. Stu had often tried to teach him the art of breaking debtors' thumbs, but Donny, finding most forms of violence unattractive, had preferred to specialize in the old newspaper business; he saw it as a kind of contemporary treasure hunt, and here was the proof: he had found Linda Mae Barker at the bottom of a rubbish container. A young girl who had given herself to *Playboy* as one might give oneself to a first lover. With enormous care, he turned to the bottom half of the centrefold to see what was going on below the waist. The pubic area was almost entirely concealed by a mound of bubbles, just showing some edges of barely shaved pubic hair, which appeared to be the same colour as her hair – an exotic touch on this nymph-like body. Donny was more and more surprised. He had seen several thousand pubic regions in his time, in every possible shape: hearts, diamonds, spades, clubs, and every shade of blue and pink, and the most usual kind were entirely shaved. He knew more about labia than his own father. Linda Mae Barker, whose left leg was raised slightly inwards, preserved her most intimate parts, kept them hidden for ever; men, and Donny in particular, would just have to imagine. He regarded this pose as both unfair and completely legitimate. In a daze, Donny got off the bus and walked a hundred yards down Josephine

171

Street. He entered a black brick building, nodded to the old Puerto Rican sitting in the hallway – he was a sort of unpaid doorman who had been there for ever – and rang the bell of Stu's ground-floor flat. While he waited, he had a last look at the astonishing twenty-one-year-old girl from back in 1972, when a hundred million Americans had seen in her the epitome of eroticism. Donny was worried by this unsettling feeling of annoyance that pervaded him – could this be what was known as arousal?

"You're just the man, Donny, I need a hand…"

Inside the apartment there was a curious combination of twilight and halogen glow. For his own reasons, Stu had decided to block off what light there was with thick shutters, which also acted as a protection against burglars. Donny had often slept there in front of the TV, his body sunk into the sofa cushions. He automatically went over to the fridge, and looked inside, without taking anything. Stu went on with what he was doing. It looked like a complicated operation, and, from a distance, reminiscent of Prohibition, a time these boys had never known.

"Can I ask what you're doing?"

"It's a parcel for Uncle Erwan."

There were ten large cups of black coffee, a packet of sugar and six bottles of pure alcohol on the table where Stu was working.

"Coffee liqueur, it's his drug, the idiot says it helps him digest. I must really love him. Just to wind me up, he won't just drink Irish coffee, like any other Irishman, the stuff you can buy in the shops, oh no, he's got to have it home-made, that's what comes of hanging out with those fucking Italians. It's a real bind, I tell you.

172

You have to mix 90% proof alcohol with sugar and coffee, but not just the sort of coffee I normally get, it's got to be espresso, the real thing, a sort of mud I get them to make at Martino's opposite. While I'm mixing the bottles, you can go to and fro, I need ten more cups like this, Martino knows. Geddit?"

"Stu, I'm in love."

"What's that to me? You, in love? Who with?"

"Linda Mae Barker."

"Don't know her."

"She's a playmate."

"Let's see."

Donny held out the magazine, and immediately regretted it, gripped by jealousy at the thought of other eyes on his beloved.

"Her? You're having me on. She looks my mom when she was at school. Take the tray and six cups, don't let them get cold, it mixes better when it's still warm."

"I want to know what happened to her."

"?…"

"…"

"She must be dead, what year is it?"

"'72."

"'72! You're crazy – you're talking about an old woman, that's disgusting."

"What happened to her? What did she become after that? Is she married, has she got kids? Did people go on saying, 'I saw you naked in *Playboy*, that was a while ago.' Did those photos change her life? For better or worse? Did she regret it? Or did she think she was lucky? What does she look like now? A woman who, for just one month, drove half the men on the planet mad – is she just growing old like all the others?"

173

Stu stopped fiddling with his bottles. He looked worried.

"It's just a stage you're going through, it's not serious, but you'd better talk to someone. I was a bit strange at your age too, but this is something else."

"I'm going to write to Hugh Hefner, he'll know what's become of her."

"Who's that?"

"The man who founded *Playboy*. He invented bunnies."

"I'd take care if I was you, with all those nuts who write in. You'll have the cops round."

"I could look on the Internet, on one of those 'Friends Reunited' sites."

"Yeah, and what about just falling for someone your own age. How about the little singer we saw at the Studio A party?"

"Linda Mae may need me just now."

"Just now I'm the one who needs you, so go and get the fucking espressos, so I can send off this fucking parcel; we'll think about your problems after that, OK?"

They finished the job, Stu put the stopper in the last bottle and then got out the wooden case in which the coffee liqueur was going to travel across the United States from West to East.

"Your Uncle Erwan, is that the garage man?"

"Are you crazy? I'd tell Uncle Dylan to go fuck himself if he asked me to do anything. Erwan's in Rykers, with the long-stay guys, he'll never get out. Idiot hasn't got any family, except me, so I'm the fool who has to make his crappy liqueur."

Stu's favourite uncle was the eldest of the Dougherty brothers. He had left Los Angeles towards the end

174

of the Sixties in pursuit of the Pasionaria of a short-lived revolutionary movement. As the only member of the armed wing of this movement, Erwan had been sentenced to life imprisonment on Rykers Island, the New York State prison, for no less than having tried to kill the President. Stu, who had never known his uncle other than behind bars, had great respect for him, not so much for his political convictions as for the length of his sentence, which gave him some kudos in the neighbourhood.

"I didn't think alcohol was allowed in jail."

"The only thing that's not allowed where he is, is credit. Anyway, he's part of the scenery there, they practically allow him to go out to buy his packet of tobacco. He plays cards with the guards, plays the mediator when there's a fight, he's always been a good spokesman. He says it's not a good example to follow."

As he talked, Stu went on packing the bottles in the box, wrapping each one in a cylinder of corrugated cardboard for protection. Failing that, a magazine rolled round a bottle did just as well. He picked up the 1972 *Playboy* to wrap the last of the six, and was stopped by Donny's horrified cry.

"Linda Mae!"

And holding his beloved against his heart, he made a momentous decision:

"Whether you help me or not, Stu, I'm going to find her. And I'll tell her what she means to me."

"Technically she could be your grandma."

Stu picked up the other magazine lying on the table and tried to read the title

"The what… *Gazette?*… What language is this crap?"

"God knows, you find everything in those containers."

175

Stu didn't enquire any further and rolled the *Jules Vallès Gazette* around the black liqueur, which was now perfectly wedged in with the five others. He stuck the address onto the box: James Thomas Centre, 14 Hazen Street, Rykers Island, NY 11370, and made two string handles for easy carrying – he'd been doing this for a while.

"Supposing you find her one day, what are you going to say to her, your Miss May 1972?"

Donny thought for a while before answering:

"That I still believe in her."

*

Rykers Island, the largest prison in Manhattan, New York, was home to seventeen thousand inmates, men and women, scattered throughout ten separate buildings. The island was a sort of state within a state, less than six miles from the Empire State Building, and it was the largest penal institution in the world. The preserve of the senior inhabitants could be found, well away from the others, in a building called the James Thomas Centre, in honour of the first African American prison guard. On this Mount Olympus of the underworld, there reigned several living legends of crime, major figures from the Mob, the last of the great mythical outlaws whom the public had never tired of hearing about. Each of them was serving sentences of up to four hundred years, long enough to die behind bars, be born and die again several times over. In order to be a member of this exclusive long-sentence club, you had to have been sent down for a minimum of two hundred and fifty years without parole.

176

And so it was that in this senior preserve, time was perceived differently to anywhere else.

These twenty inmates lived in exceptionally comfortable conditions; they were famous, and mostly rich; they had the sort of lawyers you would associate with the largest of trust funds, and their good relationship with the authorities had transformed their status into that of permanent residents rather than prisoners, and their cells into apartments comparable with the best to be found in central Manhattan. They would all die there some day, but none of them were in a particular hurry to do so.

That afternoon, two of the residents, who had been friends for four years (in their timescale, just time for a handshake), were sitting and chatting in their armchairs, smoking the ritual post-prandial cigar. The younger man, who had nonetheless been there longest, was the terrorist Erwan Dougherty; he had invited his neighbour opposite, Don Mimino, who was twenty years older than him, the godfather of all the godfathers of the Italian Mafia, who had been incarcerated for six years. Erwan was very cautious about all contact with others – he had remained in total silence for nearly eight years – and liked Don Mimino for his old-world manners, and his philosophy of life, which seemed to come from another era, as well as the quality of his conversation, which was only equalled by the quality of his silences. For the venerable Italian, the Irishman's value lay in the fact that he was the only other Catholic in the building.

"I've decided to learn my native language," announced Don Mimino.

"What do you mean?"

"I speak a sort of Sicilian dialect that was incomprehensible even in the next village. You only hear it nowadays in some parts of New Jersey! What I want to learn is the *lingua madre*, the language they speak in Siena. I want to be able to read Dante in the original. They say it's great stuff. I've worked out that if I take a course in medieval Italian, I should be able to get through the *Divina Commedia* within five or six years."

In the senior preserve, embarking on long courses of study was desirable for many reasons; most of them saw it as a better way of passing the time than exercise or television. But it wasn't just that.

"Then I'll move on to English," he continued. "I've lived here for sixty years, and all I can talk is a mixture of immigrant patois and street slang, and I'm not proud of that. My ambition is to read *Moby Dick* without having to look up words at every page."

It wasn't just a matter of killing time, it was a way of finding a meaning, or even several, to this sentence which defied any understanding. How could you envisage the next three hundred years without some kind of purpose?

"I started late with Melville," Erwan said. "When I got here, I first of all read the whole of Conrad and the whole of Dickens, then the whole of Joyce – he was from Dublin, like my parents. Then I started on a law course which took me eight years."

Law was the most popular choice, followed by psychology, with literature a poor third. Some wanted to explore the workings of the legal code, discover hidden meanings and traps, and fully grasp the details of what exactly had caused them to end up on this island. Erwan, for example, had passed his bar exams so as to

178

reopen his file and conduct his own defence. Psychology and allied subjects were also much in demand, anything concerning the mechanism of the human mind, starting with their own – indeed some simply went straight into analysis – this in order to put the troubles of the past in their place and then to be able to face the future with serenity. Psychology was also a way into other disciplines, and it helped them to understand the laws governing groups and hierarchies. In the senior section you had the opportunity to embark on a subject and expect to fully master it, exhausting it right down to the smallest detail, while taking daily care to update the sum of knowledge. Who, in the outside world, could possibly hope to achieve such thoroughness?

Other inmates studied with the sole aim of gaining good conduct points and achieving parole, which could knock ten or fifteen years off a sentence. Some of the more determined inmates had managed to reduce their sentences from a hundred and sixty to a hundred and fifty years.

Unlike the rest of the world, the Rykers seniors did not see death as the final reckoning. The final reckoning, for them, would be their first day of freedom. They had to cling on to the idea that one day, in two or three centuries' time, they would walk free and set off to discover a new world. Then there would be plenty of time to actually die.

"Then what?" Erwan asked, relighting his Romeo y Julieta.

"Well, then I might be tempted by one or two of the Asian languages. I spent so many years fighting the Japanese and Chinese Mafias that I think it might be time to start trying to understand how these guys work, and speaking their language might help."

179

"When I finished my diploma in Chinese medicine, I studied Taoism and learned about their techniques for longevity, and that led naturally on to Tai Chi. Some of the legends tell of ancient masters who lived for between nine hundred and a thousand years."

"I gave up all forms of physical activity at an early age."

"You'll come round to it, Don Mimino. Not immediately, but you'll come round to it eventually."

"We'll see. I'll study ancient medicine, and then specialize in rheumatology. My back is killing me…"

Someone knocked at the door. Unlike those of other cells, the senior ones were only closed with doors and partitions, and only had bars on the windows. "Chief" Morales, the head guard of the West Wing, which included the senior section, came in, carrying a box.

"It's my idiot nephew's regular parcel," Erwan said, cutting it open with a knife. "You'll have a drop of liqueur with us, Chief?"

"Sorry, haven't got time. Block B is playing up."

The guard, just as a formality, glanced inside the box, weighed up a couple of bottles, and left the cell. Chief Morales, despite his youth, was well respected by the inmates for his good sense and willingness to solve problems.

"We'll miss him when he retires," said Don Mimino.

Erwan opened a bottle and sniffed the still-fresh aroma of coffee.

"A guy from Milan introduced me to this when he was staying here, back in the Seventies. It's less creamy than Irish coffee, less sickly. Between you and me, I've never really liked Irish whiskey either."

Don Mimino took a sip from the little black glass his host handed to him.

180

"*Buono.*"

Erwan unpacked the five other bottles, put them in the cupboard and gathered the wrapping paper up into a pile. He was about to put them in the bin when his eye fell on the *Jules Vallès Gazette*.

"Hey, Don, is that French?"

The old Italian put on his glasses and inspected the cover.

"I think so, yes."

"I'm not much good at languages, but I might have liked French. I'll think about it."

"A lot of irregular verbs, they say."

"Suppose we did it together, Don Mimino? That's an idea! In four years we'll be fluent, and I suggest we make French the official language during liqueur time. Could be fun!"

"You're all mad, you Irish…"

They clinked glasses and knocked back their drinks. Don Mimino, out of idle curiosity, took the *Jules Vallès Gazette* back to his cell, to study it in peace. He was tempted by the idea of learning French for just one reason: he would be able to watch the films on the Classics Channel without having to read the subtitles; he found French police films from the Fifties much closer to reality than American ones from the same era. Oddly he felt himself to be closer to Jean Gabin than George Raft.

He spent the afternoon learning by heart the subjunctive endings of the auxiliary verbs *essere* and *avere*. Then he dined alone in his cell, and dozed off in front of a variety show on Rai Due which he got on satellite TV. Late that night, he woke up, worried about having insomnia, couldn't sleep, and picked up the *Jules Vallès*

Gazette. Really, he thought, it was a difficult language… Learning Chinese pictograms would be easier than this. But still, in fifty or sixty years, who knew? Before closing the magazine and trying to get back to sleep, Don Mimino's tired eyes caught sight of one line of text at the bottom of a column. Just more words, but this time in a familiar language.

Boris Godunov? If it's good enough for you, it's good enough for me!

He sat up in bed, his old vertebrae cracking. The piece was signed by a certain Warren Blake.

If it's good enough for you…

That pun belonged to him, Maurizio Gallone, known in forty states as Don Mimino.

…it's good enough for me!

The few times he had crossed paths with the son of that motherfucker Manzoni, the boy had reminded him of the joke, it had become a sort of ritual between them. Besides, they had nothing else to say to one another.

And as for the three hundred and forty-five years he had left on this island, well, he owed them to the boy's father, Giovanni Manzoni.

The Don didn't need to learn French to understand where the magazine came from: *written and edited by the pupils of the Lycée Jules Vallès, Cholong-sur-Avre, Normandy.*

He had to make a telephone call, and it was urgent.

He yelled down the corridor, waking up Chief Morales.

182

her on, like a sharp pike in the back of a condemned man. Anyway, what mattered was not the reasons for her altruistic behaviour, but its results – after all, she had no interest in what drove the other volunteers to help total strangers. At the very start of the exercise, she had been curious about their motives, and had identified several types. There were the sufferers, who devoted themselves to others in order to escape from themselves. Then there were the unhappy ones, who gave because they had never received, and the opposite – the privileged and the idle, who wanted to find a way to pass the time. There were believers, who, under a halo of self-sacrifice, worked for the poor with half an eye on their own holy reflection; these people had a special expression as they worked, a kind but controlled smile, arms wide open like vales of tears, eyes moistened by all the misery they had witnessed. You could also find the progressive thinker, looking to others to salve his conscience; the plain fact of helping the disinherited brought him an extraordinary sense of intellectual well-being. Others expected to expiate their sins by one single action. Still others went against their own natures and stopped justifying their cynicism about the decadence of the world. And there were also those who, without realizing it, were finally growing up.

Nowadays, Maggie no longer cared which of them had a real empathy for the unhappiness of others, and which felt true indignation at the sight of injustice, or whose heart beat with solidarity with his fellow man, or bled for the sins of the world. Actions trumped intentions, and every little helped. In Cholong, voluntary work was now all the rage, and there were so many new vocations that they would soon run out of needy people to help.

184

Warren treated his new fame as the recognition he deserved. The services he had performed for the younger generation had brought him respect – something he valued above all things. The father had been a traitor; it was now time for the son to assume the role and become the giver of the "alternative" justice that prevails once the law has failed. He had dropped the criminal side of Mafia behaviour, and had just retained their way of getting things done; he was now the only advocate of the forgotten ones, their only hope of gaining reparation. His justice and protection were expensive commodities, but nothing is free in this base world. Going to cry on his shoulder would put you in his debt for a long time, but what could be more precious than seeing the person who had wronged you begging for forgiveness? No price was too great for such a sight. Warren made it his business to carry out any request that seemed reasonable to him, and the other boys saw him as a hero: *Warren can help you, Warren will know what to do, ask Warren, Warren is fair, Warren is good, Warren is Warren.* His real strength lay in the fact that he never sought people out, he let them come to him; he never tried to lead, but simply accepted the authority granted to him; he never asked, just waited until it was offered. His idol, Al Capone, no less, would have been proud of him. Warren paid the price for such great power by living a secret life, as his equals had done before him. A true leader observed the law of silence, and let those who were bursting to pour out their souls come to him. *Give them what they need.* And what they needed was to be listened to. He endeavoured to get the clearest possible picture of the plaintiff's case before taking a side, or taking the case. This was the foundation of his power and the basis of his future position as leader. The structure was growing a little each day.

Although Warren had never sought followers, he had become the role model for a whole generation in Cholong, all inspired by this gift for listening, which seemed to hold the key to so many problems.

Warren had never dared question his father about his decision to become a state witness against his own people. The day would come when such a conversation could no longer be avoided, but he didn't yet feel brave enough to ask – his father was still a figure of authority despite his miserable house-bound existence.

The trauma of the trial and its repercussions had not dented Fred's extraordinarily tough inner core, which enabled him to move between the role of protector and threat as circumstances changed. The people of Cholong, in their way, were more aware of the protector in him. He would be described as a man who had knocked about the world and met the movers and shakers, who had inspired shelf-loads of books. They had a feeling that the "American" or the "writer" had the makings of a leader of men. Women turned round as he walked by, men waved at him from afar, children hero-worshipped him. He was admired for many different reasons, but all could see that what he had was natural authority. Frederick Blake was one of those rare beings people prefer to be friends with, but without quite knowing why. When he appeared in a group, they were simultaneously worried and reassured, and the chemistry changed completely: one nasty look, one handshake, and the strong were weak and the weak strong. He was the undisputed leader of the pack, the dominant male. It was a role he would happily have

186

done without, but there was nothing to be done, it had always been thus: a decision to be made, an answer given, everybody turned to Fred, without quite knowing why. His size and his chunky corpulence did not enter into it – men twice his height would bend down to him and lower their voices. Often men he'd never seen before. Who knows where such authority comes from? He himself had no idea, it was some blend of magnetism and inner aggression, combined with a certain stillness about the body, everything coming from the expression in the eyes: there was always an undeclared potential for violence in there somewhere. When he was in the town, Fred walked as though still surrounded by bodyguards, conscious of his firepower, with a private army ready to die for him. They envied him his way of expressing disagreement, without raising his voice or being unnaturally friendly. A boy brushed against an old lady with his bike? Fred would take him by the collar and make him apologize. Beer a little flat? The bartender was only too delighted to change the barrels. A gatecrasher trying to get past him? A simple movement of the finger and he was back outside. He had never been afraid of dealing with strangers when the situation required it. He had never suspected others of aggressive intentions, or felt threatened before the threat came. He couldn't understand how, out in the streets, fear had turned into cowardice, and paranoia into silent hatred. Nowadays he could feel that fear everywhere and it wasn't any use to anyone. What a waste.

The beautiful, the pure Belle, on the other hand, lived in an alternative world. Her existence was living proof that the most beautiful flowers grow on cactuses, swamps or dung heaps. Evil had given birth to grace and

187

innocence, and this grace and innocence gave pleasure to many. You saw Belle in the street and already you felt better. Hers was not a haughty, cruel beauty – it was generous, open to all, without distinction or snobbery. Everyone was accorded a kind gesture, a friendly word and angelic look, and those who weren't satisfied with that were sorry – Belle remained untouchable, and the unfortunate fools who had pushed their luck now regretted it bitterly. Her confidence added to her beauty, as it allowed her to smile at strangers and reply to compliments without lowering her head. The gloomiest of pessimists only needed a moment in her company to restore his faith in life. In her own way, she proved that humanity was capable of better things; her role as an exceptional person was to respond to cynicism and despair with goodness and hope. Good fairies really did exist, and made everybody want to be better.

That morning, she walked along the Place de la Libération, followed by the catcalls and wolf whistles of the fairground people setting up the attractions, among which was a big wheel like the one at the Foire du Trone in Paris. Belle stopped for a moment to look at the men, balancing up high, fixing the gondolas onto the wheel, and decided that she'd go up there and see what the town looked like from above as soon as the fair opened.

A countdown had begun in Cholong: only four days until the annual fair, the best in the region, twenty-four hours of non-stop festivity, the beginning of the long-awaited summer. As well as a merry-go-round with wooden horses and bumping cars, which you could find anywhere else, the big wheel attracted people from three neighbouring *départements*, and was never empty.

The town looked like a Luna Park by day, and Las Vegas by night.

Fred had announced that fairground music depressed him, and that he would spend the whole weekend on his veranda. In any case he had better things to do: chapter five of his great work dealt with the big fundamental issues of life, and answered the questions that common people asked about greater and smaller issues in the criminal world.

Every man has his price. It's not whores that are in short supply, it's money. If you can't control people with money, you've got them if you know their particular perversion, and if you don't know that, there's always their ambition. You have no idea what a businessman is capable of doing to get some business, or an actor to get a part, or a politician to get elected. I once even got a bishop to sign a forged cheque in exchange for building an orphanage which would be named after him. You sometimes get people wrong, you think they're angels – in fact they're bastards. An ambitious man can conceal an angel, and the bastard might just be ambitious – you just have to find out who went wrong at the first bribery attempt, and do it right the next time. I've seen so many men abandon their fine principles once they're shown something they've always longed for. No one can resist that. Temptation... it's often much more effective than threats. I once came across a guy, well, a couple really, who would have done anything to have a child, and...

The telephone rang, stopping him in mid-sentence. With a curse on his lips, he got up. Di Cicco, on the line, could hardly bring out the words.

"You didn't do it, Manzoni? You didn't dare!"

189

"What have I done now?"

Holding the receiver, the agent was kicking the camp bed beside him, trying to wake his colleague. Through the window he could see a figure in beige Bermuda shorts and T-shirt looking for an address in the Rue des Favorites.

"Is that your nephew outside?"

"Ben there already? I'm coming!"

He cheerfully hung up on Di Cicco and ran outside.

"Tell the boss," Di Cicco yelled at Caputo, whose dream turned into a nightmare as he watched Fred, in the middle of the street, hugging his nephew.

Benedetto Manzoni, known as Ben to the family, and "D" to his workmates, had arrived in Europe for the first time, and had been looking forward to seeing his uncle after so many years. One call had been enough to bring him over.

"Good journey?"

"A bit long, I'm not used to that."

"Have you put on weight, Ben?"

"Yeah, the girls say it suits me."

Ben was nearly thirty, but still looked like a plump adolescent – he was of medium height, with black hair, black eyes that shone like marbles, ill-shaven, with his hands deep in his pockets: he had always gone for the relaxed look – comfort for him took absolute priority over any aesthetic considerations. He kept all the essentials of his life in the multiple pockets of his famous beige shorts: papers, a few souvenirs, a survival kit. His camouflage jacket held the wherewithal for his happiness and spiritual well-being: one or two books, a few joints, a mobile phone and a video-game console. Fred, who couldn't think of anything to say, hugged his

190

nephew again, his favourite nephew, a true Manzoni, with his Manzoni looks and general attitude. Fred had always wondered about the link between uncles and nephews, that curious form of light-hearted affection, strong but without any connotations of duty and obligation. He could put on an air of authority with Ben, and would have tolerated it being mocked, but of course that had never happened.

Out of the corner of his eye, Fred saw the two shapes leaning out of the window at number 9.

"We'd better go and see the agents, get it out of the way."

Di Cicco and Caputo saw them approaching. They collapsed into their armchairs, stunned, unable to understand how Fred had managed to deceive them.

"If I'd asked your permission to invite my nephew, would you have said yes?"

"Never."

"We haven't seen each other for six years. He's practically my son! And you know perfectly well he's got no contacts with the Mob."

After the trial which had decimated the ranks of the five families, anyone called Manzoni had had to disappear as far away as possible, and stay out of the smallest corner of Mob activity. Having a turncoat uncle had cost Benedetto dear. He had lost his only friends, his honour, his name. There'll be a silver lining, people had said at the time, now he could develop a talent for some legitimate activity. Alas, Benedetto's problem was that he had no talent that could possibly be used legitimately.

"Manzoni, this is going to end badly," said Caputo. "Ever since we've been in this dump, we've done our

191

best to mop up after you. We're having trouble keeping an eye on you four, and now you've brought in a fifth."

"He's going back tomorrow, I just wanted to give him a hug. You're Italian, Caputo, you must understand."

Di Cicco tore off the fax that had just come in. It was Ben's file, and he read it out loud.

"*Benedetto D. Manzoni, thirty, son of Chiara Chiavone and Ottavio Manzoni, elder brother of Giovanni Manzoni, died 1982.* What's the D for? Dario? Delano? Dante? Daniel? What?"

He'd been asked that question a thousand times, and he'd answered it differently each time, never giving the right answer.

"How about *Disgraziato*?" Caputo suggested.

Ben decided not to respond to the FBI's sarcasm.

"Anyway, who cares," Caputo went on. "*Now living in Green Bay, Michigan, runs a small video arcade.*"

"A video arcade?" Fred exclaimed. "You mean you're the one giving out the tokens?"

Ben was silent in the face of this humiliating revelation. If Giovanni Manzoni hadn't spilled the beans six years earlier, his nephew would now have been one of the kings of the New York crime scene.

"And they say crime doesn't pay," Caputo continued.

"And what exactly brings you here?" Di Cicco asked. "And don't give me any of that crap about blood ties, we're not as stupid as you think, Manzoni."

"Call me Blake, boys, you gave me that name. Where's Quint?"

"In Paris. We've told him to come back at once."

"I'm only talking to him."

He beckoned to his nephew to follow him downstairs, and they left the house. Ben got a rucksack out of the

192

boot of his rented car, and followed his uncle. Still feeling like fools, neither Di Cicco nor Caputo asked themselves what was in the rucksack.

*

You needed to be uncommonly strong to stir the polenta. Ben stirred it in a huge copper pan with a thick stick, until it was thick enough to stand it up. At the same time he kept an eye on another pan in which some red liquid was simmering, but not yet thickening. Maggie watched him, holding a glass of wine, leaning on the work surface. She asked him for news of home.

"I've hardly been back to Newark since I moved to Green Bay. I go about every six months, but I don't stay long."

What he meant was that if any of his old fighting companions had spotted him, there would have been bloodshed. Maggie knew this, of course, but she couldn't help asking about her old friends, themselves victims of Giovanni's treachery; the earthquake caused by the trial had brought down the whole Manzoni world.

"What about my best friend, Barbara, the one who had the boutique, what happened to her?"

"Barbara? Was she the one with the boobs always hanging out?"

"No, that's Amy. Barbara's the tall, thin one, who's always laughing."

"She got a divorce after the trial. The boutique was bought by a doughnut-seller. Last I heard, she was living with a beer salesman who treats her like shit."

The boutique had been given to her by one of Gianni's sidekicks, introduced to her by Maggie. The

193

two young women had been inseparable, living through those golden years in an atmosphere of soft decadence that seemed as though it would go on for ever. Even before the betrayal, Maggie had sometimes felt dizzy with it all. Gianni Manzoni's wife – she was the First Lady of the whole area. She never had to reserve a table, and had elevated shopping to a new art form; always driven everywhere, her smallest whims were commands. Paradoxically, these women spent their time criticizing their husbands, while always respecting the hierarchy and most of the codes of conduct. If a member of the family was in disgrace, his wife or girlfriend would distance herself from her friends until the quarantine period was over. But how could one live permanently outside the clan? All those evenings amongst friends, the weekends in Atlantic City, the holidays in Miami, the intricately linked family connections. From one day to the next, love, friendship and respect had been transformed into horror and then pure hatred towards Gianni and Livia.

Rather than ponder the sad fate of her childhood friend, Maggie took a swig of Chianti. The arrival of the children back from school created an opportune diversion.

"D!" Warren shouted, jumping into his cousin's arms.

"You remember me? You were smaller than that stool!"

"His memory sometimes scares me," Maggie said. "He even remembers the day when he was bouncing on a bench and fell onto a tray of empty glasses, and his cousin Ben took the bits of glass out of his stomach one by one, while they were waiting for the ambulance."

"How could I forget that?" Warren said.

194

"You were hardly three years old," Ben added. "It was at Paulie and Linnet's wedding."

That wedding had been one of their happiest memories, before becoming one of the worst, after Gianni's evidence had sent Paulie to prison for seventeen years without parole. Linnet took to drink after that.

"I thought I could smell polenta," said Belle as she came into the kitchen. "I'd know that smell anywhere."

"Belle? Is that you, Belle?" Ben was struck dumb at the sight of his cousin.

He took her hands, held her arms wide in order to stare at her from top to toe, and then hugged her very gently, as though he was afraid of damaging her.

"The French probably don't realize how lucky they are to have you. I remember when your dad used to take you to the Beccegato restaurant. You would come into the big room and everybody would go quiet, it always happened. And us, ten great big idiots around the table, we'd try and behave properly in front of a little girl of eight."

Downstairs in the laundry room, Fred put a bowl of fresh water in front of the still-sleepy dog.

"What do dogs dream about?" he asked, stroking her.

Malavita emerged from her blanket to drink, and then lay on her back to let her master stroke her stomach. Fred gazed tenderly at her, thinking that she probably slept so much out of homesickness. The dog was probably dreaming of her homeland, the Australian bush, the birthplace of her race, of the arid land and icy nights, where her grandmothers and great-grandmothers herded and guarded the sheep. Malavita still had the physique for that way of life, all muscle and tendon, with a hard chest, short grey-black hair, and

195

sharp upright ears ready to catch the smallest sound. How could one not take refuge in sleep, when, unable to make use of natural instincts, one is so alienated from one's surroundings? Fred empathized with this suffering, and would not have wished it on anyone, even a dog. He was the only one who could imagine how useless and constrained Malavita must feel, removed to the Normandy bocage, which she refused even to explore. Fred was with her all the way, how could you blame her? He knelt down to kiss her on the nose. She let him do it, not moving. He turned out the light and went up to join the others.

"All I remember is your polenta with crayfish," Belle said, dipping a piece of bread into the sauce. "Anyway, why does polenta always have to be accompanied by elaborate sauces? Shellfish, liver sausage, sparrows…"

"Sparrows? What do you mean?" Warren said.

"Your sister's right," said Ben. "Polenta doesn't have much taste on its own, so it needs a strong sauce, you need to be inventive. In my time I did shoot sparrows in the garden with my shotgun, and then I cooked them. Belle found out and burst into tears."

"You made my daughter cry, you bastard?" said Fred, now joining the conversation. "When are we going to eat?"

Ben served his polenta according to the old family ritual. It was regarded as a reconciliation dish, a seal of family unity. And it was treated with such solemnity because it was eaten off a *scifa*, a long rectangular wooden platter, into which everybody dipped their spoon. Ben, with a few skilful movements, poured the polenta along the length of the *scifa* before it could solidify, making ditches in which to pour the sauce, with the crayfish in

196

the middle, and the game could begin. Each guest took his share with his spoon, digging a line to get to the crayfish; the greediest went first. Belle and Warren, who weren't that interested in maize flour, or even shellfish, loved the whole polenta ritual, unaware though they were that for the gangsters of New York it had a whole symbolic meaning. When a war between families was threatened, with impending bloodshed, time would always be found to discuss the matter around a *scifa*, during which each participant would dig out his share without encroaching on his neighbour. It was an elegant way of marking territory and signing a non-intervention pact. Everybody was careful not to reach the crayfish too early or too late, and to share it out fairly, as if it were booty. There was no need to exchange a single word, even less to make any plans, everything was unspoken and understood – all had given their word just by sharing the meal.

Fred, filled with thoughts of the past, stuck his spoon in like the others, but without the slightest appetite.

*

Belle and Warren, excited by the presence of their American cousin, stayed up late, until Maggie intervened, and then, finally, Fred. The three of them drank some home-made *limoncello*, which animated the conversation until late in the evening. They avoided the painful subject – the trial and its never-ending repercussions – and just talked about their everyday life, down to the last detail, illustrated with anecdotes, but never giving way to nostalgia, which might have cast a shadow over the reunion. And then suddenly, looking at the time,

197

Fred suggested to Ben that they go and "listen to the frogs partying".

"What?"

"Your uncle," Maggie said, "has found a great big muddy lake, six miles from here, where you can hear an amazing sound of frogs and toads croaking and wailing and squawking – it's an incredible racket."

"It's an orgy, I tell you, what else could it be at this time of night?"

"Can you go out whenever you like?" Ben asked, pointing at the Feds' house over his shoulder.

"You're joking! They're there twenty-four hours a day. Their light's on all night. One sleeps while the other watches TV or complains to his wife about me, as if I'd forced them to come."

"They certainly won't let you go out tonight, they're furious about Ben coming."

Fred had been waiting for this; he went over to his wife and put his arms round her, nuzzling her neck, telling her she was the love of his life.

"I hope you don't think I'm going to do what I think you want me to do…"

"Please, Maggie…"

"Fuck off."

"I need to be alone with my nephew," he begged in French. "Do your thing with the delicious momma's cooking and the olive oil, for once you'd be doing me a favour."

Ben left them on their own.

"Ever since we've been in France, I haven't been able to talk about the old business with anyone. Ben's going to tell me what happened after we left, what the FBI won't tell. And he won't say anything in front of you, Livia."

198

"Go and talk on the veranda, or in the laundry room."

"I feel I'm being spied on all the time by those two idiots opposite; I sometimes even think they've got the place bugged."

Fred led her over to the fridge, still talking.

"You know how to talk to them, you've got them eating out of your hand. The worse they think I am, the more they like you, you're the only woman looking after them on this whole continent."

Despite her husband's bad faith, Maggie felt herself weakening at the thought of the two lonely, isolated agents, cut off from everything thanks to the Manzonis.

"You can get rid of all these leftovers, the aubergines in balsamic vinegar, this end of Parmesan, the *sfogliatelle* which are falling to bits, and the remains of the polenta. You never eat it twice in one week, it's the rule."

"When I was twenty and in love with you, you could have fooled me with all this crap. Why should I be taken in now?"

"We'll only be gone an hour."

If anyone had asked, Maggie would have replied that she hadn't loved her husband for a long time now. She might have added that she often imagined living alone. All the same, she couldn't quite explain how he still managed to amuse her so much, any more than she could explain the curious way she missed him when he was out of the house.

And so, basket in hand, she crossed the road, waving to Caputo, while Fred and Ben climbed over the wall, using the propane tank, and jumped down into the weed-strewn path which separated them from their neighbour. They found Ben's car, and Fred pushed it

199

freewheeling as far as the intersection of the Rue des Favorites and the avenue Jean-de-Saumur. Two minutes later, they were driving along the edge of the moonlit forest.

Fred had been champing impatiently at the bit, waiting for a moment alone with Ben, so that he could submit him to a proper interrogation. What had become of all his friends and family, colleagues, neighbours, cousins and all the others? He claimed again that he couldn't trust the biased accounts he got from the FBI, and he asked for news of those he missed the most, and that included his mistresses. The answers were unambiguous: time had healed nothing. On the contrary, it had taken time for the Mob to lick its wounds, and its rage was that of a wounded animal. The government, by getting a big shot like Giovanni Manzoni to testify, had succeeded in cracking open the Cosa Nostra, encouraging others to sing as well and buy themselves a new life. And as long as Giovanni Manzoni remained alive, the temptation would be there. One or two more trials on that scale, and the Sicilian gangrene would itself die of gangrene.

"Stop here, we'll walk the rest of the way."

Ben parked the car next to a ditch, got the rucksack out of the boot, and followed his uncle, cutting across the fields, until they reached the Carteix factory, just visible through the darkness. With enormous care, Ben emptied the contents of the rucksack beside the entrance to the delivery car park; thirty sticks of dynamite lay on the ground like a game of pick-a-stick.

"You don't do things by halves," said Fred.

"It was from your description – you made it sound like General Motors."

Ben had tried everything in his day – TNT, plastic, Selpex, all the nitroglycerine derivatives, but in the end he found there was nothing really to compare with good old dynamite.

"The bloke who invented this stuff ought to get a prize."

He would wax lyrical, with a lot of scientific detail, about the explosive's qualities – how easy it was to handle, how stable and so on – but beneath all this serious, even solemn pontificating was the nostalgia of the schoolboy who had never grown out of playing with firecrackers. That very morning, as soon as he landed on this unknown continent, Ben had rented a car at Roissy and driven into Paris to do some shopping in DIY stores and car shops. That afternoon, before setting to work on the polenta, he had started "cooking", as he called it, watched by his uncle, a nitroglycerine paste in the Blake's laundry room. He had mixed sulphuric and nitric acid, and then bicarbonate of soda, in three receptacles surrounded by ice, with an eye on a thermometer buried in the concoction.

"It's a bit hot in here, Uncle."

"Does that matter?"

"If it goes over twenty-five degrees, there'll be nothing left, not us, not the house, not the Feds, not the street."

Fred gave his mobster chuckle, but felt a wave of heat inside him that could have wiped out the Rue des Favorites. Ben added the glycerine with a dropper and waited for it to rise to the surface before transferring it to another container. Then he had checked it with a slip of litmus paper, which had remained a fine royal-blue colour. Then he had solidified the paste by mixing it, amongst other things, with sawdust, rolled it up in pieces

201

of cardboard with a fuse in each stick. At five o'clock, a bit before the arrival of the other three Blakes, Ben had placed a quantity of dynamite sufficient to dig a second Channel Tunnel in an old biscuit tin. Then at last he was able to turn his mind to preparing the polenta, boiling it up, splashing it on the walls, beating it until his arms ached.

At the foot of the north pillar of the factory, he climbed onto the huge evacuation pipe which poured straight into the Avre; he jumped on it once or twice to test its stability. Then he went back to his uncle, who had just broken down the door between the goods-reception area and the main building. After checking with flashlights that no one was lingering there, they followed an old reflex and checked all the installations; all they found were containers containing goodness knows what, barrels of all shapes and sizes, steel piping, nothing transportable or saleable – most discouraging. They went back out and got to work. This was the interesting stage of Ben's work – deciding on the best places to plant the explosive. This was where his sixth sense came into play; his intuition could guarantee a quick and efficient outcome, depending on whether you wanted a simple collapse or a proper explosion.

"Hey, Uncle, what do you fancy? House of cards collapsing or big bang?"

Fred thought that, it being night-time and deep country, they hardly needed to be discreet.

"Let's have something spectacular – like the final explosion at the Coney Island fireworks."

The nephew couldn't help chuckling, but he took Fred's request quite seriously. If he hadn't chosen a life

202

of crime, Ben would no doubt have become one of those demolition artists who could make a whole building disappear in a fine cloud of dust. The last building he had demolished, on the orders of and in the presence of his uncle, had been an almost complete three-storey car park, with eight hundred spaces. It had been a long and tedious night, but those who had been there had, eventually, happy memories of it. Nowadays, on the exact site of the disaster, there is a small glass building, home to an import-export firm, Parker, Sampiero and Rosati.

Ready to obey his nephew's instructions, Fred watched him work with the admiration he always felt for specialists in their field. In the past he had always surrounded himself with master craftsmen, in order to beat the opposition. You needed to make a guy confess everything and denounce his mother and father? Get Kowalski. He could break a man's toes one by one without touching their neighbours – a true artist. You needed a good shot? Franck Rosello would raise his hand: he had been a decorated sniper in a war he never spoke about. His claim to fame was the single shot that had blown the head off a snitch in the van taking him to court. And even though Rosello never made the same exact shot twice, Fred had lain flat on the floor of the van when he had gone to court. To get into Manzoni's Dream Team, you had to excel in a particular field: unearthing bugging devices, getaway driving and so on. This time Fred had called on his beloved nephew because of the dynamite-handling skills that had earned him his place on the team, and, as an added bonus, a new middle initial to his name.

"Now that we're alone, tell me, Ben…"

203

"Tell you what?"

"That if they haven't forgiven me, at least the others have understood why I talked."

Ben had been dreading this conversation, and above all dreading having to tell the cruel truth. He was somewhat surprised at such a naive, hopeful question. His hero, Giovanni Manzoni, had used the word "forgiven"! Forgiven! God, he was a long way off the mark. He must be made to understand, once and for all, that whatever happened, there was never going to be any question of the Manzonis going home.

"I don't want to upset you, Zio Giovà, but you're fine here. The children are growing up, it's a nice house, you're becoming a writer."

Ben, who was in exile himself, could imagine the terrible homesickness that weighed on his uncle's heart.

"You'll never go back, just get used to that idea. It'll take two or three generations after Don Mimino's death for the name of Manzoni to be forgotten. And between now and then, as long as there remains a single henchman alive who ever received a job, a favour, a roof, whose children he was kind to, he'll empty his gun into your head without the slightest hesitation. You've become a bogeyman, Uncle; it's not just the reward, it's the honour that makes all the young ones want to kill you. Imagine the glory: *the man who killed Giovanni Manzoni, the number-one enemy of all the made men in America.* He'd be a living legend, and the younger generation would line up to kiss his hands."

As he talked, he went on taping a bunch of five sticks onto one of the outer pylons, before venturing inside the building again to deal with some aluminium beams.

204

"Icing you, Uncle, would be like finding the Loch Ness monster, or killing the great white whale, or spearing the dragon. It would be a place on Mount Olympus, drinking from the Holy Grail, washing dishonour clean with your blood."

Ben found these words painful to speak, but he felt they must be said to ensure the removal of all hope of return. Once he had placed the last charge, he took Fred by the shoulder and led him outside. They stood for a moment in the dark night, contemplating the still-intact factory; it was almost beautiful to Fred, like a bull coming into the arena, a boat about to be wrecked or a soldier going to his death. For the first time, he saw the hand of man behind such ugliness.

"You do the honours, Uncle."

Ben unrolled a long fuse, lit his Zippo lighter, and handed it to Fred. Fred hesitated for a moment, wondering for one last moment whether this really was the only possible solution to the water problem.

He had done his best to be a good citizen, he had pursued all the normal channels. He had tried to obey the rules and use what legal methods he could. He had honestly sought to behave properly and had trodden the stony path from criminal to model citizen. By allying himself to others, he had shown a gregarious side quite alien to his normal instincts. All these events had triggered a new self-awareness in him; he began to wonder if this life in hiding hadn't really changed him for ever, and awoken in him a sense of respect for the community. He had really wanted to believe that.

And now he gazed at the flame of the Zippo in his hands, still pausing, conscious of defeat. He felt

205

disappointed by society. It was not, as it claimed to be, ruled by a sense of common purpose, but rather by the single motive of profit, just like all other parallel and secret societies, starting with the one that had for so long been his own. He had given the legal world a chance to surprise him. All it had done was confirm what he had really known all along.

By lighting this fuse, he would be admitting to his impotence in the face of something that was too big to comprehend. How could one fight when the enemy is everywhere and nowhere? When it is not in anyone's interest to listen to your troubles? When those who are profiting have no faces and no addresses? When individuals are dependent on politicians, who depend on lobbies whose interests are incomprehensible to the poor jerk who places his fate in the hands of administrative procedures as long as a piece of string? Fred would unleash his own form of unreason against theirs, which suited some people so well; he would raise the stakes now with an act of violence. No doubt his life would have been simpler if he had been able to back down once he realized that the enemy was too strong and too far away, but he had never been that sort of guy. He would give them his reply on this lovely spring night, beneath the great dome of the sky, in this quiet primeval atmosphere. Fred would make the gesture on behalf of all the men in the street who could only dream of doing so.

He held the fuse in his left hand and brought the flame close to it, holding it back for one last moment.

Even the night before, he might have renounced the action and gone home, avoiding his wife's curses and Tom Quintiliani's sanctions. But tonight was different.

206

It was the first night of the rest of his life. Fred had just realized that he would never go home, that he would die, somewhere, in some senseless place, under a foreign sky, and he would be buried in rootless soil. If he allowed this pain to enter his soul tonight, it would eat into him a little more each day until he was finally devoured. He had to react without delay, and put his whole past on a bonfire, watch it go up in flames, once and for all, in a preview of the hell which he had been threatened with from an early age.

He lit the fuse and backed away about a hundred yards and waited, his eyes wide open.

The entire structure exploded in a spray of flame that rose high in the sky. The huge explosion woke him up, and the blast was like a tidal wave through his brain. The geyser of light before him lit up the horizon. A shower of metal fell for half a mile around, and Fred watched the vestiges of another era scattering before disappearing for ever. To his great surprise, he felt relieved of a burden that he had been carrying within himself for years. The conflagration died down to embers flickering on the tarmac of the surrounding parking grounds. He gave a sigh of relief.

Fred accompanied Ben back to his car, and told him how to reach the main road to Deauville, where he could get a ferry and go to London, where he could fly back to the United States.

"By the time they get their act together, you'll be in sight of the English coast. Quint will circulate your description to the airports, but actually it'll suit him quite well if you're not caught. I've made fools of them by getting you here; he won't want it to go any higher. But they won't make the same mistake again."

207

Ben didn't need a translation: they were meeting for the last time, here, on this little country lane, in an unknown country, with the sky on fire. Ben decided humour would be preferable to sentimentality.

"The owner of my video arcade is an old creep who's always boring me about the '44 landings. Now I can tell him I landed in Normandy too."

The uncle hugged his nephew, a gesture which took them both back many years. Then he got off the path to let him turn the car, waved goodbye, and watched him disappear for ever. On his way back, Fred heard the fire engines coming, and hid in the bushes.

*

The children were still asleep. Fred found his wife on the living-room sofa, sitting completely still, listening to the radio.

"You stupid Italian bastard."

He fetched a glass of bourbon from the kitchen surface, and swallowed a mouthful. Maggie wasn't going to hold back her fury for long, and so he waited quietly for the second explosion of the evening. What he got was a contained fury, in a blank, almost soft tone of voice.

"As far as I'm concerned you can blow up the whole world. I haven't got the strength to stop you any more. Your big mistake was to lie to me and manipulate me into helping with your plan. It just reminded me of things I'd rather forget, all those times when you made me your accomplice, when I was too young and stupid to know better. I spent all my time lying to the police, to our friends, to our family, to my parents, and finally to our own children. I thought we'd finished with all that."

He wasn't particularly surprised by her words. Still he awaited the verdict with a certain curiosity.

"Now listen carefully. I won't give you a sermon, Quintiliani can do that, it's not my job. I just want to remind you that our son will soon be able to look after himself, and Belle would be much better off away from us. Soon it'll just be you and me. Since I've been in France, I've found my way at last, and I can go on like this until I die, and I'm not at all sure that I need you beside me. In a few years' time, I might even be able to go home, alone, after our divorce, back to my family. But you'll die here. Not me. I'm not asking you to change, just to prepare yourself for that, Giovanni."

Without giving him time to react, she left the living room and went up to bed. Shaken by her words, he poured himself another glass and swallowed it in one gulp. He had been prepared for anything but this, the worst threat of all – that she should go home without him. It was the very first time that Maggie had considered the idea, which was after all perfectly feasible. The local radio station was reporting a fire, probably arson, at the Carteix factory. He turned off the sound and glanced outside: the street was in an uproar, the neighbours outside in their dressing gowns, sirens in the distance. Exhausted by the long day, Fred went back onto the veranda to see if a few words might spring to his fingertips. Henceforth these memoirs would be the only link between Fred Blake and Giovanni Manzoni.

His concentration was broken by a figure coming up from the garden. Quintiliani had come round the back

209

so as not to ring the bell. Fred prepared for the third sermon of the evening, after Ben's and Maggie's.

"One might have imagined, Manzoni, that the trial, the disgrace, the exile might have induced you to stop and think. Oh, I don't mean the discovery of a conscience, or any kind of true repentance, I certainly didn't expect that. Do you know why you're still capable of committing crimes like this evening's? Quite simply, it's because you haven't paid your dues. Twenty or thirty years in a six-yard-square cell might have given you the time to consider this question: was it all worth it?"

"You still believe in that crap? Paying one's debt to society?"

"With the exception of three or four well-meaning politicians, a few sociologists and the odd big-hearted social worker, nobody gives a fuck whether prison makes any difference to a creep like you, Manzoni. The whole world needs to know that you're behind bars, because if scum like you get away with it, why should anyone bust a gut obeying laws designed to suppress all liberty and pleasure?"

"Me, in prison? I'd have had followers, lots of small guys who regarded me as a legend – I'd have given them a master class. I'd have done much more damage inside than out."

"Well, from now on you're grounded. None of you can leave the house until further notice."

"The kids too?"

"Sort it out with them. After your antics last night, our arrangement may not work any more. You've been warned."

"But... Hey, Quint!"

210

The FBI agent left, relieved, but with the bulk of his work still before him: he now had to divert all lines of enquiry about the sabotage of the Carteix factory. To do that, he had to have a free hand.

Fred decided to go up to bed, but he found the bedroom door locked. He didn't insist, and instead went down to Malavita's lair – there would be no recriminations from her, at any rate. The dog woke up, surprised by this late visit, and by the noise in the street that was reaching her through the window.

Fred turned on the tap to fill her bowl with fresh water. Fresh, crystal-clear water flowed out; he couldn't resist tasting it.

He felt sure that at that same moment, throughout Cholong, dozens of people were doing exactly the same thing, and marvelling at the clearness of the water. Some of them were beginning to believe in miracles.

7

At the precise moment Benedetto D. Manzoni's plane was taking off from Heathrow to fly to America, another, travelling in the opposite direction, was coming in to land at Roissy. Amongst the mostly American passengers were ten men from the state of New York, who hadn't checked in any luggage. They all knew each other, but neither spoke nor nodded to one another. Six were of Italian origin, two Irish, and two were Puerto Ricans born in Miami. None had ever set foot in Europe. At first sight, one might have taken them for a group of lawyers come to deal with some international legal business, perhaps on behalf of some powerful multinational's global interests. In fact they were soldiers – the kind of soldiers who prefer first-class cabins to strike helicopters, and Armani suits to jungle fatigues. This was a death squad, selected in the same way as mercenaries – which is what they were.

*

Some of the Blakes regarded the curfew as a blessing, while for others it was the most unfair of punishments. Fred had already decided not to go out in order to avoid the festivities and carry on with his masterpiece. It was a point of honour to him never to be affected by sanctions. In fact the threat of punishment rarely had the desired effect on gangsters: far from scaring them, it gave them

213

an opportunity to defy the authorities and make them look ridiculous. They would insult a judge in court, spit in a federal agent's face during an interrogation, pour scorn on prison guards; they would never miss an opportunity to be provocative, and they would never bow down their heads. So Quint had consigned Fred to quarters? What a blessing. He would be able to devote himself entirely to Chapter Six, which began:

In films, people like to see violence put to the service of the just, but it's because they like violence, not because they like justice. Why do people like stories of revenge rather than forgiveness? Because men love the idea of punishment. To see the righteous hitting back, and hitting hard – that's something people never tire of and don't feel guilty about. It's the only sort of violence that's ever scared me.

On the floor above, Belle had shut herself up, to get out of sight of her family. She had been prevented from taking a role in the end-of-term show, now she wasn't allowed to go out into the town and have fun with people of her age. All she could do now was disappear into her room to try to make some sense of all this sacrifice. If she wasn't allowed to appear, she would disappear, and this time for good. She had just taken an irrevocable decision.

As for Warren, he was furious at having to pay over and over again for his father's actions. The approach of the festivities had awoken the child in him, and the punishment made him regret once more that he wasn't yet an adult. He was being punished as if he was an adult, why shouldn't he have adult status? He shut himself in his room and spent long hours in front of his

214

screen, picking up information from the Internet that would come in useful for the future he was preparing for himself. What was his plan? It was to turn back the clock, and remake history; he would change everything, and start again from scratch.

Of the four, Maggie was the most inconvenienced by the curfew. She was committed a hundred times over to helping put up and run stands at the fair, and ensure its smooth running; she would have enjoyed nothing more than making her contribution to such a popular event. She sat slumped on the sofa in front of the television, not watching it, totally discouraged and suffering from doubt. Well might she devote herself body and soul to others, she would always be dragged down in the end by Fred, and forced back into the role of Mafia wife, and what's more a discredited Mafia wife, shunned by all. For every step she made, Fred pulled her ten steps back, and as long as she remained with that creep, despite anything she might still feel for him, she would never escape from this downward spiral. She would have to talk to the one person who, after all, looked after her better than Fred ever could.

*

The town of Cholong-sur-Avre was wearing its party colours. At ten, the parents had turned up at the school hall for the concert, which had gone off without the slightest hitch – a total success and a happy moment for old and young alike. At two, the fairground people opened the fair, starting up their rides for the young people, the first of whom started to pour into the Place de la Libération. The shortest night of the year would

215

go by in a flash, the young wouldn't go to bed at all, and the less young would go to bed to the sound of fairground music. Summer had started with a bang.

Thirty-five miles away, at the Madeleine de Nonancourt roundabout, a grey Volkswagen minibus stopped to check the route. The driver, irritated by having been made to take a wrong turning outside Evreux, was encouraging his pilot to concentrate. The ten men in the back were bored stiff, staring out at a landscape that was a great deal less exotic than they had expected. The grass was green just like anywhere else, the trees were less shady than the planes in New York, and the sky seemed grey and dirty compared to the one in Miami. They had all heard of Normandy from war films, without, however, ever having felt the slightest curiosity about the place and its history. The fact was, they hadn't been curious about anything since landing at Roissy, not the climate, not the cuisine; they didn't even care about the discomfort and the travel – they only had one thought, which was how they would spend the two million dollars they would each receive when the mission was accomplished.

Six of them already imagined themselves retiring from business; at thirty or forty, they were most likely living through their very last working day. They would buy a farm, a villa with a pool, a room all the year round in Las Vegas, anything would be possible. The four others certainly didn't scorn the reward, but they were driven by another motive. They had lost brothers or fathers thanks to Manzoni's testimony, and killing him had become an obsession for them. The most motivated of all was called Matt Gallone, Don Mimino's grandson and direct heir. For the six years since the trial, Matt had

216

concentrated exclusively on avenging his grandfather. Manzoni had dispossessed him of his kingdom, of his future title of Godfather and status as demi-god. Every moment of Matt's life, every gesture was aimed at the death of Manzoni. Manzoni's death lurked behind laughter with friends, behind kisses on his children's foreheads. It was Matt's *Via Dolorosa* and for him it would be the path to freedom and rebirth.

"Follow signs to Rouen," said the pilot, his nose buried in the map.

The whole operation had been planned in New York by Matt and the *capi* of the five families, who, on this occasion, were operating as a single family. Failing any direct contacts in France, the death squad had had to organize itself via Sicily. Orders had been sent to Catania, where a local Cosa Nostra contact had arranged the logistics through one of their companies, based in Paris. The arrangements included meeting the ten men at Roissy, arranging transport and providing arms: fifteen automatic pistols and ten revolvers, six assault rifles, twenty hand grenades and a rocket-launcher. They had also been allocated a driver and an interpreter, a fellow who had previously taken part in a commando operation. Then it would be over to Matt and his men. In order to maintain team spirit during the operation and to avoid unhealthy competition, the famous twenty-million-dollar reward would be divided equally; the one who actually killed Gianni Manzoni would only receive an honorary bonus. In a few hours, he would be a millionaire and a living legend. The world would admire his actions, because the world despises a traitor. For what could be worse than to sell your own brother? The last circle of hell was reserved for such

217

people. Today, 21st June, just one of these ten would be the chosen one and would gain an everlasting place in the criminals' roll of honour. He would be written about in books long after his death.

*

Beauty had been condemned to solitude. Belle could imagine no worse fate than her own. How can you prevent a star from shining? How can you deprive the world of this gift from God? This knowledge became harder and harder to bear as she approached womanhood. She decided finally that the only thing comparable in power to her beauty was the wickedness of those who prevented her from making use of it. It was as though God himself had created such perfection with the sole purpose of depriving people of it. It was just like God to be so inhuman: to demand that you should sacrifice what you held most dear; to create temptation and sin simultaneously; to forgive the sinners and punish the good. Belle felt somehow a victim of His mysterious plan without understanding what on earth He could possibly be up to.

She sat on her bedroom floor, with a handkerchief to her eyes, thinking of all the arse-lickers she had watched lining up in the Newark house to ask a favour of her father, or to further the interests of a relation, or settle a score. The irony was that she, Belle Manzoni, his own daughter, would never have needed the slightest help. If she had just been left free to follow her own path, she would have easily reached the top on her own. She cried and cried, but all the tears in her body were not enough to console her for this virginal destiny. She might as

218

well resign herself to a life of chastity buried alive. For the very first time she cursed her mother and father for having brought her into the world, the daughter of a criminal.

But then she rebelled. Her face puffed up by tears, she told herself that it was no use agreeing to live in a manner she could never carry out. The most elegant and ultimately reasonable course of action would be to end it all as soon as possible. She ran over to the window overlooking the garden and, looking out, realized that by throwing herself out she would just end up alive but crippled. She must end it, yes, but she must do it properly, in a grand gesture, with as many witnesses to her sacrifice as possible; at last she would have a public – a public that would never forget the sight of her silhouette flying through the air to a certain death.

On reflection, she realized that she had chosen the perfect day to die, the first day of summer; the whole town at her feet in the Place de la Libération, what a great revenge it would be. She would appear at the top of the church tower and cast herself into the void. The angel's leap. They would find her broken body in front of the church door, a few drops of blood dropping from her lips onto her dress – it would be a sublime vision. But why the church, anyway? Why mix God up in this? What had He done to deserve such a sacrifice? To die in His house was to accord Him too much honour. In any case, God didn't exist, you just had to study the evidence. Or else He too was a victim of the Peter Principle and had met the limits of His power when faced with Belle's destiny. She closed her eyes to visualize the Place de la Libération and its buildings, but none seemed high enough. Unless… Why not? The big wheel!

Of course, the big wheel! That would be her grand finale. And what a great symbol, the big wheel, turning for evermore without her, much more powerful than the church. Relieved, she opened her cupboard and got out her one-shouldered Goddess Diana dress, her silk scarf and her white sandals. She would be fixed in people's memories as a kind of pagan Madonna, too beautiful for such a cruel and ugly world. Her photo would be in the papers, and millions of people would imagine her death, adding details, creating a Belle mythology, a whole legend. Like the romantic heroines of old, she would inspire the poets, who would write songs about her that would be sung by other young women for generations to come. Who knows, perhaps one day a film would be made about the life of Belle Blake, a great Hollywood film that would draw tears on five continents. She put a little foundation on her cheeks, and a touch of eyeliner, and imagined all the merchandising that would go with the film: the posters, the dolls in her effigy, the effigy of an icon of the future.

She looked for one last time at her face in the mirror. Her only regret in killing herself was that she would not be able to watch her body defying the laws of ageing over the years. At thirty her beauty would have gained in elegance, at forty in nobility and at fifty there would be glowing maturity – Belle would conquer the ravages of time. What a pity not to have had the chance to demonstrate this to the world. She scribbled a note, which she left on a corner of the desk, which read: *Carry on without me.*

In the next-door room, Warren too was preparing his great escape. Quintiliani's curfew had simply accelerated his original plan. In the earlier scenario, he would have

220

risen on an August morning, had breakfast in the usual way, and then would have invented some pretext for leaving early and returning late, say a bicycle ride with his friends. Instead of which he would have gone to the Cholong station and caught the 10.10 express to Paris. Two months ahead of time, he was going to leave this FBI-guarded prison at once, and his disappearance would last for several years, until he came back to his family, or brought them back to him in his new role as Godfather.

He picked up the notes he had made on the different stages of his planned journey. In a few minutes he would set off to the station and catch the 14.51 train to Paris Montparnasse. From there he would proceed to the Gare de Lyon, where he would wait for the overnight Naples Express, which would easily get him over the frontier at Domodossola. In Naples he would go straight to the San Gregorio quarter, where he would mention the name of Ciro Lucchesi, boss of a branch of the Camorra working in New York. Without him needing to ask, he would be taken straight to meet Gennaro Esposito, the *capo* of the whole region, a man who was never seen, but whose shadow hung over all of Naples. And he would introduce himself as the son of the traitor Giovanni Manzoni.

Gennaro would be amazed and ask why the son of the most famous rat in the world had come into the lion's den... Warren would then remind him of the enormous debt Ciro Lucchesi owed his father, who had sabotaged an FBI inquiry that would have sent Ciro down for a hundred years. Now the traitor's son was offering Lucchesi the chance to settle this debt by arranging his transport from Naples to the United States. Lucchesi would be forced to agree to this, and Warren would

221

find himself arriving in New York harbour a few days later, as his great-grandfather had done at the same age, all those years ago. And then everything would begin again. He would find a place, rebuild an empire and cleanse the name of Manzoni. What were sons for, if not to repair the sins of the fathers?

Once he had landed on his native soil, he would have to be as discreet as possible, travel short distances only, speak English and French alternately, behave like a young tourist about to meet his parents, learn the names of the towns and areas he travelled through, so as to be able to describe his trip if ever he was questioned. He tucked several maps and tourist information gathered from the Internet into his jacket, to provide himself with a story to tell the authorities if necessary. Then he packed his toiletries into a plastic bag: if he didn't want to be taken for a vagabond, cleanliness must be a priority. He would wash and sleep as often as possible, so as to remain fresh and healthy. As for money, he had plenty of that, thanks to all the services he had performed for his school friends; everything had to be paid for, either with other services, or more often in ready money. The money would be useful for greasing palms, buying clothes, sleeping in hotels when necessary, eating decently, buying drinks for people who might be useful and handing out tips. He turned off his computer, gave it a tap, as though saying goodbye to an old friend, and left the room. The first stage of the journey was tricky. He needed to go quietly into the garden, around the veranda, and, when he had reached the garden shed, slide between two sheets of metal, pull up a bit of wire netting and slide underneath it into the neighbour's garden, climb over his fence and head for the station.

222

From then on, he would be an outlaw. And he would soon find out if he really had the makings of one.

He came face to face with his sister in the corridor. Like him, she was cautiously tiptoeing downstairs. Belle's plan was just as acrobatic as Warren's: she would get into the garden by the laundry-room window, climb onto the wood pile against the party wall, over into the neighbour's house and go straight out from there. She was much too concerned with her own problems to notice Warren's conspiratorial manner, and he likewise noticed nothing of his sister's solemn demeanour.

"Where are you going?" he said first.

"Nowhere, what about you?"

Warren wasn't going to see Belle again for many years. One day he would come back to fetch her, and then he would offer her Hollywood on a plate, and the world at her feet. He clenched his jaw, holding back his tears. Belle took him in her arms, so as to leave him with a last image of his loving sister. He kissed her with the sort of affection he had never yet felt for anyone.

"I really love you, Belle."

"I want you to know that I'll always be proud of you, wherever you are – never forget that."

And they kissed each other again.

On the ground floor, Fred, cloistered in his veranda, was a thousand miles from imagining this outbreak of sibling affection. He was stuck, because of some memory lapse, in the middle of a chapter describing the initiation ceremonies of the *Onorevole Società*. Before becoming a made man, recognized and accepted by the brotherhood, the petitioner would be summoned to a ceremony presided over by the ancients, the form of which had not changed for centuries. His forefinger

223

would be pricked with a needle, drawing a drop of blood, and a holy picture would be placed in his hands and set on fire. He would then have to repeat: *May my flesh burn like this saint if I fail to keep my oath...* Fred couldn't remember the rest, and yet how many times had he heard the oath, after having spoken it himself thirty years previously? How did it go... *May my flesh burn...* what, in God's name? Something came next... What could explain this sudden lapse, just at the wrong moment, just when his inspiration was in mid-flight? Nothing would come, only the image of himself burning up like the holy image.

He yelled his wife's name several times, and then started to look for her in the house. When he didn't see her on the sofa, which she had hardly left for several days, he had a strange premonition and began to search each room, one by one, including those upstairs. There he found his children, and didn't even notice the fact that they were entwined with one another, with tears in their eyes.

"Anyone seen your mother?"

They shook their heads and watched him go down to the laundry room, where he circled the sleeping dog before coming back up to the living room.

"MAGGIE!!!"

Had she disobeyed Quintiliani's orders? That was unthinkable. She would rather have died than attract more sanctions. So what?

There must be some explanation, perhaps the worst of all.

*

224

Less than a mile and a half outside Cholong, the minibus turned into the Beaufort forest and parked alongside the Avre. The men got out and stretched their numb legs, as silent and concentrated as ever. The chauffeur gave a noisy sigh of exhaustion, and stood by the river to pee. The guide, who was acting as interpreter, brought out large plastic bags full of new clothes, which he placed on the ground for the team to choose from. Matt had given very strict orders about the clothes they were to wear; they were to look like all those Americans who had been coming to the region since 1945. This was easy for some, but looking like that type of American was a bit more complicated for those who had always modelled their appearance on gangsters in films.

The younger ones were quite capable of watching a film ten times over in order to spot a particular make of jacket or shoe. And if some, once they had been made, gave up the costume, for others it was like a second skin. Without questioning this, the men had no idea how to interpret the order to "look like those Americans". What exactly did that mean? Try and look like an idiot? Look as ordinary as possible? Attract attention? Not attract attention? Should they dress like adolescents, Texan rednecks, or homeless New Yorkers? Which particular sort of bad taste was required? There were so many to choose from.

And so designer jackets, tailor-made trousers and silk shirts were shed to make way for T-shirts, Bermuda shorts, short-sleeved shirts with soft collars; they put on shapeless, synthetic, patterned garments and caps. What did it matter, soon they would be consoling themselves with two million dollars to spend on Madison and Fifth. Matt set the example by going first: he pulled on pale

225

pleated trousers, a red T-shirt and a beige jacket. Greg Sanfelice chose washed-out jeans and a University of Colorado T-shirt. Guy Barber squeezed his crotch into some tight-fitting black jeans, and added a navy-blue cotton shirt practically open to the waist. The rest of the gang crowded around the bags. Julio Guzman provided a running commentary for each of his team-mates.

"Jerry, it's crazy – you look just like an American!"

"You – you crazy Puerto Rican – you know what you look like? A fucking American!"

The men gradually relaxed and joined in the fun: "Stupid American bastard…" "Shut up, Yank." "You Americans, you're such idiots…"

Matt then brought out the four cases containing the arms. The men went quiet again, feeling a bit strange in their new clothes, and shared the handguns out between them. They had the choice between a semi-automatic Magnum Research .44 pistol and a Smith & Wesson Ultra-Lite .38 Special revolver. The first was very dependable if you were shooting at a moving target from a distance, and the other was ideal for an execution at close quarters – it just depended on individual methods of operation, particular habits and skills. Not all of them had been recruited for their talents as killers. Some were genuinely thrilled by an untouched weapon, its smooth uncorrupted surface, its smell as yet unsullied by cordite, the shiny blue steel; while others felt sad at the thought of their old familiar gun, their life's companion, which had kept them alive, which now had had to be left behind. It was now time to perform a few ritual gestures, loading the barrels, engaging the magazine, aiming, pulling the gun in and out of the belt or the holster, sticking it in the back of

226

the trousers, on the stomach, under the armpit and so on. Then Matt took them down to the edge of the river for a final warm-up session of shooting practice, loosening up and running in their weapons. Nicholas Bongusto started shooting, aiming at imaginary targets on the opposite bank, before spotting a fisherman's cabin a few yards upstream, with a jetty on stilts sticking out into the water. He took aim at this structure. Soon all ten men were standing in a row, emptying their guns in the direction of the little shack. After a good five minutes of non-stop firing, the tin roof had slid down into the water and the wooden walls, now peppered with bullets, were beginning to collapse. The game now was to aim for the stilts holding up the jetty, so that the whole structure would collapse into the river – which soon happened. The guns were in perfect working condition by now, and each gang member had taken great pleasure in breaking in his weapon.

Matt distributed ready cash and mobile phones, and then had a word with the interpreter, who was also the driver and guide, who suggested that they follow the banks of the Avre on foot until they reached the town. After some last-minute words to his troops, Matt led the march on Cholong.

As they got nearer to the town, strange and yet somehow familiar sounds began to reach them: a well-known racket, loud shouts and fairground music, the universal sound of a funfair. The death squad began to imagine the most absurd hypotheses.

"A welcoming committee?" Julio suggested to try and relax the atmosphere.

"Wouldn't be surprised," said Nick. "I've seen black-and-white films of that. In Normandy, as soon as they

227

see a group of Americans approaching, they bring out the marching bands, and the girls and the firecrackers too, it's a sort of tradition."

Matt signalled to them to stop, when they were about to cross the bridge which marked the entrance to Cholong.

"What's all this crap?" he asked the guide.

The guide went up to a poster stuck to a tree, which provided the answer. He explained as well as he could that it was the festival of Saint Jean.

"Well, perhaps we're in luck," said Matt.

*

"I'll do whatever you want, but get me away from this monster, Quint. What happened on Thursday will happen again and again, he'll find other Carteix factories, whether you watch him or not. He'll set the whole town on fire, he'll take over the businesses for his rackets, he'll start some secret gambling den, he'll terrorize the local council with a baseball bat. Giovanni was born with destruction in his soul, and when he finally dies his last thought will be a curse, or if he regrets anything it'll only be not having wreaked enough destruction."

Fred, sitting under the kitchen window outside the Feds' house, was sobbing bitterly. His intuition had been right: Maggie had gone over to the enemy. He was making a superhuman effort to turn the geyser of rage that he felt rising within him against himself and not them. His life had been thrown to the dogs, and by his lifetime companion. He stopped himself from banging his head against the stone, in case it made the

228

wall shake and alerted them to his presence. Quint had become the strong man of the Manzoni family, perhaps even its saviour.

"Belle and Warren are doomed as long as they live alongside that son of a bitch," she continued. "It's him Don Mimino wants, not us."

Fred bit his hand, and only unclenched his jaw when his incisors had broken the flesh, but even then the pain was not enough to numb the pain Maggie was inflicting on him. Quintiliani was going to take such sadistic pleasure in separating him from his loved ones; Fred would be stripped of all dignity and pride, until he was prepared for any abasement and humiliation, just for the sake of hearing their voices on the telephone. The king of agents, himself so long separated from his own children, hadn't expected such a bonus; Maggie had just supplied him with the sweetest revenge of all. Fred, desperate to relieve this searing pain, was again tempted to knock himself out by banging his head on the ground. Who on earth could put up with such agony? Fred was probably the only person on earth who didn't know the answer to that question. It was the victims.

*

The town was turned upside down: it was a good moment to avoid attention. Nobody would notice them in the general confusion. Matt sent two groups of men on patrol through the town and suggested that the five others should melt into the crowd and try and pick up information as to the whereabouts of the Blakes. The latter were suspicious at first at being sent into the kind of action they weren't expecting. Most thought it was funny.

229

The caretaker at the Jules Vallès *Lycée* had deserted his post in order to go to the funfair with his family, and so Joey Wine and Nick Bongusto easily got into the school. All they had to do was put their foot on the electronic locking mechanism and vault over the gate; then they stopped and tried to decipher the school signposts. Joey followed the arrows that said Reception, Office and School Hall, and advised his colleague to head for Refectory, Nurse and Gymnasium.

He smashed down a glass door and got into a corridor which led to the school offices. Joey had been quite prepared to do some terrorizing in order to find out little Warren Blake's address, and was somewhat disappointed to find himself alone in this long grey pebble-dash building. Instead of just breaking a couple of arms, he was going to have to open the metal filing cabinets himself and riffle through them. Bored and exhausted after the first drawer, he knocked the others over and then pulled the cupboards down too. Then he went into the headmaster's office, sat down in his chair and looked through his drawers; one was locked, so he forced it open with a paper-cutter. He found several notes which he automatically pushed into his pocket. Then he wandered on until he came to a classroom, which he couldn't resist going into.

Had Joey ever been to school? On reflection, he had probably missed some good times on the benches of the Cherry Hill public school in New Jersey, a school he would avoid each morning in order to join up with the gang on Ronaldo Terrace. He had never seen a blackboard so close up, and the smell of chalk meant nothing to him. He scratched a piece of chalk on the board; it made a strange noise which made his skin tingle. So was it this

230

little white stick that made all the difference? Did this little white stick contain all the knowledge in the world? Could it demonstrate everything, prove that God did or didn't exist, that parallel lines meet in infinity, that the poets knew it all? He couldn't think what to leave as his mark, what word, number or drawing, so, after a little hesitation he wrote in large letters JOEY WAS HERE, as he had done so often before in the toilets of bar rooms and nightclubs.

Bongusto, after crossing the playground, went into the gymnasium, where he yelled a few obscenities, which echoed around the space. He rolled a cigarette and began a tour of the equipment; he hung from the railings, tried to climb a fifteen-foot knotted rope, inspected the shelves full of football shirts; then he picked up a basketball and examined its profiling. He thought it looked incredibly like a world globe. The strange thing was that Nick had never held a ball before. He had watched hundreds of games over many years. He had waited for young basketball players at the entrance to playgrounds, in order to offer them all kinds of substance in pill or sachet form, but he had never joined them for a bit of shooting practice. Later in the arenas, he had organized the betting and watched the stars in action, he had even got to know some of them, at times when he had been in charge of bending them or scaring them shitless, depending on the instructions he had been given. He knew the rules and the players better than anyone, and he could have been a player himself, with his physique, his height, those huge platter-shaped hands, that shaved head. And yet he had never felt the rough rubbery texture of that red ball between his hands. He held it now and took it out to

231

the basketball court in the playground, stood at the top of the key and took a deep last puff of his cigarette stub. He had a difficult choice before him: either he could shoot the first basket of his life, or he could remain the only American never to score once. Joey watched him through the window striking a basketball player's pose, and whistled encouragement.

Paul Gizzi and Julio Guzman, for their part, felt lost in a ghost town, wandering around empty streets past shuttered shops. They had never seen streets like these, narrow and slightly sloping, edged with couch grass and ivy, with branches of apple trees leaning over the walls, fragrant shady streets with unpronounceable names. They stopped in front of the only shop whose name they understood: SOUVENIRS.

Gizzi, at forty, had retained his bad-boy look. He had straight, short, pale-brown hair, with a quiff in the middle of his head, hazel eyes and a dimple in his chin. He took a little camera, which he always carried with him, out of the inside pocket of his green jacket, pointed it at a little white ceramic well and took photos of it from several angles.

"What the fuck are you doing?" Guzman asked.

"Can't you see? I want a souvenir of a souvenir. I know someone who'll like that."

Guzman, a chunky little bulldog-like figure, who had been impatient since birth, grabbed the butt of his rifle and hit the window, smashing it with a few blows.

"There you are, take it."

"Guzman, you're sick."

"Me, the sick one?"

Gizzi had taken the photo for his sister, Alma, who was fifteen years older than him, who had remained a spinster because of a fiancé who had left town when he

232

heard that the Gizzis had very close links with the Staten Island family. A little reluctantly he picked the object out of the broken glass and blew the dust off. He could already see Alma's smile.

Franck Rosello, on the Place de la Libération, his usual taciturn self, was wandering around the stands, unused to such activity. He stopped for a moment in front of a display of pottery and plaster figures representing religious or bucolic figures. Then, seeing all the children stuffing themselves with sweet things, he took a fancy to a red toffee apple dripping with caramel. Without forgetting the ever present possibility of running into his old boss, Manzoni himself, he made sure none of his colleagues could see him approaching the candy van. He was a childhood friend of Matt's, adopted by Don Mimino's family and brought up as a Gallone. He had developed his talent as a sharpshooter in Giovanni's gang, and had become a specialist in the elimination of witnesses. He had thus been instrumental in the cancellation of several trials and in saving the skins of several high-up bosses of the Cosa Nostra. The brotherhood was indebted to him and treated him like a hero. He was paid by the sack-load for each contract, and had never spent a single day behind bars; he had a clean sheet despite twenty years of loyal service. His head count included several famous snitches, such as Cesare Tortaglia and Pippo l'Abruzzese; he had only had one failure, and that was Giovanni Manzoni. If the circumstances were right and Matt was planning a long-distance shot, Franck would get a second chance. His mouth stuffed with toffee apple, he stopped in front of the shooting stall, which reminded him of the one at the funfair in Atlantic City, where he had been born.

233

"Three euros for five genuine bullets," the man said. "You can win ten to fourteen points with each shot, fifty if you hit the red, and a hundred if you hit the bull's-eye. Four hundred points, you get a teddy bear. You American?"

Franck only understood the last word and put a five-euro note on the counter; he picked up a rifle and took aim. Without adjusting his aim, he pulled the trigger five times. The man showed him four scattered holes, the fifth having gone off the target. The next time, Franck was able to correct the parallax caused by a slight curve in the barrel and achieve a total of four hundred and fifty points.

The stall-keeper hesitated before surrendering to the evidence. Four hundred and fifty? At a second go? Nobody had ever had such a score. Even he, with all his own equipment, wouldn't have been able to do it. And yet, holding the card up to the light, he could count four strikes in the bull's-eye and one on the red. Franck was about to leave the stand without his prize when he saw, standing at his knee, a little girl on her own, fixing him with a stony look. Franck saw an indignant message in those huge still eyes, which left no doubt as to its meaning. He lifted the little girl up to face the stuffed animals hanging messily above the range. Without hesitating, she pointed at the biggest of all, a gorilla five times her size.

"You need eight hundred points for that one," said the man, exasperated.

Franck lined up a few coins and totalled five hundred points with five bullets; the holes joined together in the bull's-eye like the petals of a single flower. Once again the gypsy studied the card with disbelief, and could

234

only see three holes – where were the two others? The American had the devil's own luck, but that didn't mean he was going to get the show prize – it had certainly never happened before. Franck showed him how two bullets had been superimposed on the previous ones, you just had to look and show a bit of good faith to see that, the target proved it, what was the point of making a fuss? Passers-by were beginning to gather, and Franck couldn't understand why the stakes had suddenly risen. His mission and the need for discretion inhibited him slightly, but it was too late now to deprive the little girl of her trophy. He made sure she couldn't see what was happening, discreetly grabbed the stall-keeper's arm, twisted it behind his back, telling him to keep quiet, and stuck the muzzle of a rifle into his mouth. The man raised his arm in shocked surrender. A minute later the little girl grabbed her monkey in her arms, and at last gave in and smiled. Before letting her go, Franck could not resist running his hands through her long fine gold-speckled hair. Something told him she would never forget him.

Rosello was not the only one showing off his talents amongst the fairground attractions. Hector Sosa, known as Chi-Chi, the elder of the two Puerto Ricans, stopped in front of a punchball surrounded by a gang of young lads. Hector had always been capable of knocking out men three times larger than himself, and had made a speciality of charging head first towards the biggest and strongest, his bravery bordering on foolhardiness. He had become famous ten years previously, during the world middleweight championship in Santa Fe; employed as bodyguard to the reigning champion, Chi-Chi had reacted badly to a ticking-off, and put him

235

out of any condition to fight. During his two months of detention behind bars in San Quentin, the toughest and cruellest prisoners had treated him with the greatest of respect. Now, by breaking the machine with one blow of his fist, he had become a hero to the youth of Cholong.

A few yards from there, Joey's older brother, Jerry Wine, ace driver, the one every gang wanted as a getaway driver for the big jobs, couldn't resist a turn on the dodgems, and was having a whale of a time. The object was to crash into as many people as possible, bing, bang, smashing into every obstacle, charging head down into the traffic jams, sparing nobody. What could be more fun for a guy who was capable of finding an escape route through the middle of a group of ten police cars, or of driving through a parking lot at forty miles per hour without touching a single lamp post? He spotted a group of trouble-makers who seemed a little annoyed by his driving, and decided to annoy them further with his little red car.

Guy Barber – real name Guido Barbagallo – for his part was glued to the lottery stand, where he was driving the operator mad by using several number combinations he had perfected in the Las Vegas casinos. The smallest event could trigger his passion for gambling, making him lose all sense of time and reality. Guy was an expert at inventing new ways of gambling, and would bet on anything, from numbers on banknotes to car licence plates or street posters. The most astonishing thing was that he always ended up by finding some logic in the most random sequences of numbers. At that level of obsession no one ever enquired whether this gift enabled his addiction or vice versa.

The only one, apart from Matt, who remained focused on the object of the mission, was Gregorio Sanfelice. Gregorio, a heavy-arms specialist, had been chosen by Don Mimino himself for his absolute trustworthiness. Greg was the exact opposite to a Manzoni, the opposite to a snitch – this was a man who had chosen to take five years in jail when the FBI were offering him his freedom in exchange for three or four names, in complete secrecy, without a trial, in such a way that nobody in the Mob would have suspected any treachery. While he waited for orders, leaning on a table in the drinks tent, he finished a carton of chips and a glass of beer. He wore a cap and was dressed entirely in blue denim. As he watched the local people coming and going around the surrounding stands, he thought only of the new man he would become once he got his two million dollars. Now that he was fifty, Greg felt it was about time to hang up his boots and return to the woman in his life, the mother of his children; he would swear to her that he would never risk death or prison again. He would make up for lost time, buy them a house near Bear Mountain, in the middle of the woods, and would spend the rest of his days reassuring them and taking care of them. They would never have anything more to fear. Once Manzoni had been sorted out, he would fly home with his colleagues, claim his money as soon as they had landed at JFK, and there and then, he would salute them, shake hands for the last time, and take a taxi to Zeke's at the corner of 52nd and 11th, where Michelle worked as a waitress. He would tell her to leave there and then, they would go and get the children out of school, and everything would begin again for them, somewhere far away. As he dreamed of this imminent

237

future, he wiped a trace of foam off his big pistolero moustache, and took a last mouthful of beer. He rose from the table, and came face to face with a ghost.

Without showing any surprise, Greg lowered his cap over his face, left a few coins on the counter and went over to a row of game consoles. As he slid a coin into a pinball machine, he kept his eyes glued to the ghost, who was wearing an open-necked Hawaiian shirt over a white T-shirt and wandering around the fairground with his hands in his pockets. Greg didn't have to think very hard to remember him: that was the motherfucker who had almost sent him down for twenty years. The bastard, whose name was something like Di Morro or Di Cicco, had managed, ten years ago, to infiltrate a gang of robbers who were preparing a heist on a bank in Seattle. He had put on an incredibly effective performance and, in a feat almost unknown for an undercover agent, the fucker had succeeded in gaining Greg's trust through drinking sessions in the company of friendly nightclub hostesses; they had almost become friends. But Di Cicco had turned out to be a better actor than cop; he had successfully passed himself off as a gangster amongst real gangsters, but he had blown the operation through lack of coordination with his colleagues, and Greg had escaped by the skin of his teeth. Di Cicco's presence in this backwater was proof that Manzoni was there too. Greg, keeping an eye on the FBI agent, made a sign to Franck Rosello to warn Matt, who in turn felt a surge of adrenalin at this news. And then a sort of ballet began to take place around Di Cicco and Caputo, without either of them being aware of anything untoward.

While Jerry drove the minibus into the centre of town, Greg and Chi-Chi waited for the precise moment when

238

the two agents would leave the Place de la Libération. Matt wanted to avoid unnecessary risks, and preferred to neutralize them immediately so he could work them over. Caputo, who was walking behind his partner, had a sudden premonition of trouble as they turned the corner of the Rue du Pont Fort. He couldn't have described what it was that had entered his mind, which was numbed by the fairground music, the beer and the sunshine. When this sort of thing happened, he simply handed himself over to his instinct for survival, something he called upon more often than others did. It was an instinct that had been honed by the ever present fear of death, in particular the fear of a stupid and pointless death, brought about by carelessness. To die fighting was one thing, but to die in an ambush was to die a rat's death, with no glory. However, with or without the premonition, there was no time to warn Richard or to reach for his gun: they both found themselves with a gun stuck in the back of the neck, and they raised their hands. Greg, pointing his at Di Cicco, was about to satisfy an unhoped-for personal vengeance. Chi-Chi searched Caputo, relieved him of his gun and silenced him with a blow on the back of the neck from his rifle butt. Matt, Guy and Franck joined them at the corner of the Allée des Madriers, and the minibus drove in silence through the empty streets of Cholong, bearing six members of the Cosa Nostra and two federal agents, who fully understood the purpose of the visit. Matt cocked his gun.

"Now – which one of you is prepared to die for Giovanni Manzoni?"

*

239

Five minutes later, Jerry parked the minibus at the corner of the Rue des Favorites, with the Blakes' house in their sights, fifty yards away.

Hit hard and without warning. No chance should be missed to destroy Manzoni at the first opportunity, making maximum use of the element of surprise. Strategy must be sacrificed to impact. Sanfelice got out the wooden box containing the AT-4 Viper, and set to work preparing the rocket.

"Penetration power fifteen inches of armoured steel, speed three hundred and thirty yards per second, light, easy handling, dependable, our GIs love it," he said, putting it on his shoulder. "Get back behind me, you guys, if you don't want to look like a pizza for the rest of your lives."

Matt Gallone, Franck Rosello, Guy Barber and Jerry Wine all stood beside him, watching. Hector Sosa, in the minibus, kept an eye on the agents, who had made no attempt to resist. Matt was right: Feds they might be, but they had no desire to die for the sake of a Manzoni. Sooner or later, Don Mimino's men would have found the Rue des Favorites, and nothing could have prevented what was about to happen. To croak just in order to delay the operation would have been a professional mistake. They had been taught that during their training: don't die uselessly.

Hector couldn't help looking away from them to watch the spectacle. The rocket flew straight, softly piercing the façade of the house before exploding inside, throwing the walls outwards, opening the whole building up like a flower, so that the roof and the first floor collapsed in one block, down to the ground. Sprays of brick flew up and crashed down in a hundred-yard perimeter

240

around the point of impact. A thick cloud of dust, like poisonous fog, hung over it for several seconds, before dissolving and gradually letting the light of day return to the Rue des Favorites.

"Don't go there yet. The temperature inside will be up to two thousand degrees."

Greg knew the AT-4 Viper of old. He had used it during an attack on a bullion convoy: it had completely melted the driver's cabin, like something in a cartoon. For this one brilliant single shot he had spent days training in a bus graveyard in the middle of the Nevada desert. Considering his contribution over, he packed the launcher back into its container. All he had to do now was wait for confirmation of a single fact – that Giovanni Manzoni had been destroyed.

A second before the conflagration, Fred had been lying on the ground, his eyes sore from so much crying. He had made the terrible decision to leave Cholong immediately and break out of the Witness Protection Programme, to give up expecting any help from the American government. After Maggie's denunciation, all that was left for him was to flee, leaving his family to live out in the open, without the awful sensation of being watched night and day by a third party. By going it alone, he would be removing his family from danger, giving them back their lives. He just needed to go by the house to fetch a few things before evaporating into the background. Then came the explosion, so sudden and so intense that he stopped dead, frozen to the spot. Feeling weightless, he slid along the side of Quint's headquarters to have a look down the street; he saw that the very spot in which he had spent most of the last few months was now no more than a dusty

241

cavity, a hole filled with rubble. Suddenly he heard a strangled cry, which he recognized. He ran into the Feds' house, where he saw a hysterical Maggie trying to escape from Quint's grasp. He was holding her flat on the ground, his hand over her mouth. Fred threw himself down to help him put his wife out of action, and prevent her from screaming for help. Quint pulled his hand back and stunned Maggie with a blow on the back of the neck. Then he placed her head carefully down on a corner of the carpet. He left the room for a moment and returned with a first-aid kit, from which he drew a metal box containing a syringe. Maggie had to be protected from herself, and straight away.

"She'll sleep for at least six hours."

They crawled a few yards over to the window, and raised themselves up just enough to glimpse, at an angle, a minibus surrounded by a handful of armed men who were about to approach the rubble.

"Apart from Matt Gallone and Franck Rosello, I don't know the others," Fred muttered.

"The little dark one is Jerry Wine, and the one putting away the RPG is Greg Sanfelice."

Quint wondered how these lowlifes had found their way to the Manzonis. Six years of work had been wiped out before his very eyes. He couldn't believe that anyone in Washington or Quantico would have talked, and put the problem off until later. How many were there? Five? Ten? Twenty? More? However many they were, he knew that this was the elite, and that Don Mimino's men would blindly obey any order they were given. If it had been established in New York that that rat Manzoni was living in a little town in Normandy, France, they would raze the little town in Normandy, France to the ground

242

and carry on from there. Much as Thomas Quintiliani hated the Mafia, he couldn't help respecting men who pursued their aims with such determination. Don Mimino lived according to his own rules, you had to give him that.

Once the dust cloud had evaporated, Matt rushed over to the ruins, with his Smith & Wesson in his hand. Greg was adamant about it: if there had been anything alive at the moment of the conflagration, whatever it was was now truly dead and already buried, so what was the problem? But Matt was determined to obey his grandfather's orders to the letter, not to leave the premises until he had spat on the body of his enemy. If it hadn't been for possible problems with customs, Don Mimino wouldn't have said no to a little souvenir for himself, Manzoni's heart in a jar of formaldehyde, for example. It would have been something to show to anyone who might have been considering following in his footsteps, and it might also have been a nice decorative piece for one of the shelves in his prison cell. Matt told the men to come and help clear up so as to be certain. Jerry brought the picks and spades out of the boot.

Quintiliani, still crouching on the ground, was trying to call his men, but neither Caputo nor Di Cicco were picking up, and he drew his own conclusions. Fred remained spellbound by the spectacle of these men, some of whom he had known, and loved like brothers, now digging in the ruins of his house, searching for his body.

"I'm going to try and get reinforcements, but for the moment we can only count on ourselves," said Quintiliani, with astonishing sangfroid.

243

Jerry, with his pickaxe in hand, was bending over the pile of stones that, ten minutes before, had been a kitchen, when he heard a ghostly wailing sound. He alerted Matt.

"Sounds like a kid crying."

From the depths of the pit came a voice not strong enough to scream, but which refused to stop. Greg, who had been the cause of many types of scream during his career, had never heard such a heartbreaking sound. Guy wanted to bring it to an end before even finding out what it came from. They pulled back several pieces from walls reduced to rubble, pulled out a metal sink, picked up some kitchen equipment and hacked into the floorboards. They were just pulling back some breeze blocks, when suddenly the whole floor gave way, and they found themselves buried up to the waist. Jerry helped pull them out of this trap, but the unbearable wailing continued unabated, indeed it seemed that the creature had regained hope that someone would rescue it.

Malavita, in her lair, had survived the explosion. A form of life that had once resembled a dog emerged from the bowels of the earth. She finally emerged into the fresh air, exhausted, her flanks pouring with blood. Her bleeding, broken body was covered in cuts. As soon as she saw the men standing still, watching her, she recognized them as her torturers and gazed at them with a pleading stare.

Matt sneered at Sanfelice's great confidence: "Nothing left alive" – here was something alive that had emerged from the cataclysm. And so might not Manzoni himself be in there too, that scum who had been defying them for all these years? In a fury, he attacked the dog, all that trouble for this motherfucking pooch! He grabbed

244

to respect non-interference pacts would be taken in hand by independent soldiers, the Mafia equivalent of the blue helmets, who only took orders from the committee. Then he would impose on each family a system of filial law in which women would play a much more important part. The stronger the family ties, the less betrayal there would be: it is always much harder to betray a mother or a sister. Making the organization more woman-friendly would have many other virtues and would reinforce the sense of community. The old retrograde, ossified Mediterranean model had reached the limits of its usefulness. They would, once and for all, leave the Middle Ages behind them and introduce a real sense of equality by giving women the power they so richly deserved. The next stage, probably the most delicate one, would be to steer the Mafia in a more "ecumenical" direction – that word kept coming into his head. Through the use of diplomacy, he might perhaps succeed where all other attempts at unity had failed: other races and religions would be accepted without distinction and integrated according to strictly observed quotas. The Mob had been decimated by wars against the Chinese and the Puerto Ricans – those days must now be over for ever. Apart from all these changes, the basic structure of the organization would remain the same: one boss for every three lieutenants, each of which would have ten men beneath him. The number of bosses would vary according to the region; a group of bosses would form a family, each family with its godfather, and the group of godfathers would form the top level of authority, itself presided over by the *capo di tutti i capi*. And that role was one Warren was perfectly happy to see himself in, in the fullness of time.

246

He suddenly saw two shapes on the freight tracks a hundred yards away; they appeared from between two grain wagons, part of an interminably long train that seemed to have been abandoned there. The men, in their forties, dressed in sporty clothes, were clearly lost, and in a hurry to find their way back to where they came from. They hurried towards him. Warren noticed something familiar about their demeanour, from several small clues: heads slightly pulled into the shoulders, a sort of awkward stoop, along with great speed of movement and a powerful physical presence. When they got close enough, Warren, his heart pounding now, recognized their features as those of his fellow countrymen. One, he could swear blind, was Italian, and the other could only be a pure-bred Irishman, a fucking mick, a paddy, a harp, quite unmistakeable. Warren felt the joy of someone meeting his countrymen on foreign soil, that feeling of instinctive solidarity, that brotherly link that passes beyond frontiers. These were his homeboys. He could see himself again when he was very young, playing at the feet of these tall men in dark suits who used to pat him gently on the head. They had been his role models – there would never be any better ones. And one day he would be one of them.

His initial enthusiasm was suddenly assailed by doubt, however. Why had these ghosts from the past suddenly appeared, just as he was making his plans for the future? Why had New Jersey come to him, and not the other way around? Warren lowered his eyes, suddenly realizing that these guys could only have got lost in Cholong-sur-Avre for one good reason, a reason that might not be good news for the Manzonis.

Nick Bongusto and Joey Wine had come out of the school. Break was over. Matt had rung them to tell them

247

about the fiasco at the Manzonis' house and to order them to get back to the minibus, which was parked on the edge of the Place de la Libération. The whole business was turning out to be more complicated than they had thought. Time to set to work, and really earn those two million dollars. They climbed onto the Paris platform and finally found a person to ask – a young man standing alone, staring at the ground. Young Blake had had time now to remember the ghastly story of the snitch's son, who had been taken hostage by the Mob to prevent his father from testifying. The father had testified, and, a few days later, what remained of the son had been found by the FBI at the bottom of a barrel of acid. Warren, seeing the two men approaching him, felt a stab in his guts, from the memory of all the threats he had heard about since childhood. It was at the root of everything, it was the basic tool, the touchstone of the whole Mafia operation – pure terror. His head felt as though it was held in a vice, his breathing stopped, his neck stiffened in pain. He felt an icy stab in his churning gut; it drained him of all strength and paralysed him; he couldn't prevent a thin dribble of urine trickling down his leg. He, who a moment ago had seen himself as the supreme chief of organized crime, was now prepared to go down on his knees and pray for his father to appear on the platform and save him.

"Downtown?" Joey asked.

Terrified of betraying himself, Warren wondered if this was a trap. Was Joey really looking for the town centre, or was he just confirming his intuition? If he got it wrong, Warren could already imagine himself thrown onto the tracks and reduced to pulp by the oncoming train. He hesitated and then responded, pointing his hand in the

248

right direction. The loudspeaker announced that the express was coming into the station. A few people got out. The ghosts had disappeared.

He was now marked for ever by the fear of death. Nothing would ever be the same. Now he was confronted with the first real choice of his new life as an adult: should he go off and conquer the New World, or should he stay with his family now, at this, the moment of truth? The train drew out of Cholong, leaving Warren standing on the platform.

*

Back on the Place de la Libération, right in the middle of the festive crowd, Belle was allowing herself a few last moments of wandering around. She envied all these families exercising their right to happiness. If only she had had the good luck to be born into an underprivileged family, to a life of suffering, or to mad people, living outside reason, or even retarded ones, with no clear thoughts about the world around them. Instead, Fate had decreed something different for her, and she had been dealt a father who was capable of sticking a man's fingers in a door and then slamming that door. This same father, who had been so gifted at that type of activity, had risen through the ranks to control a whole territory, like a mayor or a deputy – but feared a great deal more than either of those, since he had the power of life or death over anyone who crossed his path. And to cap it all, he had decided to denounce this parallel world to the authorities, condemning himself and his family to live like hunted creatures. Belle had been both exiled and banished, and there was no place left for her on this earth.

249

She laughed happily at the surrounding gaiety, and then headed towards the big wheel. Its thirty-six baskets, filled with people, would soon empty out to make way for the next lot of passengers. Without worrying about the practical technicalities of her plan (How would she get under the safety bar? What would be the right moment to climb onto the edge and jump from the highest point? Where would she hit the ground?), she was filled with a strange sense of elation. She would only get one shot at it, but her suicide would as be as great a success as everything else she did. She would take her revenge on a cruel and cynical world with this supremely romantic gesture. She approached the turnstile, bought her ticket and waited for the wheel to stop.

*

Matt and his troop, furious at not having found Giovanni's body, joined up with the four other members of the gang in the Place de la Libération. The time had come for a council of war. Jerry thought they should use what was known as the Brazilian method of spreading terror in a city centre with a trapped population: this consisted in opening fire on a public building, preferably a police station or town hall, and, as they had done with the fishing hut, firing on it until the whole building caved in on itself. Greg even suggested that they should save time by simply firing a second rocket from the AT-4 Viper. Franck and Hector said they'd rather avoid going that far: perhaps they could proceed *mano a mano*, and send a general appeal to people's goodwill rather than spreading panic. This fucking funfair could be turned

250

to good use. They had spotted the deputy, the mayor, the chief of police and his six men, all in uniform: all they needed to do was neutralize them and then make use of them. As far as the rest of the population was concerned, Franck suggested sticking to the usual recipe for obtaining information: two thirds intimidation, one third bribery.

During this phase of the operation, the men were able to really express themselves, and make full use of their skills. In Le Daufin restaurant, which opened onto the square, the mayor of Cholong, the deputy for the Eure and the police chief were forced to interrupt their aperitif by the sight of five revolvers pointing at them. They thought at first that this was some sort of practical joke, but then Matt showed them, through the window, what had become of the forces of law and order: six uneasy-looking gendarmes had already accepted the status of hostage, under the threat of an MP5 9mm submachine gun. To the question "Where shall we put them?" Jerry had a jokey answer that Matt, to his surprise, thought was brilliant. And so the inhabitants of Cholong, unable to react in any way to such a strange situation, were treated to the sight of a curious procession filing through the funfair: the grandees and the gendarmes, surrounded *manu militari* by a handful of untidy tourists. How could one imagine that these shabby tourists were capable of emptying tower blocks with baseball bats, and of taking possession of entire districts as if they were a battalion of GIs, or of controlling, for security purposes, all the comings and goings around several buildings during a summit meeting? Matt instructed them to place the muzzle of a .38 Special against the head of the big-wheel operator, just to ensure his cooperation. The previous

251

passengers disembarked, still reeling from their ride. Hector and Jerry, doubled up laughing, pushed each hostage into a basket.

Belle, her ticket in her hand, found herself ejected from the platform, along with all the others waiting their turn. Like her brother before her, she immediately recognized this form of violence. And like her brother before her, she suddenly felt surrounded by ghosts. These were the guys who used to treat her like a princess, escorting her wherever she wanted to go. If she'd asked them for the moon when she was ten, they would have thrown in the sun as well. And now these same guys were sabotaging her suicide bid? Was her life just going to be a never-ending hell, with God on their side, determined to do her in?

Matt waited until the wheel started turning, and then instructed his interpreter to take over. The latter stepped up to the loudspeaker. His voice echoed over the whole square. He issued a warning to the public: there was no threat to the inhabitants of Cholong, and everything would go quite smoothly as long as there was no resistance to the actions of this small group of Americans – he didn't quite know how to describe them, and the word "delegation" came to mind. As well as this, there would be a reward of two hundred thousand euros for anyone who helped capture the American writer known as Frederick Blake, dead or alive. During the announcement, Chi-Chi and Guy passed around the notorious *Times* article about the Manzoni trial, which they had photocopied and were now distributing like a tract. Finally Matt told the interpreter to drive around the town making the same announcement from the candyfloss van.

There were some, however, who stepped forwards, wanting some explanations about this "state of siege". Matt suggested to Hector and Greg that it might be an idea to prove that they meant business. The latter, holding their MP5 9mms, asked the doubters to move aside as fast as possible, and then emptied their guns into the local artists' stands. Vases and clay pots, glazed sculptures, glass lampshades – all flew up in thousands of pieces. Seascapes and portraits were perforated through and through under the helpless gaze of their artists. The charity stall, which Maggie was in charge of, was reduced to dust. There followed a terrified stampede out of the square; the music and the roundabouts fell silent, giving way to cries of panic which took a long time to die down. After a while, all that could now be heard was the rusty metallic creak of the baskets on the big wheel going round and round.

*

Giovanni Manzoni had never suffered such a cruel reversal, even at the height of the wars between the families.

His work had been destroyed before being completed. It had been still-born.

All those hours he had spent at work, pondering every comma, carefully considering each verb before using it. He had even gone so far as to open a dictionary. All the love that had gone into this work, the fruit of his loins, the mirror of his soul, the song of his heart, all gone for ever. All that determination to seek out the truth about himself, without hiding anything – he had been offering his readers the gift of his entire life. And now

253

it had all been reduced to dust in a few seconds, dust and rubble.

This was worse than looking death in the face. Fred felt as though he had never even existed.

Earlier on, listening to his wife's curses, he thought he had touched rock bottom. Now he understood that all pain is relative. You think you've lost everything, and then you find there's so much more to lose. In less than an hour, Fred had buried his future, and a moment later his past had disappeared as well.

As he felt his strength ebbing, he suffered a strange hallucination.

A cohort of zombies filed through the room, men of all ages, with caved-in skulls, bodies riddled with oozing holes, drowned men with eyes popping out of their heads, a great parade of all the victims, direct and indirect, of Giovanni Manzoni and his gang. These ghosts bent over Fred, who lay prostrated on the floor, and gave him a little tap on the shoulder, enjoying this divine moment of revenge. They had waited so many years in silence, in Limbo or under the ground, waiting to reappear at the right moment. They had come to tell Fred that, by attacking innocent people, Gianni Manzoni had shattered the natural order of the universe, and the time had come to set that right.

Quintiliani, who had never been strong on retaliation, didn't have the heart to attack Fred: *What you're going through is nothing compared to what you've inflicted so many times on strangers who didn't fall in with your tyrannical ways. So how do you feel now, deep down, Don Manzoni?*

"Say something, Fred. Just one word."

"Vendetta."

"What do you mean?"

254

"We're going in there, Quint. You and me."

"?..."

"We'll get them, you and me. There can't be more than ten of them."

"Are you mad, Manzoni?"

"Don't count on any reinforcements. If we don't get them, they're going to get us. And until then they're going to do a bit of damage."

"..."

"Don't think about it, it's an opportunity you'll never get again. No trial, no years of gathering evidence to lock them up with, no lawyers to discredit your evidence. This is your one chance to finally wipe out the flower of organized crime. You'll enjoy it, and you'll be promoted for it. It will be a case of *force majeure*, and everyone will be happy."

"There are a lot of them, Fred, and they're well equipped."

"You've spent twenty years studying these guys' methods, and I've spent twenty years training and leading them, who's better qualified than us two?"

Quintiliani pretended to think it over, and made a show of indignation, but he had taken the decision from the moment he had requested the reinforcements: it had been made quite clear to him that the special forces would not intervene as long as the hostages were dangling in the air with guns trained on them. They had even actually made the suggestion that, as an FBI officer, he should operate at his own discretion.

The federal agent now had the opportunity to behave, with complete impunity, in just the same way as those Mafia scumbags – how could he turn down such an opportunity? He, Thomas Quintiliani, would grab this

255

chance to act according to his own set of rules, to be judge and executioner, to pull the trigger without the slightest compunction, or ethical doubts. As a boy, he had, like all the teenagers who hung out on Mulberry, been tempted to join a gang. They were the heroes, not the guys in blue who patrolled the streets with their coshes. And although once he grew up he had finally chosen his side, he had never forgotten his fascination with the made men, the goodfellas. And now here was Fate offering him a chance to exorcise a demon that sometimes reappeared in his most shameful dreams.

Fred, for his part, was also fulfilling an old fantasy: to pull the trigger with a good conscience, on the right side of the law and with the blessing of Uncle Sam. With a bit of luck, he might get a medal. All good things come to those who wait.

*

Some of the townspeople had fled to neighbouring towns to get help, others had gathered in the centre to try and decide how to react to the siege, but most of the population had simply gone home, turned on TVs and radios and started ringing round. When it very soon became clear that there was nothing more to hope for from the authorities, despite all the procedures and high-level communications, the inhabitants of Cholong finally understood, no doubt for the first time in their lives, that they were on their own.

In a café in the La Chapelle district, thirty people tried to address the situation, and to find some way of reacting to the threat. Some wanted to analyse it, while

256

others called for immediate action before the situation reached a point of no return.

In the meeting room, a hundred others listened to a translation of the *Times* piece being read out loud, and heard about the Blake/Manzoni past. All felt betrayed. A mafioso! They had welcomed criminals into their midst, opened their school to the spawn of the Devil. The French state must have been complicit, as well as the CIA, the FBI, Interpol, the Pentagon, the UN, and they had all picked on Cholong-sur-Avre! On top of it all, the fête had been ruined and their lives put in danger all because of that cursed family. As indignation reached boiling point, a group of men formed a militia to track down the bastard and hand him over as soon as possible to those hunting him down.

A few individuals chose to act alone, in the secret hope of getting the reward, which would be enough to keep them secure for a very long time.

The odd individual was observed, here and there, behaving strangely, but to no particular effect. Some saw this upheaval as a temporary crisis and rapidly discovered ways of profiting from the situation. Old grudges were brought to light by the urgency and the danger; this could be the perfect moment to settle a personal score.

For the older inhabitants, grim memories of terrible impotence in the face of an occupying power were reawakened. The word "war" was mentioned.

A war indeed, and one no one could ever have predicted here, in this peaceful township, where, just the day before, people were enjoying the good life. A town of seven thousand inhabitants, identical in every way to the neighbouring town, touched by history, but never

257

very hard, evolving slowly through the ages. No better and no worse than their neighbours, the people were simultaneously home-loving and restless. If you believed the statistics, they obeyed all the demographic and seasonal norms, the national averages. A sociologist, at the risk of dying of boredom, could have used Cholong as the basis for the archetypal provincial town. And it all would have continued like this until the end of time if the Cholongais hadn't suddenly been dragged into a war that was not of their own making.

*

Having lived through what I am about to relate is no help.

But if I hadn't lived through it, I couldn't have made it up.

There are surely some things that can't be invented and that one couldn't describe without having been there. Without having felt it all in one's guts. Quint has to keep quiet, that's his job. The story he's told the world, well, I'm the only one who knows what's true and what's made up. Apart from him, I'm the only witness.

I just couldn't resist it. I had to sit down again in front of a blank sheet of paper and tell what really happened, even if nobody ever reads these words. Reader, before you decide that I'm completely mad, just let me tell you the story of how me and Quint tried to restore order to that little town.

First of all, try to imagine what it's like to make a pact with your worst enemy to kill your own brother. Me, Giovanni Manzoni, team up with a man whose death I had dreamed about so often? When I think about it now, long after it all happened, I still feel sick. I'll try and hold back all the swear words that come to mind when I have to mention that mother-fucking cop (of course it's tempting, but one mustn't become too

258

repetitive). I'll just call him by his name, Tom Quint, originally Tommaso Quintiliani. One day they'll make me change all the names in this story, but until then...

If only he'd been a product of my imagination, a fictional character. I could have made him do or say anything I wanted. Then I could have paid him back for everything he's made me suffer in the last few years. But Tom is all too real. You can't predict what he's going to do, and I have no idea what makes him tick. Tom is a true dispenser of justice. Can you imagine that? He's not just the good cop who's a part of the neighbourhood, the ordinary human being, a bit fallible, you know the type (I certainly do, I've killed several of them). He comes from another species altogether. It may sound crazy, but avengers still exist. Tom is the worst type of cop, because he's the best. It took him four years to finally get me, not a day less, but he got there in the end. Those Bureau guys, they don't live like other people. You know, a bit of fun, a few dollars in your pocket. Take your kids to the cinema, take care of your bored wife, that kind of thing. No, for them, as soon as they wake up in the morning, all they can think of is the guy they're chasing. They talk about him a hundred times a day. Putting him in a cell would be, like, the crowning achievement of their lives. As though there weren't other, worthier aims in life. You start wondering if they're really human, with those dark glasses so you can't see where they're looking. And how about those earpieces? I always wondered what they could hear in those things. Some kind of higher being that the rest of us mere mortals can't hear?

No, no one knows how a guy like Quint functions. But he claims to know how a Manzoni functions. Compared to Tom Quint, you can see right through me. He caught me by anticipating all my movements, it was as though he could read my mind. If you believe the Feds, they think people like me are thick, limited, predictable – and plenty more sneering words like that.

259

I'd rather he kept his dark glasses on when he talks to me. On the rare moments when he takes them off, I can't bear seeing myself in his eyes. I see things... How can I put it?... On good days I'm a psychopath, but most of the time I'm just an animal. He stares at me as one might stare at an animal. A dinosaur, some kind of extinct species, some creature that you only see in a delirious nightmare. And instead of not caring, it puts me in a rage. I don't know where that rage comes from, and I don't know how to get rid of it. So I keep it bottled up inside me, and it scares me. Truth scares me, it's the only thing that does.

You should have seen the look on his face when I told him I was writing! There must be a word for it – something between scorn and mockery. "You, Fred?..." I'd have preferred it if he'd spat in my face. Me, write? Giovanni Manzoni? How could that be? The story of my life? It was a wretched idea, they all thought so, even my family. Why did they all get so worked up about it? I wasn't asking anything from anybody. I wasn't doing any harm. I just disappeared onto the veranda every day. They didn't have to worry any more about any other stupid thing I might be getting up to. You should have seen them, instead of just fucking off and leaving me alone, the children laughed at me, and Livia – the whole thing made her nervous – she shouted at me worse than ever. Quint ratted on me to his bosses. Everyone got their wind up, all because of me. But I carried on, despite all the bad will. You know when I finally realized what a horrific thing it was for me to write my memoirs? It was when they destroyed them with a bazooka.

Sure, I was traumatized then. If I hadn't seen it with my own eyes, I would never have believed a catastrophe like that could really happen. And even seeing it, the whole scene right in front of my eyes, hearing everything, I still refused to believe it. You see it, but the brain can't take it in. The story of my life going up in smoke. When something like that happens, you

260

start imagining things, you look for signs, you try to make some sense of the whole thing. You have to really, otherwise you'd go mad. I decided that, by writing my life story, I had unleashed supernatural powers. I had annoyed the gods, like in the Roman and Greek times. Perhaps it was written: my story should never be told, my memoirs must remain just hovering above my head. It was a way of telling me: Giovanni, who's interested in this so-called truth? Who gives a fuck about your life? Your story, it's about the customs of a time gone by, it's of no interest to people now. You belong to a species that's heading for extinction, the race will die out with you. In any case, who would be stupid enough to believe in a single one of those days you spent in New Jersey? Even Livia has no idea of what went on. Quint could testify, and how. No one else would have believed me. It all had to be suppressed, probably just as well in the end.

Maybe one day, when everything's settled down, they might let me publish this, with the word "novel" on the cover, and I'll have pulled it off. I'll change everything, the places, the names, the timescale, everything except the actual truth. No one will notice anything, no one will suspect anything, it won't set off any disastrous reaction. The reader will just say to himself "It's fiction", and as soon as the book's closed, he'll have forgotten about it. I myself don't even want to be believed any more. I just want to tell the story, page after page, one thing after another, and then the next thing, on and on to the end. A novel, for Christ's sake. With heroes and villains, comedy and tragedy – you just have to call it fiction. No need to try and be serious, or to believe that what one's doing is important. No need to be clever, just tell the story, say what comes next. I've learned from experience to wait for what comes next. So many things happened from one year to the next, sometimes from one hour to the next. And while you're waiting for "The End", all sorts of things could happen, good and bad, things that seemed good,

261

but got complicated, fuck-ups that proved to be helpful. You just had to wait and see.

Me and Quint, we decided to get them, these Newark executioners. They were crazy to have left Newark, that wise-guy paradise, that perfect world where anything goes. Those long grey streets, those rows of low-rise buildings, with odd gaps everywhere like missing teeth. You had to get up early to see anything attractive about it, even if you had been born there. And yet it was more real than anywhere else – friends were friends for life, the pasta tasted better, the women were more passionate, even the blood seemed redder. And you understood the hidden meanings in people's words. If you haven't known Newark, you're like a wild animal who has been born in the zoo.

God made temptation, the Devil made hell, and Man made Newark. And when you're cast out of Newark, the rest of the world is like a deep dark hole.

Yes, they were crazy to have set off from there to come and sort me out. I should say, eliminate me. In the real sense of the word. Don Mimino, their patron saint, who was rotting in jail at Rykers, had instructed them to dissect me and make a useful travelling vanity case out of my skin. But since the old guy's travelling days were over, he changed his mind in the end; he'd started reading books, and old ones too, so he thought new bindings might be a better idea. (Apparently Don Mimino had decided to take advantage of his stretch in jail to tackle the whole of Shakespeare – he would read it all, understand it all, and then begin again, until he finally got to the bottom of it and sucked out every drop of meaning – after all, he had all the time in the world to do it in.) What could be more thrilling than to read Hamlet, *holding between your fingers the cured and tanned skin of the man who caused your downfall? The Don hadn't stinted on the expenses, and the families from the*

262

Five Boroughs had sent their best men, each one hand-picked for his speciality. I was, of course, flattered by this gathering of talent on my behalf.

"How many are there, you reckon?" Quint asked.

"Something between the Magnificent Seven and the Dirty Dozen."

He and I set off arm in arm through the streets of Cholong – you had to see it to believe it. (Talking of which, I'd like to say, just as an aside, that I've always found the name Cholong unpronounceable, especially for an American like me, so I've renamed it So Long.) Tom had his weapons hidden under a long coat loosely done up around the middle because of the submachine gun attached to his front. You should have seen his cool expression! Trying to look normal when he was carrying a fourteen-pound long-range rifle as well, slung across his shoulder – it was a sniper rifle, the sort of thing with a shape that's hard to pass off as anything other than a fourteen-pound sniper rifle.

"We ought to make a plan, Fred."

"Plan? What plan? The only plan I've got is to shoot on sight, and shoot well."

"I wonder if I'm making a big mistake sticking with you. You go by the La Chapelle district, I'll come through the square, we'll meet in half an hour behind the Town Hall."

"Just one piece of advice they may not have given you at Quantico. If you kill one of them, kill him a second time. It might seem odd at first to shoot a dead body, but you've no idea how useful it can turn out to be."

He went off and I heaved a sigh of relief. It was the first time he'd left me alone for a long time. Out of his control. And armed to the teeth! Forget Fred Blake, I was back to being Gianni, the real me. Giovanni Manzoni! I would have shouted it in the streets if I could. It had been a long and painful wait. But

263

I had never given up. Every minute of those six years, I had imagined starting over like before. It's what had kept me going, the hope that one day I'd get my real life back again. And that day had finally come.

The fact is, ordinary life, the everyday life that other people lead, is beyond me. Everyday life for everyday people, it's a mystery: what could possibly be going on in their heads and in their hearts? How could they trust in a world that had to be obeyed? What did honest people do? How could they live with feeling so vulnerable? What does it do to you to be a victim? A victim of your neighbour, of the world around you, of the state? How could anyone accept such an idea, and accommodate himself to it for his whole life? What do honest men do when you show them they're tilting at windmills? That they will never be able to move mountains?

There's nothing to protect you, little man. You may think there is, but you're wrong. Did no one ever explain to you that you're a straw figure at the mercy of bastards like me? And there are so many of us bent on harming you, even fine men who are on the right side of the law, but to whom you mean nothing except an opportunity to make a profit. I'm sorry for you, truly I am. Before all this, I knew you were suffering, but I had no idea how much misery there really was in the world. And yet God knows you try – I've watched you. You retain your faith in humanity, you try and sort things out, to do your best. And then all your efforts come to nothing, ruined by all those who couldn't care less about your faith in humanity. You cry – who's going to listen to you? Who's going to bust a gut to help you and your little family? So you say everyone's got troubles, often a lot worse than yours, and you sink your head between your shoulders, and you march on, little man, because you're a little soldier and you have to endure. Until the next time.

264

I've tried it myself. Couldn't do it. Never had that sort of courage.

My head full of all these problems, I came around a corner and found myself face to face with one of the killers who were after me. And this was one I knew well – we had been inseparable as teenagers. Nick and me, we'd smashed a lot of heads in together. Sometimes we'd be together for forty-eight hours at a time. We'd look out for one another if ever we strayed into another gang's territory. That sort of thing creates a bond in the end.

When Nick saw me, he didn't have time to get out his gun, and neither did I. So we smiled at each other, and shook hands – You look well, how are you, what's become of you since the old days – each waiting for the right moment to draw, and the moment didn't come. Boxers call this the "vista" (the vista determining whether they should take a risk or not), and so there we were, face to face, neither of us lowering our defences. But the odd thing was that our friendly chit-chat was perfectly sincere. We reminded each other of a secret we had in common.

We were twenty, and we were hungry. We were as fierce as Rottweilers, and ambitious too – yes, we were ready to turn the world upside down. But, pending that, we ran errands for the boss of the Polsinelli clan – we did all his dirty work. That time, we had been told to track down a bookie who had scarpered with the twenty-five per cent cut he owed the boss (business had been good for the last three years). The crazy thing was, the little fellow had gone to hide at his parents' house! Nick and me, we couldn't believe it! The biggest cretin in the world couldn't have done anything stupider. It was a little house in some dump in Mercer County, exactly two hours' drive from the taxi depot that served as Polsinelli's headquarters. The weird thing was, when Nick and me rolled up, the parents, a retired couple, asked us in, and suggested we wait for the boy to come back from some errand in town. Taken by surprise, Nick and I found

265

ourselves being served coffee and biscuits, the little old couple really happy to meet some friends of their son, and telling us all sorts of stories about his childhood and all that. So obviously, when he finally turned up, nobody knew what to do. The son knew at once why the two guys on the sofa were waiting for him. And you've got to hand it to him, Nick put on a good show, he gave the guy a big hug and so did I. He let us do it, and the parents were happy to see the friends reunited. Nick suggested we go and have a drink in the town, and the guy got in the car without any fuss. He said goodbye to his parents, trying not to cry, and the mother had even thought it a bit odd that her son should kiss her when he was just going off for a cup of coffee at the corner. Once he was in the car, the guy hadn't tried pleading for his life, or saying he'd pay the money back – he knew perfectly well it was too late for all that. I was sitting on the passenger seat, not feeling very proud of myself, and I looked at Nick, who wasn't happy either. It was the little old couple who had ruined everything with their stale biscuits. You should have seen the mother's expression, so happy that her son had such well-dressed and polite friends. What were we going to do now?

"Get out. We never saw you."

"?…"

"Get out before we change our minds, asshole."

I told him in great detail what we'd do to him if we ever heard of him again, or if he ever reappeared in his old haunts. On the way home, Nick and I, we didn't say anything. We would be bound together by this secret until the day we died.

And now that day had come for one of us in this street in So Long, so many years later. We both knew that one of us was going to cop it. It did us good to reminisce about that story, a story that only ourselves and the reprieved victim would ever know about. We wondered what on earth could have become of

266

that guy, and we started laughing, and that was when I saw a split-second gap, the split-second we had both been waiting for, just enough for me to draw my gun and blow Nick's head off.

As I looked at his body lying on the pavement, I wondered to myself about questions of friendship. Is the concept of friendship amongst made men different from that of other people? If it has to end one day, surely any true friendship can and must only end in bloodshed.

All this time, Tom was taking cover on the top floor of a building. I say "taking cover", he wasn't actually taking cover, he was living out an old fantasy, and watching the world through a gun sight.

If anyone had asked him, when he was a child, what he wanted to do when he grew up, he would have replied "sniper" without any hesitation.

Sniping, for him, was a quite different thing from dirty and squalid murder. Crime that involved smells and noises was fine for animals like us, he thought. He, Tom Quintiliani, was way above all that sort of thing, in this case quite literally: he had found the highest point in the centre of town (apart from the tower above the church, which, he later confessed to me, he had tried unsuccessfully to break into – no respect...) On his terrace, he just had to pivot around to catch all the different parts of So Long in his sights. They all looked so close through the scope, almost within a hand's reach. Surveillance screens never showed anything as clearly as this.

Sniping had a metaphysical dimension for him too. It represented silence, time, distance, concentration, understanding, seeing. The sniper was the personification of death, striking at the most unexpected moment, from far away, invisibly. Like God Himself. He felt as though he was everywhere at once. He was right about one thing: you get your reward if you wait long enough. And beyond your wildest dreams.

267

Julio Guzman and Paul Gizzi had paused on their patrol to drink some water from the fountain under the covered market at the north end of the square.

At the other end, a mile and a half to the south, Franck Rosello sat on a bench in the square opposite the Town Hall and unfolded a map of the town. For an occasional sniper like Tom, it was an honour to have this living legend amongst sharpshooters in his sights.

But the closest of all his targets was Greg Sanfelice, sitting in one of the baskets of the big wheel, watching over his hostages like a mother hen.

Tom was wondering which one to choose. A real sniper would never have asked himself that question.

After he had drunk at the fountain, Paul Gizzi moved aside to let Julio Guzman take his place: he was already lying on the ground, where he had dropped down like a dead leaf. Tom had aimed at his heart.

A second later, Franck Rosello slumped down on his bench, without having looked death in the face, just like the victims of his own shootings. Every time he had pressed the trigger, he had thought that he too would like to die like that. To be hit without warning, without time for fear or regrets. Tom had just made his wish come true.

Franck's arm had no sooner touched the grass than Greg's head exploded into the air. Close shot on a moving target. Tom was earning a place in the pantheon of elite marksmen.

After a moment of pride, he suffered a sudden churning fear in his gut, a terror he found it hard to describe to me later (his hands were trembling so much, the only way to stop them was to sit on them – I'm not joking). It wasn't his first dead body, no it wasn't that. But to have shot three men almost at the same time in three different places; that was "supernatural" – that was the word he used. That idiot wanted metaphysics – well,

268

he got them. Still, when he came down from his perch, he swore he'd never touch a long-distance rifle again.

We met up at the rendezvous. He suggested getting rid of Paul Gizzi, who was now alone in the market square. We would work a simple manoeuvre: one would be the bait, the other would grab the guy; it didn't take long (apart from deciding who would be the tethered goat, Quint being uncooperative again...) I had never met Paul Gizzi until then. When I shot the bullet into his brain, I was sorry not to have had time to get to know him, and to compliment him on the famous "Gizzi move".

It was a good ten years ago, at the end of a winter afternoon. Gizzi had plunged the whole business section of San Francisco into darkness, with a four-hour blackout. There had been a general panic, leaving him four hours to operate in. The result was he cleaned out three banks of sixty per cent of their liquid cash. All the members of the gang had agreed not to share out the proceeds for a year. Not a single one ever boasted about the job, and not a single one was ever caught. That's the secret: keeping your mouth shut. I would love to have asked him a thousand questions about the logistics of the operation, and make him cough up his secrets.

That's my greatest fault: I prefer the backstage details to the show itself. I hate not knowing about the tricks and the strings. Once, one evening in Las Vegas, I was with some other Mob guys watching the greatest magic show on earth. The man on the stage kept appearing and disappearing, flying through the air, and everybody was amazed by the magician's genius. I was dying of curiosity like the others, but, unlike them, I couldn't leave it at that. I couldn't resist it. As the next show began, I slipped backstage and managed to silence all the bodyguards who were trying to do what bodyguards do. I went into the magician's dressing room to make him explain how he became invisible in front of a hundred people. The guy thought I was

269

joking at first, and then he invoked the magician's code of honour, according to which you never reveal your methods. It was only when I suggested some disappearing tricks of my own – how to make a magician's body vanish in the Nevada desert, how to make all his teeth drop out at once, how to lock him in a trunk with a rattlesnake – that the greatest magician in the world finally spilled the beans.

And here I was that day, two paces from the drinking fountain in the market square at So Long, and I hadn't had time to say to Paul: "I really admire what you do!" – to tell him how much his work had always been a point of reference for all of us. But time was short and we had to get on with getting rid of these guys without having to mull over the good old days each time. So now no one would ever know how Paul had pulled off his "Gizzi move", his very own secret weapon. His secret would go with him to the grave.

In crime, just like any other part of life, it's the champions who get the respect. People love great exploits, it's the thing people go on dreaming of right up to the end. What does discipline matter in the face of genius? Each of these gangsters who wanted to kill me deserved whole volumes telling their life stories and analysing their methods. They pushed themselves that bit further, breaking new barriers of excellence. Look at me, for example – I always carry a photo of John Dillinger in my wallet. He was the only really great figure of the Thirties. Even Baby Face Nelson and the boys from the Barrow gang, much as I respect them, couldn't reach his knee. That was the time of artists and poets, the true idealists. Dillinger respected human life and didn't like leaving innocent victims. At that time, wolf only killed wolf, the sheep didn't come into it, except when it came to being fleeced.

The thing is, to tell the truth, if there's one thing I can't stand, it's amateurism. Crime should be left to criminals.

270

Professional killers are the only ones I respect. The others, the occasional assassins, the retarded delinquents, the avengers of lost causes, the crazy serial killers, the fanatical terrorists, the loudmouth murderers, the small time gangsters – all those who haven't been trained in the skills of death, they only deserve my undying contempt. Let the shooters shoot, for God's sake, and stick to your own quiet little life, you'll see, you'll gain from it in the end. Stop annoying those around you, it's not your job, and if you should happen to try playing the gang boss, you'll pay with your life. Crime, real crime, is a vocation. You pay a high price if you devote your life to it, and it's a price few men are prepared to pay.

Tom Quint, who's a predator too, but on the right side of the law, says the same: let us work in peace, all you other young idiots tempted by this career. Let the big boys play in their play-ground, and go home. Your families will mourn for you and you will suffer when human justice turns against you. And divine justice won't be any kinder towards you – it hates amateurs.

He and I had decided to walk back up towards the Place de la Libération in order to hit the head of the squad, Matt Gallone, and cause a bit of havoc in the rest of the gang. No luck – no sooner had we had the idea than we got ourselves nabbed, me and Tom, like amateurs. No way of escaping, no bargaining, nothing. When you hear the crackle of machine-gun fire and a guy tells you to kneel down, well, you kneel down, especially when you have no idea where he's coming from, or who he is, a cop or a killer. You just kneel down and put your hands on your head, without even being asked. We looked pretty clever, both of us side by side on the sidewalk, about to be killed without even knowing who was going to do it (I thought I heard Jerry Wine's voice, but I didn't quite have the nerve to ask). There wasn't time for anything, no wisecracks, no last wish, no prayer, no last insult for the killer, or thought for a loved one, nothing.

271

Tom and me threw our arms down and waited for a quick clean death.

What happened next? There was a burst of gunfire – but it wasn't for us. Amazed at still being alive, we heard screams, and turned around to see Jerry Wine and Guy Barber, their legs riddled with bullets, rolling around in agony on the ground. The person who had shot them was a little guy, about fourteen. I didn't recognize him immediately.

Like all kids, he had grown up without me noticing it. When he was just so high and could hardly talk, he used to gaze at me with such adoration – at me, his rascal of a father. It was a different kind of admiration to what I was used to; that had been the admiration I got from killers and courtiers, based on other things, fear mainly, but also envy and jealousy – everybody had plenty of reason to admire me and fear me. All except this little fellow who hung on to my leg and clung on as though I was a giant. That sort of admiration came from pure love. I can still remember Warren's inventiveness when he wanted to make me happy: during games of Monopoly he would slip money to me under the table when I got into debt. His elder sister couldn't understand why he did that. "It's only a game," she'd say. But the kid insisted. His dad had to win, and that was that. And the more I was myself, with all the faults his mother would point out, the more he loved me for being myself. For him I was the perfect father, and everything about me was exceptional. And then suddenly, one day, that trusting look in his eyes just disappeared. I never understood why.

I asked him where he'd got the machine gun from. He said: "It was by Julio Guzman's body, by the drinking fountain." I saw Quint preparing to finish off Jerry Wine and Guy Barber, so I took the kid by the shoulder to spare him the sight of a summary execution. As soon as we got round the corner, we fell into each other's arms.

272

It was good to talk again, to let ourselves go.

I said to myself, why deny him his vocation if it's his destiny to go back there and reconquer my kingdom, and once more raise the family flag? Nobody should stand in his way.

Maybe my son would succeed where I had failed.

My fatherly role would now be to help him overcome obstacles – he could benefit from my experience.

But I was one step behind. Warren no longer wanted this inheritance. He wanted no part of this barbarity, a word he used several times. He had realized this an hour earlier at the So Long station. I couldn't quite tell if this made him sad or relieved. In any case, there was no anger in his voice.

What he had just lived through had, in just a few seconds, aged him by ten years. I suppose that's what's meant by growing up, becoming an adult, but then he asked me the worst question ever: he asked me if I thought that society would one day manage to finally get rid of people like me. Whether there was any hope at all for the world in which he was going to grow up, and perhaps be a father himself.

Anyone who has been a father will recognize this moment – the day your kid questions everything you stand for. You tell yourself that it's just an adolescent phase, that he'll understand eventually and come round to your way of thinking. The difference here was that I knew that Warren would never come round.

He'd asked the question. I had to answer. After all, it was probably the last time he'd ever listen to me. I was tempted to lie, and give him a bit of paternal reassurance. But, out of respect for the man he would become, I went ahead and told him what I truly thought: "No, my son, the world will never get rid of guys like me. Because for every new law there's a wise guy ready to break it. And so long as there's a middle way, there'll be those who opt for the margins. And so long as men have vices,

273

there'll be other men prepared to supply them. Still, maybe in a thousand years or so, who knows?"

Tom felt a bit awkward interrupting this tête-à-tête, but he managed to convey to me that there was still some work to do. Warren and I shook hands in a manly fashion. He said he'd never touch a gun again, but that he didn't regret having done so just once, and not just to save me – in a way it was to restore me to life, and pay off the debt that all sons owe to their progenitor. The slate was now wiped clean. He could henceforth live the life of an honest man with nothing dragging him back, no millstone round his ankle.

And then? What can I say about what happened next?

What happened next gave the word "barbarity" its full meaning once more. Tom and I decided to separate again. So I was going back up towards the Place de la Libération, and I found myself alone in an empty bar, up against Hector Sosa. I had to face him empty-handed, although I would have been more than happy to get rid of him with a couple of bullets. A fist fight was the worst possible option – there was nothing Hector liked better than crushing noses with his fists. Well, everything went into that fucking fight, bottles smashed on the skull, chairs, even tables. This level of damage usually came with a full gang fight, but there were just the two of us. Anything went – we both liked a straight fight, no weapons, just fists. I had held on to my temper for too long (it was what I used to save in the past for the bad payers, the ones who had to be beaten up, but kept alive in the hope of an eventual payment). To tell the truth, I launched into this fight in a rage, but it was a beneficial rage, it unwound me, relaxed me, rather like yoga, or Zen, or a seawater cure. It cleared the mind of a whole lot of grudges and unresolved issues. There's no better therapy for a guy like myself. But all the same, I soon got fed up with it. I was getting my face smashed up, and really, this saloon-bar brawl

274

had gone on long enough. But my opponent wouldn't go down; it seemed impossible to knock him out once and for all.

Still, in the end, there's got to be one left standing and one on the ground, that's the way things are. Did one of us have more to lose than the other? That's the only possible explanation for what happened. Hector stared at me, between two streams of blood trickling down his face. He was dumbfounded. He had notched up heavyweights and middleweights in his time, and he could not understand how this Manzoni guy could still be standing. It was beyond anything he could possibly understand. He collapsed on the ground after a whiplash blow from a chair, and then sank into unconsciousness, which looked as though it might last for ever.

For his part, Tom Quint had got rid of Joey Wine, Jerry's brother, without too much trouble. I'd gladly have swapped jobs. Joey's problem was his addiction, and his addiction was banks. He couldn't resist a bank. And if you've got an addiction you can't resist, it'll get you in the end – all the warnings, sermons and enforced or voluntary treatments in the world won't stop you. Where Gizzi would sometimes spend several months preparing a bank job, Joey would break in to a bank in the same way as you might suddenly take a pee. While Paul would embark on a long courtship, Joey would slap his hand on the victim's ass. He'd get himself beaten up, but it never changed anything, he'd just start all over again even more enthusiastically. I can still remember the day Joey was let out after serving a four-year sentence for robbing a branch of Chase. After coming out of San Quentin, he drove for two hours, thinking about his wife and two daughters, whom he hadn't kissed for years, and the friends with whom he was planning a celebration that night. Then he found himself driving through a little deserted town. A little bank in the high street "called out to him", as he put it.

275

Who knows if was the pain of having missed something for so many abstemious years, but Joey sat in his car for an hour, gazing rapturously at this beautiful little bank, a small voice inside him insisting: "Carry on driving, you fool, you know perfectly well how this will end up, think of your daughters, do you really want to go straight back to that hellhole?" and another voice saying: "Isn't she beautiful! If you miss this chance, you'll regret it all your life." In the end, the temptation was too great, and within two days he was back in his cell, with an extended reoffender's sentence. You can't help truly sick people like Joey. One day it would all end badly.

As Tom walked past the biggest bank in So Long, on the corner of the Place de la Libération, he glimpsed an odd sight through the window: there was Joey, on the other side of the counter, hurling himself like a madman against a connecting door. For Tom, it was almost painful to see the guy, with his incurable illness, losing all contact with reality, and he even paused for a second before wasting him, wondering to himself if these villains actually preferred the theft itself to the money, the sensation being more important than the reward.

We'd had that conversation a hundred times over. Tom wanted to make me admit that I'd become a mobster because of the adrenalin rush, in the same way as a gambler who is equally excited by winning or losing. I would insist that the only thing that drove us was money. "But how can you love money to such a point?" he would say, and I would try to explain to him that we Cosa Nostra thugs were obsessed by money, but how can such an obsession be explained? Just the thought that our money was piling up somewhere, that it was flooding in, that soon we'd need another place to pile up all those banknotes, that was our obsession, our passion. OK, sometimes we used it to buy stuff, to give pleasure to our families, but that sure wasn't the object of the exercise. In any

276

case, nobody was worse than we were at spending it. I admit it: we only liked showy stuff. If it was shiny or gold, we'd buy it. Expensive? Priceless? We had to have it. The best stuff was always the most expensive.

The funny thing was that we enjoyed spending just as much as getting stuff for free. That was another passion of ours, just as strong as our love of money: gifts, stuff fallen off the backs of trucks, payments in kind, whether we needed them or not. If we were protecting a guy whose pizza chain was doing well, we'd go off with a few thousand dollars and a couple of pizzas for the road. Same with furriers or bathroom shops. We'd load ourselves up with rubbish that we'd end up throwing away. Tom couldn't understand this: "What, it's really worth rotting in jail for that? Or getting a bullet between the eyes? Killing guys? Having trouble around you every day of your life? Ruining your families?" The cop, he just didn't get it. And I gave up trying to explain it all, because, to tell the truth, I didn't really understand it myself.

Anyway, Joey finally got three bullets in the kisser, just at the moment the door he was breaking down, the door to God knows what, finally collapsed. Tom then came and joined me on the Place de la Libération. I waited for him, sitting on the merry-go-round, which was still going round.

*

By the evening, So Long had become the centre of the universe. I found myself reliving the nightmare of the trial: an army of journalists from all over the world, interviewing anyone they could, politicians, "observers", intellectuals, VIPs, popular singers – as well as the man in the street, whom they found in the street, and who was all too delighted to offer his opinion on the affair. Everybody had something to say about my story, my

277

testifying, my betrayal; some wanted answers from me. I felt I was being tried by the whole of humanity.

That was almost literally true! They poured in from all over the place: TV trucks, helicopters, private jets. A swarm of CNN people, hundreds of reporters, thousands of eager spectators hemmed in by police forces from the four neighbouring départements, *as well as special detachments sent in from Paris. All this to try and make sense of what had happened that day in this unknown little dump in Normandy.*

The American networks had shared the material they had on my trial, and it was being played over and over again now on European TV. The snitch's whole history was being retold, and by nine o'clock, everybody knew everything – or at least they thought they did. What was worrying me most was that among the corpses being swept up in the streets, one was missing, the worst one of them all.

Matt Gallone had disappeared. Knowing Matt, there was nothing surprising about that. He was never where you expected him to be. A beat was organized, with a dozen volunteers; his description was circulated; roadblocks were put up. Matt had always dreamed of being public enemy number one, and the great day had come. Quint seemed so sure of himself – he'll go south, he said. He said that if Matt managed to make it to Sicily, he'd be taken care of by the Cosa Nostra for as long as necessary, years maybe, before going back to the States. He was right, of course, but I dreaded another possible scenario: that he might still be in So Long. Nobody in Europe knew him as well as I did. As long as there was a single breath left in his body, he would continue to carry out his grandfather's orders. He would choose a thousand deaths rather than one minute of shame, after this day that marked the final downfall of the Gallone clan. I swear to you, I'd have been happy to be wrong about that.

278

They put me in quarantine while they decided what to do with me. The hotlines between Washington and Paris were buzzing, and the most unlikely authorities quarrelled over who should be in charge of prisoner Manzoni, claiming reasons of state and security. The American government, the secret services, the FBI, but also all the different branches of the French police, right down to the little captain of the So Long gendarmerie who had been one of the hostages on the big wheel (he claimed that he might never recover from the humiliation of that experience). It was a legal, political and diplomatic headache, to say the least. Myself, I gave up trying to understand anything. I'd been kept in hiding for years, everything possible had been done to keep me invisible, and suddenly my face was all over the place, and everybody wanted a piece of me. Luckily I'm the vicious sort – if I had any goodness in me, I'd have gone mad.

They all agreed on one point: the whole world wanted me, and the whole world must be satisfied. That would be the only way to avoid a political and PR disaster, and to keep the public at bay. People must have the chance to SEE Giovanni Manzoni, and hear him too. Whether I was a living legend, or a criminal bastard, I was obliged to make an appearance. After that, they said, everything would settle down again, and justice could be allowed to take its course.

Tom Quint, more than anyone, was determined to show that I had survived the So Long reprisals. He was the overall winner in the whole affair: in half a day he had got rid of the elite of several branches of organized crime, and the Witness Protection Programme was now famous throughout the world, and shown to be successful – after all, it had protected the life of a snitch with all the ferocity of a pit bull terrier. Already dozens of mafiosi were on the line from all parts of the United States offering to testify. This was the apogee of Tom's career. But to achieve a completely successful outcome to the operation, I had to agree to appear before the cameras.

279

And all I wanted to do was to tell them to go hang. I had just been given permission to join my family in the basement of the Town Hall, and I had no desire to be exhibited before a million viewers. I really didn't feel like being an object of rage and disgust to a whole lot of strangers. The irony was, I aroused a lot of other feelings in the public mind: curiosity of course, but sympathy too, compassion even. And of course a whole gamut of other reactions, from indignation to pure hatred. But indifference – never. And indifference was all I wanted at that moment. I knew already how the little TV interview would play out. I would be bombarded with negative waves and bad vibrations (I believe in that sort of thing), and I didn't think I'd be able to deal with the consequences of all that hatred.

"You haven't got the choice," Tom said. "If you don't do it, we'll both be lynched. Let's get it over with, this day's gone on long enough. Then I'll buy you a drink."

I asked him if there was any way to get out of that, at least. He burst out laughing and led me up to the cameras. You can picture the scene – a little platform with microphones on it, a hundred journalists, and the whole world watching.

"Gotta do it, Fred."

"You sure?"

In other words, are you sure you want to exhibit that hardened villain Giovanni Manzoni to the world? I was exhausted by life in general and in particular by the battle I had just fought. I was about to arouse more reflexes of hatred from all sides. All of humanity was about to curse me in every language, spit on the ground, threaten me, point me out to their children. From east to west, north to south, at sea and on the land, in deserts and cities, among the rich and the poor. Surely the world didn't need this – in fact what it needed was the exact opposite.

That's when I had my idea.

Belle, my diamond, my princess.

280

I really would be a proper writer if I could find the right words to describe my daughter's look. But who could do such a thing?

She said yes at once when I suggested that she take my place – I couldn't understand why she agreed, but we'd all be the winners. Her face lit up even before she came under the spotlights. And the people saw it, that inner light; they felt it, that inner peace in her heart. When she smiled, each man thought that smile was for him alone. She's a miracle, Belle. A Madonna like her is made to be seen.

She gave good news about the family, and especially about her dad. It was as though she was reassuring the population of five continents about my fate. For a minute Belle was the most famous and the most watched girl in the world. She left the stage, more glowing than ever, with a little gesture that seemed to promise a return.

*

Night finally fell on So Long, and everything returned to normality. The inhabitants returned to their beds after this day of madness, trucks began loading up again, and even the police lay low, awaiting new orders. Tom installed camp beds for my little family at number 9 Rue des Favorites, the Feds' villa. His two lieutenants, each with a pump-action gun, stood guard in the sitting room, while Tom and me leaned on the window sill, knocking back the bourbon we'd been dreaming of all day.

Malavita was trying to sleep, next to the boiler in the basement, wrapped in several metres of bandage. She had had quite enough of this fucking day. The state they'd found her in – who would do such a thing to a dog? When I saw her in that condition, I just wanted to look after her, to help her to recover, and then take her for walks in the forest, play with her in the garden, teach her

281

a few tricks, let her come and go freely, in short give her back a taste for life. I think she felt the same way.

But before that she had a score to settle, and as quickly as possible. And that's exactly what happened that very night, after everyone had gone to sleep. They say revenge is a dish best served cold. Not for her it wasn't. It fell into her mouth, freshly cooked.

She heard the basement window squeaking, and felt someone's presence, and then saw a shape in the dark. The intruder had no idea that the dog was there, in the dark, still alive. She recognized him by his smell, or maybe just by instinct. How could she forget him? You never forget, and you never forgive. What people say about all that is just crap.

In the dark, Matt had found the stairs that would take him up to me. He was prepared to die just to get my guts, and avenge the honour of his family and every other mafioso. Omertà *would have the final word.*

He must have frozen when he heard the growl. A fucking dog? Yes, it was that fucking dog he'd beaten up that afternoon. He didn't even know what it was called.

Malavita.

One of the many names Sicilians call the Mafia. Malavita, *lowlife. I always thought it had a more melodious sound than "Mafia",* "Onorevole Società", *"the Octopus", or the "Cosa Nostra". The* Malavita.

Since I'd been forbidden to refer to my secret society under any name whatsoever, I could still call my dog anything I wanted, and shout her name everywhere, just for old times' sake.

From the condition of the body when they found it the next morning, it seemed that Malavita had leaped at Matt's throat and torn it out with one bite. And I'll lay a bet that she then went straight back to huddle against the boiler and go to sleep, content at last.

282

Epilogue

An American family, the Browns, moved into an abandoned house in the small town of Baldenwihr, in Alsace.

As soon as they moved in, Bill, the father, found a little shed at the bottom of the garden, and decided to make it his study.

FRAMED

Tonino Benacquista

"One of France's leading crime and mystery authors."
Guardian

Antoine's life is good. During the day he hangs pictures for the most fashionable art galleries in Paris. Evenings he dedicates to the silky moves and subtle tactics of billiards, his true passion. But when Antoine is attacked by an art thief in a gallery his world begins to fall apart. His maverick investigation triggers two murders – he finds himself the prime suspect for one of them – as he uncovers a cesspool of art fraud. A game of billiards decides the outcome of this violently funny tale, laced with brilliant riffs about the world of modern art and the parasites that infest it.

In 2004 Bitter Lemon Press introduced Tonino Benacquista to English-speaking readers with the critically acclaimed novel *Holy Smoke.*

PRAISE FOR *FRAMED*

"Screenwriter for the award-winning French crime movie *The Beat That My Heart Skipped*, Tonino Benacquista is also a wonderful observer of everyday life, petty evil and the ordinariness of crime. The pace never falters as personal grief collides with outrageous humour and a biting running commentary on the crooked world of modern art."
Guardian

"Edgy, offbeat black comedy." *The Times*

"Flip and frantic foray into art galleries and billiards halls of modern Paris." *Evening Standard*

"A black comedy that is set in Paris but reflects its author's boisterous Italian sensibility. The manic tale is told by an apprentice picture-hanger who encounters a thief in a fashionable art gallery and becomes so caught up in a case of art fraud that he himself 'touches up' a Kandinsky."
New York Times

£9.99/$14.95
Crime paperback original
ISBN 1–904738–16–8/978–1904738–16–9
www.bitterlemonpress.com

SOMEONE ELSE

Tonino Benacquista

Who hasn't wanted to become "someone else"? The person you've always wanted to be . . . the person who won't give up half way to your dreams and desires?

One evening two men who have just met at a Paris tennis club make a bet: they give each other exactly three years to radically alter their lives. Thierry, a picture framer with a steady clientele, has always wanted to be a private investigator. Nicolas is a shy, teetotal executive trying not to fall off the corporate ladder. But becoming someone else is not without risk; at the very least, the risk of finding yourself.

£9.99/$14.95
Crime paperback original
ISBN 1–904738–12–5/978–1904738–12–1
www.bitterlemonpress.com